A GLIMMER OF HOPE

Copyright © 2010 Beth Davis

All rights reserved. No part of this book may be used or reproduced or transmitted in any form or by any means, electronic, or mechanical, including photocopying, recording, or by any information storage and retrieval system, without the permission of the Publisher.

Beth Davis -
A Glimmer Of Hope

www.bethdavisfl.com

Library of Congress Control Number: submitted

ISBN: 978-0-615-38318

Published by Writerjax Publishing
P.O. Box 56321
Jacksonville, FL 32241

Printed in the United States of America

Cover Design by Nicole Schott
Cover Photography by Jodi Stobe
Author's Photo by Brian Shields (Lumen Entertainment)
Book design by Caroline Blochlinger *(www.cbAdvertising.com)*

This is a work of fiction. Names, characters, places, and incidents are the product of the author's imagination or are used fictitiously. Any resemblance to actual events, locales, or persons, alive or deceased, is entirely coincidental.

Dear John,
Nice meeting you
at RAM!
Cheers!
Beth
Davis

A GLIMMER OF HOPE

Beth Davis

To my father, Jack Kelley, for teaching me the beauty of language and storytelling. I love you always.

☙

ACKNOWLEDGEMENTS

This novel began as a short story, created after Mass on a Sunday afternoon when a wave of creativity hit me. I added characters, twists and turns and four years later, I had a finished novel. Then I spent two years revamping it and working with my editor to get it as close to perfect as possible. But this book has been anything but my work alone. There have been so many hundreds of friends and family who have given me facts, opinions, prayers, support and time along the way and without them, this book would not exist. I need to acknowledge them here:

To Jodi Stobe, for taking such an amazing photograph for my cover. You are terrific! To my niece, Nicole Schott, for creating such a wonderful book cover. You are a magnificent artist! To Emily Carmain of Noteworthy Editing Services for bringing new eyes to my manuscript and being an amazing partner on this journey. To Sergeant Rick Hike of the Jacksonville Sheriff's Office – you took time to help me make my characters and story believable and real. You helped me come up with a fantastic ending. Thank you for all your continued encouragement and support.

To Caroline Blochlinger of CB Advertising Services, for formatting my manuscript. Thank you for your talent and time. To Brian Shields of Lumen Entertainment for taking my author photo. To the staff at Lightning Source for helping me navigate the unknown road of publishing. To all the members of the Florida Writers Association for their fellowship. To Vic Digenti for your support and all the classes you set up for FWA. I learned so much!

To my college buddy Dan Myers, who showed me it is possible to write and publish your own book. To all my professors at the University of South Carolina's College of Mass Communications and Information Studies for your patience, guidance and instruction. To Henry Price, Pat McNeely, Phillip Milano, Bruce Hamilton, Boaz Dvir and all the editors I've worked with – you each taught me lessons I'll carry always.

To Glenda Booth, retired Amber Alert Coordinator for SC Law Enforcement Division. Thank you for your expertise and your support.

To my college professor, advisor and friend, Ernie Wiggins – you were there when I debated leaving the newspaper industry. Just as you did in college, you gave me your best advice, which led me to write this book. Thank you for teaching me how to write a great story and for being my friend. To all my friends and family who have supported me during this seven year project. Your interest in my story and progress propelled me toward this finished book.

Most importantly, I want to thank my husband, Ted, my sons, Ted III and Brad, and my daughter, Amanda, for supporting me these seven years by listening to me ramble about my characters and their lives. I love you all so very much!

1

"I've been thinking about you a lot lately. I have something to ask you, and I'm just going to go for it. Can we be lovers again? We had something electric when we were together, and I miss it. I've been remembering how it felt when you held me tight against your chest and I felt your heart beating. Looking into your blue eyes and feeling your lips on mine are part of my dreams.

You made me feel like the sexiest woman alive when your fingers caressed my skin and you whispered in my ear. We were the only two people on the planet those afternoons together. No man has ever made me feel the way you did, and I want those feelings again. I felt alive and beautiful and so comfortable with myself as a woman when I was with you.

I'll take one day a month, a meeting here and there, a stolen moment, whatever you can give. When I think of you, I start to tremble. I remember all those times we were together and how it felt to touch you and spend time with you. I want that back.

I know it's not right, but connections like ours don't happen every day. Please, I'm begging you, let me back in. Open your heart and let me back in."

"Professor?"

Claire Bennett looked up from the pile of compositions on her lectern and watched a young man approach her on the stage. He wore the traditional college student uniform: knee-length tan shorts, a black t-shirt advertising his favorite rock band, and faded black discount-store flip-flops. His backpack dangled from one shoulder, and he held his cell phone in one hand and a sheet of paper in the other.

"I'm a little confused about this assignment," he muttered, holding out the paper. She took it and glanced over the scribbled cursive.

"What in particular is confusing to you, Mr. ...?"

"Jones. Tony Jones," he said a little louder, glancing at her through long brown lashes. The kid looked barely sixteen. "I'm just wondering—this is an English class, but the first day, we're writing an essay for you? Are we going to be doing a lot of writing for this class? I'm not a very creative person, to tell you the truth."

She read the first few lines, trying not to grimace openly; she hoped Mr. Jones was a better reader than writer. Claire looked back at him and saw that he was waving to a curvy blond in the second row.

"Mr. Jones," she said, bringing his attention back to the stage, "I asked you and your classmates to write a short essay this morning to determine what difficulties or challenges you face in your writing. The assignment was to write a persuasive essay about a topic you feel strongly about, and I see you wrote about," she looked at his paper again and frowned, "the need for higher speed limits. You believe South Carolina drivers aren't moving fast enough?"

"Well, I know I drive pretty well and I pass people on the highway like they're standing still. It wasn't like that in Nevada where I used to live."

He smiled at a brunette by the exit door, then looked back at Claire with a smirk. "Cops in the desert don't mind if you fly a little."

"Well," Claire shook her head slightly, "maybe you could write a short piece about desert driving for your lab instructor tomorrow."

"Lab?" He looked at her as if she'd started a new conversation without him. "What lab?"

"This class meets five days a week, Mr. Jones. The lecture portion of this class is Monday, Wednesday and Friday. You have a smaller lab section with one of my teaching assistants Tuesday and Thursday." Seeing his eyes start to glaze over, she added, "Do you have your schedule with you?"

He reached into the bottom of his backpack and pulled out a crumpled paper with doodles all over the margins. Five minutes and several deep sighs later, the deflated student left the stage, his shoulders a little more slumped than when he arrived.

Claire wondered how he hadn't noticed the lab on his schedule, but the thought left her mind when she heard someone behind her call her name. Ian Thomas walked across the stage with a sense of authority and confidence that she knew she'd never have.

"So, Claire, how was your first class with our newest students?" he asked, checking his Blackberry. "Have any gems in your classes so far?"

"I don't know if I'd say gems," she said, glancing over her shoulder at Mr. Jones, leaving with an arm wrapped around the blond from the second row, "but I'm sure I'll have an interesting year."

"You sure you're up to the challenge of teaching and handling your new administrative duties? As the liberal arts dean, I want to make sure you're not stretching yourself too thin." Ian clipped his Blackberry to his belt.

"Ian, I've taught at this college for fifteen years, covering almost every class we offer in the English department. Stepping into the position of department chair while the search continues for Paul's replacement isn't a big deal." She realized as the words left her lips that he wasn't the only one she was trying to convince. "Paul Geller was a good man, and I'm happy to do what I can to make this department run smoothly, just as he would have wanted."

"I just can't believe he's gone," Ian said. "He was the picture of health. Lisa and I went hiking with him and Janet upstate just two weeks ago, and then he dies of a heart attack. He was only fifty-five." He shook his head. "So you sure you're ready to handle all the added responsibility of department chair?"

She looked him straight in the eye and heard herself say, "No problem at all."

As the words left her lips, images of recent sleepless nights and hours spent at the computer fixing student and faculty scheduling problems, before moving on to prepare her own lessons, swept through her mind. She had bought a new spiral planner weeks earlier, although finding the time to fill in the pages was her current challenge. The department secretary had offered to order a Blackberry for her, but new gadgets did nothing but confuse her. Paper was good enough.

"Glad to hear it. Let me know if there's anything I can do to help." He started to walk down the steps off the stage, but turned. "I'll see you tonight at the department's orientation meeting for the graduate student teachers. Seven o'clock in the conference room. You'll be there, right?"

"Of course. See you then."

Ian followed in the direction of Mr. Jones and Claire exhaled deeply. She had completely forgotten about the meeting.

She returned her attention to the composition on the top of her stack of papers and read the name Becky Overton. The girl's words seemed so heartfelt and emotional. Claire imagined the young woman writing this love letter with tears rolling down her cheeks, thoughts of her lover streaming through her mind. Either that, or Ms. Overton had an amazing imagination and creativity beyond her teenage years.

Suddenly, she realized she only had ten minutes before she was due at her next class three buildings away. Quickly gathering up grade books and papers and placing them in her briefcase, she made a mental note to seek out Becky Overton through her teaching assistants to see how she was handling her class load.

Outside the faculty entrance at the back of the auditorium, she noticed a small cardinal sitting in a nest in the tree near the door. Sudden gusts of wind swayed the branch, and Claire watched as the bird struggled to stay in the tree.

I wonder if I'm taking on too much, she thought. She watched oak branches blow, dropping leaves on the students below. Across the sidewalk, a petite woman with short blond hair, with her back to Claire, stood talking to a female student.

As Claire walked toward them, the coed glanced at her over the other woman's shoulder with a pleading look.

Claire chuckled to herself. "Annie Gordon, aren't you supposed to be teaching class right about now?"

When Annie turned to face Claire, the student slipped away down the sidewalk.

"Hi, Claire. Just a minute." She turned back to find her student rushing down the walkway, making a cell phone call.

"Were you talking that girl to death about some historical figure that she just had to read about?" Claire made a face as she finished the line and couldn't help but laugh at Annie's stubborn glare.

"Like you don't do the same thing when one of these kids shows the slightest interest in literature?" The two women smiled at each other, then Annie shook her head and looked up and down the sidewalk at the kids around them.

"You met any Einsteins yet?" she asked Claire with a grin.

"You're the second person that's asked me about my students today. I've only had one class so far." Annie stared at her until Claire laughed out loud. "Okay, no Einsteins, but I did meet the actual reincarnation of Casanova." They began walking toward the campus library, and Annie put her arm around Claire's shoulder.

"So this Casanova: what's his deal? Just out to impress the girls or does he actually have something going on upstairs?"

"Oh, Annie, you should've seen this kid. He comes up to me to talk about class work and a second later, he's practically blowing kisses to girls in the class. He's probably in there right now," she said, pointing to the library, "with a girl giggling on each side."

"Are you telling me you never cuddled up to some hottie in the basement of your college library?" Annie stopped and looked at her friend. "That's where I spent most of my freshman year." She made a face like she was thinking back, and then laughed. "I dated some real losers. Thank God I didn't stay with any of them. It's so hard, as a college student, to know who's real."

Claire thought back to Becky's paper. She couldn't help wondering whether Becky's words were sincere. If so, she had a tough time ahead.

"Hello?" Annie waved her hand in front of Claire's face. "Where'd you go?"

"Just thinking of someone I know who's dealing with a loser like that right now." She shook her head as the words floated from her mind. "Listen, I've got to get to class. Want to meet for lunch later?"

"I'll have to call you, babe. Gotta go bore some more kids with history. Watch out for Casanova."

Claire waved to her friend and headed off to her next class. Clouds that had been light and puffy an hour earlier were getting dark to the west. A storm must be coming, she thought, as she moved quickly past a rowdy pack of students.

2

‿〇◟

The gray clouds to the west blew across the sky as Dennis Kincaid watched the people on the street below struggling to keep their coats closed as they walked into the wind and rain. A stocky man across the street used his umbrella as a weapon, leaning into the rain, which was blowing sideways in sheets.

Dennis could almost feel the raindrops hitting the back of his neck, when Donna knocked on his office door.

"Mr. Kincaid, your nine o'clock is here," his assistant said, leaning in.

"Thank you. Please tell him I'll be with him in just a moment." He fought off a shiver.

Dennis watched Donna leave his office and heard her deliver the message to his visitor in a muffled voice. He realized his heart was racing and took several deep breaths, trying to calm himself. Can't let them see you sweat, he thought. But the truth was, he was worried. His heart was pounding, his palms were sweaty, and he dreaded this appointment. Rodney Landis could ruin Dennis with one phone call.

Dennis first met with Rodney six months earlier. The forty-year-old accountant was injured in a car accident and it appeared clear that it was the other driver's fault. When Dennis had read the notes on the case, he assumed it would be an open-and-shut case with a significant award for Rodney. But now the greedy bastard had a hold on Dennis that he couldn't shake.

He took a deep breath, then picked up the phone, dialing a few numbers.

"Donna, please bring Mr. Landis in."

A few seconds later, Donna opened the door and entered the room. Rodney reluctantly took his eyes off Donna's back side and looked over at Dennis.

"Good to see you again, Dennis."

He shook Dennis' hand firmly and moved confidently into the office. Before Dennis could say anything, Rodney carried his large leather briefcase to the nearest chair and walked to the windows.

"Darlin', why don't you make sure Mr. Kincaid and I aren't disturbed? This shouldn't take long."

He turned and raised his eyebrows at the two of them, threw his coat jacket over the back of a nearby chair, then turned back to the storm outside.

Feeling Donna would hear the pounding of his heart, he nodded at her, knowing full well he would hear about it later. She closed the door behind her.

He turned to Rodney and tried to control his temper. Six months ago, this dirt-bag had walked into Dennis' firm with a foam pad around his neck and his tail between his legs, and now he was ordering Dennis' assistant around like he owned the place?

"I have those records I told you about." Rodney's voice echoed off the glass as Dennis watched him lean his forehead against the window and look down at the street. "I thought you might like to see them."

Dennis forced himself to move across the room toward his desk. His mind was racing, but he concentrated on steadying his breathing.

"You don't have anything on me." Dennis hoped his words sounded as confident to Rodney as they did in his own head. The coincidence was too far-fetched. Rodney's story didn't make any sense.

Rodney opened his eyes wide. "What we have here is a failure to communicate, Dennis." He walked to his briefcase, snapped the fasteners open and looked at Dennis. "I see you don't believe me and I don't blame you. Trust me, getting these billing records took some time, but I had to protect myself. I'm sure you understand that."

Rodney leafed through the papers, glancing at each sheet. Dennis looked around his office, trying to think how this could have happened. He had been so careful at his first firm after law school. It had been fifteen years ago and he was just starting out. To make the contacts he needed, he had bought clients' dinners and first-class flights and golf excursions. But he'd pulled in a record number of cases that first year. The partners had even recognized him for his efforts.

He hadn't liked taking the money, but it was a little here and a little there. And now this idiot accountant thought he had the upper hand?

"Ah, here it is." Rodney pulled out a few sheets of paper and handed them across the desk. "A listing of all the money you stole from our old company. As you can see, I have it listed by date. And I have hundreds of pages of proof at home. I just brought the totals and dates for you to see." He sat back in the chair and adjusted his tie.

"You were a busy man, Dennis. Working all those clients and your boss at the same time."

Dennis looked down the numbers to the bottom total. His stomach turned when he saw all the digits and recognized some of the larger totals. Rodney had something on him, but this wasn't over yet. There was no proof. He threw the papers across the desk at Rodney, sending them flying onto the floor.

"How dare you?" He stood, leaning over the desk. "I win your case for you, win you tens of thousands of dollars for a neck injury that appears to have healed itself, and now you come into my office, ordering my staff around and accusing me of embezzling money from the first firm I worked at?"

He'd expected Rodney to recoil from his attack, but he sat calmly, hands folded in his lap. His smile stayed constant and his eyes never wavered from Dennis'.

"It was both of our first jobs. You, the hotshot attorney, and me, the new junior accountant. I remember meeting you, Dennis, and for the first few months, your billing looked fine. But then, small charges didn't add up. Then they became more and more frequent and you were taking all those trips with clients and becoming the favorite of the very people you were robbing," Rodney said.

"I didn't show anyone, but I made copies to protect myself and show it wasn't my fault if anyone ever confronted me."

He stood to his full six feet and put his knuckles on the desk, leaning in toward Dennis.

"I'd forgotten about it all until the car accident and I saw you were practicing here in town. I signed on with you right away. I knew even if I didn't win my case, we could work something out."

He snapped his briefcase shut. He glanced at the

paperwork on the floor. "I'm going to leave this with you for your review. I'll be in touch." In a matter of seconds, he had crossed the room and left the office.

After staring out the window for several minutes, Dennis walked around the desk and gathered the papers. The thought crept into his mind that Rodney might actually have documentation of the theft. If he did, Dennis' world would crumble. He and Zach would be forced into bankruptcy, all because of bad choices he'd made when he was so young and stupid. Choices he thought no one knew about.

He jumped slightly at Donna's knock.

"Claire called," she said quietly. "She said to let you know she has a dinner meeting on campus and won't be home until late. You should pick up dinner for yourself."

He nodded. Standing, he placed the papers in the chair and walked to the window. On the street below, a young woman was trying to open her umbrella and had dropped her briefcase. He thought of Claire and wondered where she was right then.

He thought back to that morning when she'd raced out the door with her briefcase strap over one shoulder, juggling her keys and coffee mug in one hand and stray papers in the other and tried to open the car door. He'd tried to help her, but she told him in no uncertain terms that she didn't need or want his assistance.

Of course, there had been problems between them lately. He'd been traveling a lot more this year than last, but she knew travel was part of his job. The weeklong trip to New York in April and a long weekend in the Keys for the South Carolina Trial Lawyers Association Convention in June were necessary to keep legal contacts updated. She had to understand the importance of networking. Sometimes it also meant after-dinner drinks or a golf game on Saturday morning with a colleague. Whatever it took to get ahead in the world.

"How'd it go with Landis?"

Dennis turned to see Zach Grossbart, his law partner, in the doorway. The former high school linebacker somehow filled the space without being intimidating.

"Nothing out of the ordinary," Dennis lied. "Just following up on some of his paperwork."

"Oh, yeah, that car accident case. Everything finished with that?" He handed Dennis a mug of coffee.

"No problems. He just stopped by to thank us for our help." Lying to Zach was getting easier and easier, and he hated himself for it.

"You seem a little nervous yourself." Zach moved the papers Rodney had just delivered to the desk and sat in the chair. "Everything okay? You seem a little off."

Dennis nodded. "I was just thinking about Jane, that's all."

"That woman was nothing to you—you've said yourself she was a whore and an addict. And she's been dead for almost twenty years now, Dennis. Why waste your time?"

"She was still my mother." Dennis turned to his best friend with a look of resignation. "She did what she could. Things didn't get really bad until high school."

"If that's what you want to remember. I'm amazed you survived. If it hadn't been for your grandmother's agreement with Namington allowing your mother and you to live on his property, God knows what might have happened to you."

"Come on. I know my childhood wasn't the greatest, but up until she met Jack and got hooked on heroin, it wasn't that bad. She used to take me bowling, I remember that."

"Man, that was in fifth grade." Zach leaned back in his

chair and laced his fingers behind his head. "I remember quite a few fights I got into freshman year because I heard people calling you names or talking bad about you and Jane. This scar," he pointed to a small scar on his right arm, "that was from Donald Spencer. Remember him? He made some crack about your mom leaving you alone for days at a time. That suspension was long, but worth it. I think I knocked a couple teeth loose, if I remember correctly."

Dennis stared at his friend, then sipped his coffee. "Kids in high school can be cruel. I'm just glad I had your family as backup. Your mom saved me with her cooking."

"She does make a mean pot roast," Zach said. "Listen, I don't know exactly what you went through. I do know George Namington helped you become the man you are today. Hell, the man paid your full ticket through Columbia University and gave you the background to get your first job at a law firm. If I were you, I'd forget Jane and look where you are now."

Zach picked up a picture from Dennis' desk. "Hey, I've never noticed this before."

Dennis took it from Zach's hands.

"It used to be on the credenza. It was taken on our wedding day." Claire wore her blond hair in long curls in those days. The veil was pinned to a tiara with gold and sapphire stones. The color so closely matched her eyes that at one point during the ceremony, he didn't hear the minister's question. There were so many shades of blue in her eyes and just a hint of green. She was exquisite.

These days, those eyes were red and puffy from late nights grading papers in the lamplight, and the long curls had been cut years before. She claimed wearing her hair short made it easier to get ready in the morning, but she was still always in a rush.

"There you go again, out in la-la-land," Zach said. He stood up and walked toward the door. "Why don't you take some time off? Maybe take a couple days to sleep in. I'm sure Donna could clear your schedule. I need you ready for the videoconference with Thomasville's board members later this week."

"I'll let you know."

His partner left the room and Dennis turned to his computer. He did need a vacation, but this wasn't the time to take it. The firm was picking up clients right and left and now Rodney was threatening to blow his life to smithereens. He jumped every time the phone rang. He signed back on to his computer and stared at the beach scene background on the screen.

He was sure Rodney didn't have the paperwork to back up his claim. He couldn't let the little prick ruin his life. He had to get on with the rest of his day. A few short meetings, some reports to type, a workout at the gym to blow off some steam, and then he'd go to the country club for dinner.

As he sorted through his e-mail, he thought of Claire and made a mental note to try to call her that afternoon. That morning, he'd noticed dark circles under her eyes. He'd ask Donna what she did for relaxation. Maybe there was a spa she could recommend for Claire. He smiled as he thought of offering the spa trip for his wife and a girlfriend. She could go while he was in Vegas this weekend golfing with clients, he thought, as he began typing a response to the first of dozens of e-mails from the night before.

3

He'd have to remember to buy better shoes and a briefcase, Luke Rosentino thought as he tried to find a comfortable way to carry all his papers and textbooks. He couldn't believe the trek from the faculty parking lot to the middle of campus. Shading his eyes, he realized he'd have to pick up some sunglasses, too. This sun seemed brighter here than up north.

Things had changed so much since he was in college, he mused as he walked toward a group of students who were taking up the whole sidewalk, forcing him to detour onto the grass to get around. They acted like they owned the campus, lost in conversation with friends, oblivious to everyone else around them. Or these days, he noted, they scurried along with their heads down, eyes glued to a tiny LCD screen and keyboard or programming the playlist on an iPod.

Anyone who might get in their way should just suffer the consequences. If he didn't keep the pace, he might get trampled under someone's Nikes. And God forbid any of them found out he was a new professor. He didn't know which was worse—the stares or being flattened by a sophomore running to catch up with his drinking buddies.

Luke looked at his campus map that Monday morning for what seemed like the fortieth time. Whoever put this together must be six feet under by now. None of the buildings were where they were supposed to be according to this worthless scrap of paper, and he was supposed to be in the history department to meet Catherine Schneider, the history department chair, in less than ten minutes.

How in the world did they expect him to reach his building on time when faculty parking was half a mile away and his only guide was this century-old map on a tiny brochure?

It was really his fault, though. He should have made a dry run the night before, but he'd forgotten how much work was involved with moving, even when it was only one person. Unpacking boxes, waiting for phone and cable hookups and the inevitable search for the pan he remembered packing in the kitchen boxes.

He was turning the map at different angles and looking to his left at what he thought might be the liberal arts building when something smacked into him from the right, knocking him to the ground. His papers and books flew out of his hands, and the college map landed in the bushes. It took him a moment to catch his breath and realize he had just passed the corner of a building.

Behind him, he saw a slender, blond woman on her knees, trying to get to her feet. Her books and papers lay in a row down the sidewalk in front of her. She wore a dark blue suit and heels. He assumed she was a faculty member and was very glad she wasn't Catherine; this woman had a quiet beauty Catherine lacked.

"Oh, my God, are you okay?" he asked her.

She turned to look at him. He thought she looked a little disoriented, brushing the grass off her arm.

"Yeah, I guess," she said as she picked up her papers and

shook them off. Ignoring the pain from the freshly-raw skin on the palm of his hand and scrape on his arm, he quickly came to her side and helped her gather her things.

"I'm really so sorry. I didn't see you coming around the corner. Please forgive me," he said.

"It was totally my fault," she said, picking up the last papers. "I should have known better after working my way through the maze of students for so many years."

"No, it was completely my fault," Luke replied. "They should have stop lights at the ends of the buildings for newcomers like me walking around with half a brain."

She smiled at him. "Let me help you gather your things."

He realized he had been staring at her so intently, he'd forgotten that his books and papers were lying in the grass, rapidly soaking up the water from the nearby sprinklers.

Luke smacked his forehead in a playful way. "Strike two. Yes, getting my teacher edition textbooks out of the wet grass would be a very smart move. Glad you thought of it."

She smiled and helped him gather his books. Luckily, most of them landed with their covers in the grass and only a few of the papers were damp. His workbook, *A History of the United States and Its Wars*, however, was not so lucky.

As he picked it up from a puddle at the edge of the grass, what seemed like a gallon of water fell from its pages. They both laughed as the water hit the ground and made its own puddle. He shook his head.

"I deserve this. I don't even look where I'm going, I run smack into a colleague, knocking her books and papers everywhere. The least I should get is a soggy workbook."

"How about some nasty cuts as well?" she said, grimacing as she pointed to his arm. He looked and realized the stinging actually was a rather nasty cut, which was now bleeding profusely. Looking at the ground, he noticed a broken bottle. He must have caught a shard in the fall.

"Not a problem. Just a little blood." He took a handkerchief from his back pocket. "But if I faint and start to fall, push me away from the glass, okay?"

She laughed again. "Fair enough. One problem, though. When I carry you to the clinic and they ask me your name, what should I say?"

"Strike three. I didn't introduce myself."

"Blame it on post-traumatic stress syndrome."

"A very possible diagnosis," he said. He smiled at her and realized that in addition to being beautiful, this was one very smart woman.

"Luke Rosentino, new history professor, at your disservice." He half-bowed to her, almost dropping the workbook into the puddle again. She grabbed the book right before it hit the water.

"I think one soaking per book is enough." She handed the book to him and extended her hand. "I'm Claire Bennett, English department chair."

He took her small hand in his and shook it slightly. He watched her face flush and she pulled back. "So you're working with Catherine Schneider. Lucky man. She's highly respected in her field—you'll learn a lot from her."

"That's what I'm hoping." Then it hit him: the time. "And I have to meet her for our initial conference in exactly," he glanced at his watch, "four minutes. Could you possibly point me in the direction of her office?"

"It's in the next building, second floor," she said, pointing to an ivy-covered tan building to his left. "And I happen to know there is a bathroom just down the hall from her office so you can clean up. Tell her you ran into me outside the building." She laughed at her words.

"Can I tell her you're uninjured from our 'running into each other'?"

"Yes, I'm fine. And if she's unsure of whether she should

have hired you, after you talk for a while, have her call me and I'll explain our diagnosis to her."

"Okay."

He started running toward the building, wondering if she was watching him.

∾ ∾ ∾

It had already been a stressful morning and now Claire had blindsided a complete stranger on campus. But he had been so nice about it, even taking the responsibility on himself for her clumsiness.

She stood there a moment and watched the tall man approach the building and take the steps two at a time. He had long legs and an athletic build. She liked his looks— short brown hair, light green eyes and a beautiful smile. That smile had made her forget she was having a bad day. It actually made her mind wander places it hadn't gone in months.

Suddenly, she shook her head. What was she doing? She was a married woman! She arranged her bags and books and walked toward her next class.

∾ ∾ ∾

Luke arrived at Catherine's office and asked her assistant for a five-minute delay due to injury. She fussed over him and sent him down the hall to the bathroom with a box of Band-Aids, assuring him she would explain his tardiness to Catherine.

Five minutes later, breathing easier and with wounds still stinging, but clean and covered, he knocked on Catherine's door and shook his new supervisor's hand. They had connected immediately over the phone during his initial interview three months earlier.

He remembered from the final set of interviews a much more rigid, severe woman than the one sitting across from him that morning. She was relaxed, sipping hot apple-cinnamon tea from her college mug. Today's conversation flowed easily, from her thoughts on his transition from a small college to a large university to his teaching style. "Since you're teaching freshman and sophomore history, your smallest class will probably have about fifty students, so keep that in mind if you don't get the class participation you had in Ohio," she said, leaning back in her chair after they covered the department basics and her expectation that he make himself available to students in person and by e-mail.

"And don't let it bother you if you don't know all of your students, even after several weeks. There will be kids you might see in your class once. Your job is to teach the ones who show up. That's all we can really do."

Walking through the maze of halls in the building basement an hour later, he realized finding his office would be his first task. The history department shared the space with the criminal justice and sociology departments, and room 15 continued to elude him. He passed an office covered in Florida Gators paraphernalia, and one that had symphony music coming from a radio on the desk; another had stuffed animals arranged on a corner cabinet.

The last room at the end of the hall had a light smell of lemon in the air. It was bigger than his office in Ohio, but there had only been five thousand students at his last college. Now he had almost twenty thousand young people to inspire with his history lessons—at the very least, he hoped to inspire them to stay awake in class.

An oak desk sat at one end of the room with a filing cabinet next to it. On the other end sat a large bookcase and two comfortable armchairs. He had just laid his books on the desk when there was a knock on the door. He turned around to see a familiar face.

"Hey, guy, I was wondering if you'd ever get here," Annie Gordon said, leaning against the door frame.

"Hey, babe!" Luke walked over to her and picked her up in a giant hug.

The two hugged tightly for a few moments, before he set her down. "You look great, kiddo. How are ya? Here, grab a chair." He gestured to one of the armchairs and moved the chairs to face each other.

"I'm sorry I couldn't get together on any of your visits to town in the past few months. How long has it been since I've actually laid eyes on you?" She squinted and then grinned.

"Well, you came up to Ohio for Christmas two years ago," he replied, studying her face. "Honestly, Annie, you don't look any different than you did on graduation day fifteen years ago. Let's see," he said, rubbing his chin. "If I remember correctly, I was the one in the gown. You were wearing this flat, square hat—"

"Very funny."

"You didn't let me finish." He leaned back in the chair. "We went to dinner afterward at that little Italian place, the one with the football-field-length meatball subs. We shared one, you got sauce all down the front of your silk blouse, and we went to my apartment to get you cleaned up ... What an interesting night!" he said, raising his eyebrows at her.

She chuckled to herself and he noticed her face turned red a second later.

"You weren't that great—kind of disappointing from what I remember," she said. He laughed out loud and mimed an arrow to his heart.

"I think we were both nervous." He breathed deep, feeling truly relaxed for the first time since he'd woken up that morning.

"Who would have thought that fifteen years later, we would be teaching at the same college and still be the best of friends?"

"I certainly never would have thought it." He rested his elbows on his knees and his chin in his hands, leaning toward her. "But I'm glad we are."

They talked for what seemed like an hour, until Annie looked at her watch and got up to leave.

"I've got a class to teach. I would imagine you have one too."

"Mine don't start until tonight, thankfully. I haven't even had a chance to tour campus or get my office organized. I didn't get into town until two days ago, and the movers just arrived yesterday—I was beginning to think I might have to put them up for the night. It seemed like midnight before they finally got everything unloaded, and I got to bed," he said. "Hey, if I didn't mention it, thanks for putting the good word in for me on this position."

"You bet, buddy. By the way, how's Elizabeth? Has she started school yet?"

Luke pulled out his wallet and handed over a small picture of his daughter. "She's supposed to start first grade next week. Patty moved last month, and there's a great Catholic elementary school less than a mile from her condo."

Annie looked up from the picture. "How are you taking the split?"

"I'm fine. It was time, Annie. We had been together for seven years and she's wanted to get married for about half of that time." Annie handed him the photo and he put it back into his wallet. "I knew that wasn't what I wanted, so we sat down and talked and agreed a split was best for the whole family."

He looked up to see Annie's baffled expression. "I know that sounds funny, but we'd been fighting a lot in the months prior to the split. I didn't want Elizabeth being raised in that environment. I want for her what I had."

"I've seen your family," Annie said, walking toward the door. "Seventy-six cousins and twenty aunts and uncles always hugging and eating and talking. It's a wonder you don't weigh three hundred pounds with your mother's cooking."

"The good part is Patty's condo is only five miles from Mom's, so Elizabeth can have Mom's ravioli whenever she wants."

"Well, I'm just three doors down if you get bored. I'm the one with the stuffed animals."

"Great seeing ya, Annie," he said as he hugged her goodbye. "Maybe we can have lunch this week." He watched her practically skip down the hall and slip into her office.

He went back to his desk and sat down. When his elbow touched the wood, he winced in pain. He had to find out more about Claire Bennett. He had been struck by her soft demeanor, her slender body—but more than that, it was something in her eyes that caught his attention. Almost as if the moment they met was supposed to have happened a long time ago and now everything was right. He knew it sounded corny, but he couldn't get her out of his mind.

He thought about grilling Annie for information, but there would be endless questions if he did. As he logged onto his computer, he knew he had to find a way to bump into Claire again...just not so hard this time.

4

⨘

The second day of classes loomed in front of Claire. She had stayed up until three in the morning reading the compositions, but they were graded and recorded in her book. Grad students were going to teach the labs starting today. She had taken one of the labs herself so no one could say she wasn't staying connected with the students. She'd seen several professors move to administrative positions and forget how to teach.

Traffic on the oak- and pine-lined county road seemed light that morning as she maneuvered her new red Audi around a minivan. She needed the solitude of the open road in the foggy early morning hours.

Driving the thirty miles to school, she normally listened to jazz or blues with the breeze blowing through her hair from the open windows. She needed to forget the confrontation she had with Dennis at the house that morning. They had been fighting for days.

⨘⨘⨘

When she had gotten home after having dinner with Annie the Friday before school started, the house was dark and there was no message from Dennis. After making herself some tea, she had fallen asleep almost immediately in their bedroom and woke to sunlight streaming through the lace curtains of the second-floor window.

She'd rolled over to drape her arm across Dennis, only to find he wasn't there.

The clock read nine o'clock. She climbed out of bed, slid into her satin robe and went downstairs. She looked in the garage and seeing his car was gone, imagined he had gone to his office in the city to work like he did many Saturday mornings.

She hadn't thought any more of it as she ran errands and worked out at the gym. By mid-afternoon, though, there were no messages and she was beginning to worry. She had called his cell phone but got only his voicemail. She tried to remember if he had told her of any business trips he had scheduled, but none came to mind.

She spent Saturday evening working on her lesson plans for the first week of school and watched a rented movie in bed. She woke suddenly to a dark room and the sound of the garage door going up. The alarm clock read three a.m.

She could tell without seeing him that he was drunk. His routine was to come in right away and come upstairs, but that night, he let the engine run for about five minutes, then turned it off, and it was another ten before she heard the garage door close. It sounded like he stumbled over something, then cursed before he closed the door of the guest room on the first floor. Dennis had slept in the guest room several times in the past month to avoid waking her when he came home late.

Sunday morning, she woke up wondering if she should demand to know where he had been since Friday. Dressing for church, she decided to play it cool and see what his mood was before saying anything.

She walked downstairs and found the guest room door open and the bed made; he was gone. There was no note telling her anything. She didn't hear from him until late Sunday afternoon when he called from his cell phone. She was very cool to him as she asked where he had been all weekend.

"What do you mean? Where have I been? Don't you remember? I left for the conference in Charlotte Friday right from work. I told you about it weeks ago. Our golf tournament starts in a couple of minutes. I just called to tell you I'm having dinner with my clients. Don't wait up. I've got to go. It's my turn to tee off. Everything else okay?"

She said nothing and hung up, but spent the evening thinking of all the things she should have said. She lay awake for hours after he came in at one a.m. and spent another night in the guest room. He's going through something at work and that's why he's been so distant, she thought.

Things had been good until about a year earlier. He was spending more and more time at his office and was less and less communicative with her. She knew they both had busy schedules with her working at a college thirty miles away and him working sometimes eighty hours a week in the city. But most people managed to call at least once a day to see how their partner was doing.

She had woken up Monday morning angry; she had a right to a better life than this. She dressed and went downstairs to get her coffee. He sat at the dining room table, reading the paper like nothing was wrong.

She glared at him over her coffee mug and said nothing when he said hello. He put the paper down and glanced at her.

"What's the matter with you?"

She told herself to stay in control. "You think there is something wrong with me for wanting to know where my husband has been for the past three or four days?" She heard her voice rise in volume. "You know that I've had a lot on my mind with the department chair appointment and all my extra responsibilities. You don't think it's possible I forgot about a weekend away that you probably told me about a month ago?

"Were you so busy that you couldn't call for one minute and leave me a message on the machine?" She realized she was standing and screaming.

"I don't know what you want me to tell you." He looked at her blankly. "I told you about the conference and the tournament weeks ago. You sounded like you had a busy weekend lined up so I figured we'd just catch up this week."

"Oh, you mean you thought this week would be different from the last few months and we might actually talk? Sometimes I feel like I don't even know you!" She had stormed out. He had come home late Monday night and they had avoided each other, then started right back up this morning.

How had things changed so quickly between them? She remembered back to when they were first married and how they would talk every evening over dinner, narrating the day's events to each other. They would go to parties and go to dinner with other couples and enjoyed being together. She wondered what it would be like to be single again, then reproached herself for the thought. Every couple has difficult periods in their marriage. This was just something they would have to work out.

A nagging question came at her as she turned into the college parking lot. Did she really want to work it out? The decision to improve a marriage had to be something both parties wanted. This morning when they argued, she stared across the mahogany table at him. His expression was not one of a man who saw the need for a solution. Maybe this weekend had happened for a reason. Maybe she needed a jolt. She was complacent with her marriage.

Suddenly, she remembered her parents, and a feeling of shame washed over her. They had stuck together through two daughters and all the drama that includes for more than forty years.

A memory seeped into her mind. It had been a few days before she left for college, on a Saturday night. Coming out of her room upstairs, anxious to get to the party her friends were throwing for her, she heard it. Her parents were arguing in the living room at the bottom of the steps.

"I don't understand what you want, Rose," her father said in a frustrated tone.

"I don't want to be the whiny wife, Bill. I just need you to understand what I'm feeling." Claire caught her breath and listened. "Our oldest daughter is moving away and I don't know that I'm ready for that." Claire could hear her mother crying now. "What if she's not ready to move out and live on her own? Have we kept her too sheltered? I'm so worried about her."

"I think we've done everything we can do, Rose. She's a good girl and she knows what we expect of her. I'm not sure where this is coming from."

"I knew I shouldn't have started this. I should have kept this to myself," her mother said. "I'll work it out. Don't worry, I'll work it out myself."

She heard her mother's footsteps on the tile in the kitchen and water running in the sink. She tiptoed down the stairs, peeked around the corner and watched her father walk to the sink and put his arms around his wife from behind and hold her. Her mother's tears came strong and hard as Claire watched her frame wither in her father's grip.

"Everything will be fine, Rose. I promise. She's going to be fine. She's only going to be at school a few hours away. If she needs us, she knows we'll be here for her."

Claire stood against the wall in the hallway, not sure what to do. She ended up going back upstairs for ten minutes, then loudly making her exit known, hoping not to embarrass her mother.

She should try harder to understand Dennis' needs and wants. It was all so confusing, but she didn't have time to think about it now. She gathered her books and locked her car.

Her English 101 lab was in half an hour and she still had to put together her PowerPoint presentation. They would be revealing their persuasive essays in class and she was hoping to meet Becky Overton this morning.

Compared to the other essays, Becky's was heart-wrenching and Claire wanted to make sure it was fiction.

∾ ∾ ∾

"Beck, wake up! You're going to be late," Julie said, throwing a pillow across the dorm room. The green ball of fluff hit its target and the body under the cover stirred. "Your alarm clock didn't go off and lab starts in thirty minutes."

Kicking the covers off her dorm bed, Becky Overton glared at her roommate.

"Remind me again why I signed up for an eight a.m. lab?" she moaned.

"I believe it was because all the other times were taken, but remember, it's only twice a week," Julie said, as she buttered her toasted bagel.

Becky swung her legs over the side of the bed, stood up, and arched backward, trying to get the kinks out of her back. She had moved into the dorms a week earlier and her back was paying the price for sleeping on what seemed to be a twenty-year-old mattress.

She had hoped to get a run in before class like yesterday. She'd had one of the dreams again and running seemed to clear her head. The summer had been exciting with graduation and her summer job, but the way it ended had been difficult.

"God, the lab's on the other side of campus. I've got to grab a quick shower. Will I see you later?"

"More than likely. I've got a sorority meeting tonight, but I should be back after that. Gotta go. See ya!"

"Thanks for the pillow alarm. I promise I'll do better."

The warm water and the sensation of the bubbly soap on her skin helped wake her up a little, but the dream had shaken her more than she realized. She'd been having the same dream since leaving her job two weeks earlier. She was seated at the end of a long table and men in suits lined the table, all of them staring at her.

An older man at the opposite end of the room was yelling and pointing at her. She couldn't tell who he was and she couldn't hear words, just yelling, but there was no doubt that everyone at the table was accusing her of something. She knew she had made some bad decisions this summer, but how could people know? The whole situation had been handled very discreetly and she'd never told anyone. She just wanted to know what the man across the room was saying. She toweled off, letting the dream slip away. Then she saw the time and quickly dressed.

Fifteen minutes later, Becky found room 160 and quietly opened the door. The room had theater seating, but wasn't much larger than the average classroom. There were only ten people in the room when she arrived.

She took a seat in the back of the room. Not much noise, a small group, lots of empty seats and, hopefully, the professor wouldn't expect too much this morning. Julie said Bennett was the department chair and that sometimes those could be the worst teachers because they hadn't taught in years.

A few more students staggered in and at two till eight, the door opened and Becky watched as Professor Bennett entered the room. She was blond and not very tall, but she walked straight and proud, as though she knew a secret the rest of them didn't know. Becky guessed her to be in her late thirties. She carried a stack of papers and books that looked like it might topple any minute, but she made it to the desk, set the books down and looked at the class.

"Well, it looks like everyone made it," the professor said, after a silent head count. "Fifteen of you—that's the maximum. My name is Professor Claire Bennett and I will be teaching this lab as well as the main class, so you get the joy of seeing me every day."

"This morning, I wanted to go over the essays you turned in yesterday. I want you to take us through your writing process and tell us how you came up with your stories. I'm hoping we can have some lively discussions this semester. Last semester, I had mostly guys and I couldn't get them to discuss anything deeply unless someone brought up the latest football scores."

Becky felt her heart pound. She couldn't be serious. She had written that essay yesterday with the hopes to never see it again. It hurt writing it. She debated whether to leave the room, but instead sank into the chair.

"We'll start with Susan Pemberton." The other fourteen sat back and relaxed.

∾ ∾ ∾

An hour, some laughter and tears later, the students gathered their belongings. Claire had achieved her goal. They had worked through some issues, some about writing and some of the heart, three of the girls in front seemed to have bonded and she discovered who Becky Overton was by process of elimination. The tall slender teen sat in the back throughout class, watching the others share their stories.

"Excuse me, Ms. Overton?" Claire asked hesitantly as the other students worked their way toward the door. "Can I speak to you for a minute?"

Becky paused at the step at the door, looking as though she wanted to get lost in the small crowd that was leaving.

"Is something wrong with my essay, Professor?" Becky asked.

"I give this assignment every semester on one topic or another, Ms. Overton. Most of them are usually written in a hurry. After all the years I've been teaching, I can pick those out in a heartbeat. This, on the other hand, is one of the best I've read in a long time."

The young woman looked into Claire's eyes and smiled. She looks so young and innocent, Claire thought. I hope she hasn't lived this essay.

"I'm very impressed. Taking a vague assignment like this and writing a piece that moves your reader is no small feat, especially as a freshman in college before school even starts. Do you like writing?"

Becky looked down and nodded. Claire wasn't sure, but she thought Becky's eyes seemed bright.

"I don't mean to pry, but there was so much emotion in your composition. How did you prepare to write this? Did you base this on the experiences of someone you knew or just write from your heart?"

"A friend of mine had been seeing someone special over the summer and he ended it two weeks ago," Becky said, looking at the floor. "I've been spending a lot of time with her lately."

"Well, her loss got you an A-plus," Claire said, trying to make eye contact with Becky. She felt maternal for the first time in her life, wishing she could lift Becky's chin and her spirits. She wasn't sure if she was telling the truth, but at least they had met. "I'd like to submit your essay to a national contest for fiction writers if you don't mind. What do you say?"

For a moment, she wasn't sure Becky had heard her question, but then Becky looked up at her.

"You want to enter my composition in a contest? Wow! Yeah, that would be great. Thank you."

"I hope I didn't keep you from your next class."

The two women studied each other for a split second.

"If you need any help with anything, let me know what I can do for you," Claire said. "I know a lot of people on this campus and would love to make this first semester as smooth as possible for you."

She watched as Becky rolled a ruby ring around her right finger and bit her lip. "I'd like that."

5

❧

Luke moved forward through the throng leaving the cafeteria. A short redhead turned just as he passed and her backpack smacked him in the arm.

"Oops, sorry, sir." The girl put her hand over her mouth as he held his arm and she moved away quickly with her friends. He heard her giggle and call him "Too Tall" under her breath to her friends. So creative, he thought as he finally made it through the crowd.

Luke stopped and had to laugh. It was like stepping back in time. Student council members had decorated the room with movie posters from "The Girls on the Beach," "Gidget Goes Hawaiian" and "Blue Hawaii" for the opening week beach party that night in the main courtyard. Balloons and streamers were everywhere. He walked toward Annie, shaking his head.

"What's wrong with your arm?

"Hmmm. Oh, nothing, just a short student's backpack got a little out of control." They walked toward the lunch line.

"This beach theme makes me want to dig out my suit and shades, get in my convertible and head down to Kiawah

Island." He looked over his shoulder at her. "Remember that trip we took summer before senior year and you met that guy with the red Corvette? What was his name? Steve?"

"Memories," she sang. She picked up a tuna sandwich wrapped in plastic. "Just make sure they're not Speedos you're wearing. You don't want to traumatize these kids."

"Very funny. What about you and your bikini?"

"I'd get a standing ovation."

He rolled his eyes at her and he made himself a salad, then poured a glass of tea.

"Whatever. Thank God the first day's over. How was it for you, Professor Gordon?"

"Pretty good, Professor Rosentino, except American History 101 in the afternoon." She chuckled. "You know how it is. You stick two hundred teenagers in a room after lunch and make them listen to your expectations for the semester and pretty soon, you're talking over the snores."

They chose a table near the window and sat down with their trays.

"How about you? First day teaching at a new college can be a little unnerving."

"Not too bad," he said. "I had a European History at eight this morning and Introduction to Latin American Civilization at ten. The ten o'clock wasn't too bad because..."

He looked out the window and saw Claire. She was walking toward the back of a group of students approaching the cafeteria, talking and gesturing with a young male student. Luke followed her with his eyes. Her blond hair swayed across her neck as she walked. Her red sweater and black slacks fit her body perfectly. But more than that, her smile captivated him. He felt himself grin as she laughed at the student's joke.

Suddenly, he was aware of something moving in front

of him. He turned and watched Annie wave her hand in front of his eyes.

"Huh? Oh, yeah." He took a bite of salad. "It wasn't too bad because they were juniors and—"

"Were you just staring at Claire?"

Luke looked across the table at Annie. She was staring at him with one eyebrow raised, waiting for an answer. If he told her of crashing into Claire yesterday, he'd never live it down. He could just tell her they had met and ask her how well she knew Claire, but he'd have to be careful. Annie had a unique talent for knowing instantly when he was interested in a woman, sometimes even before he did.

"I met her yesterday. She helped me find the history building. She seemed nice."

He watched as Annie waved Claire toward their table. He heard her approach from behind and tried to calm his breathing. Annie was surely picking up on his reaction, which was the last thing he wanted. She would love nothing more than to play Cupid and try to set him up with women from every corner of campus. He could get his own dates.

He turned in his chair as she reached the table and spoke.

"Hi, Annie. I hope I'm not interrupting anything."

"No, not at all. I just feel a formal introduction is in order. Claire Bennett, I would like you to meet Luke Rosentino, the newest member of our history department. Luke and I went to college together. We've been best friends for almost fifteen years."

"It's nice to see you again. Has Annie showed you the campus?"

"As a matter of fact, not yet." He looked into her eyes. He hadn't seen that color blue since he and Patty had taken that Caribbean cruise two years earlier. He forced himself to look at Annie and swallow.

"It's been a busy week with the movers and getting the house set up. I'm sure she'll come through for me toward the end of the week." He winked at Annie.

"Well, if she doesn't fulfill her duty as best friend, let me know. I could show you the high points. If that's okay, Annie?" Luke watched her face flush.

"So, English department chair. The fine world of literature," he said, sitting back in the seat, looking at Claire. "Who's your favorite writer?"

Her stance relaxed and she smiled wide. "I really enjoy Edgar Allan Poe, but they're all wonderful. I think the best writers create characters you remember years after finishing the story. Someone who has been painted with words in front of your eyes, paragraph by paragraph, until you can anticipate their every move."

He nodded. "I feel the same way when I read about historic figures. I read their biographies so I can get inside their heads and figure out why they made their great, and sometimes, tragic decisions."

The two looked at each other and, for an instant, the sounds of the cash registers and students' conversations all dimmed. Luke hadn't felt this chemistry since the day he had met Patty. He couldn't stop looking at Claire, but he knew Annie would grill him when he saw her grin.

Claire glanced at her watch.

"I've got to run," Claire said. "Got a class in ten minutes, just time for a small salad to go. Nice seeing you again, Luke."

As she walked toward the lunch line, he noticed he'd been holding his breath. He slowly let it out and turned to face the music.

"What?"

"You've got it bad."

"What? You think—come on, Annie. I was just being nice."

"Well, buddy, I hate to tell you, but she's married."

"Whatever. You know me. I like to talk to people. And she's a friend of yours, so I'm sure we'll talk on occasion." He forced a forkful of lettuce in his mouth. Oh, God, she was married. He felt like a balloon that Annie had just popped. How could he feel this way and she be married? A minute ago, he felt a connection with a woman that he would remember for years and now it was gone.

"Uh huh. If you say so," she said.

"I do. Now tell me about your students, Gordon. Why do you keep putting them to sleep?"

6

❦

"Excuse me, is your dinner partner on his way?"

Annie looked up from her menu to see the waiter with a tray in his hand.

"Excuse me?"

"You're waiting for someone. Would you like another glass of wine while you wait?"

Annie glanced at her watch. This was the last time she would let herself be set up on a blind date by girlfriends, only to be stood up.

"That would be great. Chardonnay, please." He brought her the glass and she was suddenly glad she'd thought to bring a book with her. There was nothing worse than waiting for someone with nothing to do.

She looked out over the restaurant from her table near the door. The space was quiet and slightly dark, but Annie saw it as full of life. Couples sat across from each other in the glow of candlelight, whispering and sharing their personal stories. All except the couple in a booth in the opposite corner.

Annie could only see the woman, but from the look on her face, it was obvious this was not a happy occasion.

She guessed the girl was about twenty, and she used her hands to make a point to her companion, but would then put them down as if stopped in mid-sentence. Annie was sure she could see tears in the candle's glow.

After about five minutes of arguing, the girl's dinner partner stood up and walked toward the door. Annie drew in her breath as she held the menu in front of her face.

What was Dennis Kincaid doing here and who was that woman? Why was he having drinks at a restaurant almost an hour from home with this young girl and why was she crying?

Dennis walked out of the building in a hurry, followed by the girl, who wore a short denim skirt and button-down silk shirt. Her heels clicked on the tile floor as she pushed the door open.

Annie tried to see out the window, but the pair turned the corner. This doesn't look right, she thought as she paid the bill and walked out. She needed to find out what was going on.

∾ ∾ ∾

"Listen, I told you I don't have anything else to say to you," Dennis said over his shoulder. "I told you this is over."

"It can't be," Becky said. "All those times we were together talking, dancing, making love—didn't it mean anything to you?"

They reached his car, parked in the back of the lot under some aging oak trees, and he looked over the car roof at her. She was very pretty, but it couldn't continue. The affair had been exciting, knowing that no one else knew about their times together in the conference room after work, but she didn't work there anymore and the excitement was gone.

"I'm sorry, I've got to go."

"Can't we talk in the car for a minute? It's starting to rain." She looked at him with pleading eyes, and suddenly he didn't have the heart to turn her down.

"Get in."

They got into his Mercedes and he glanced at her. She had completed an internship at his firm during the summer and he had been instantly attracted to her. She was eighteen—he'd made sure of that—and he couldn't stop watching her as she moved around the office.

Two weeks after she started work, he had pulled her close in his office and kissed her. She hadn't fought him and they'd had sex on his desk that night.

The affair lasted most of the summer. They met after work in his office, a conference room and sometimes at the company apartment downtown on the weekends. She made him feel young and alive.

She leaned toward him and laid her hand on his leg. "Dennis, I just want to be with you."

He looked at her and realized she had undone another button on her shirt. Her touch sparked his imagination, making it difficult to think clearly.

"You wore that shirt and short skirt on purpose, didn't you? You know how I get when you wear that outfit." Maybe just one more time, he thought as he leaned over and kissed her neck and unbuttoned her blouse. God, she smells good. He ran his fingers along the edge of her bra. I'll make sure she understands this has to be the last time, he thought.

She slowly slid her hand up his pants leg until she reached his crotch. He let out a moan as she caressed him through the material. He kissed her, running his hand through her long brown hair, then placed his hand on the back of her neck, pulling her closer. He hadn't meant for the affair to start, but there was so much chemistry between them. At least he had made reservations a few towns away where no one knew them.

He pulled her blouse off her shoulders and unhooked her bra. He couldn't understand why she wanted him. She was so young and beautiful; she could have any man. The thought came and went as he brushed his lips over her breast and felt her arch toward him.

Her fingers ran though his blond hair. Unbuttoning his shirt, he felt her hot breath on his skin as her fingers slid from his stomach into his slacks.

He looked into her face and saw desire and passion in her eyes. He pushed his seat back, undid his belt and zipper and guided her onto his lap.

A few moments later, her skirt was around her waist and they were together, moving in perfect rhythm. They held onto each other tightly as the rhythm increased and their breathing became heavier. Waves of heat moved through his body as they kissed each other hungrily and he finally cried out as one last pulsing wave crashed over them both.

"Baby," she sighed as she caught her breath. "Amazing. Wow." She kissed his face and held him close.

He pulled her back and brushed the long dark hair out of her face. He had to end it. "That felt great. It's been great every time but you know this has to be the end, Becky."

She laid her head on his shoulder. He held her on his lap and watched through the rain as a blue pickup truck left the parking lot. It had been parked across the aisle from them the whole time. He was suddenly glad they'd met so far from home. At least no one they knew would be any wiser.

7

∾⟫⟪∾

Becky pulled into the dorm parking space, shut off her car and stepped out into the misty air. He said their relationship was over, but he'd said that before. Pulling on the metal door of her building, she sniffed the sleeve of her shirt and breathed in his cologne. The sexual energy when they were near each other sapped her of any clear thoughts. All she could think about was spending time with him, wrapped around him.

There had been two other boys during her senior year, but they were so immature compared to Dennis. They'd only wanted a notch in their bedpost, or more accurately, their cars' back seats. Dennis took time with her and brought her to heights she had only read about in women's magazines.

There was something in his eyes tonight that told her he didn't really mean what he said. Once inside the car, the chemistry had filled the air and she knew she had to have him. The sex was incredible. When they were together, all that existed was their breath, lips and the sensation of their bodies touching.

She stepped into her dorm room and closed the door behind her. She took off her blouse, held it to her nose and inhaled. His cologne was light and manly, and when she closed her eyes, she could imagine him standing next to her.

She opened her eyes and saw that the light sprinkle outside the window was now a downpour. She pulled on an oversized sweatshirt of Dennis' and sat on her bed, holding her knees close to her chest.

"Whew, what a night." Becky turned to see Julie come through the door and head straight for the bathroom, taking off her jacket and shaking it over the tub. "I was at my parents' house for dinner with my brothers and it started coming down heavy on the highway. What a mess. I'm going to take a shower."

As Julie shut the door, Becky tried to imagine a real home, one without drinking or arguing, one where people hugged and said that they loved each other. The dorm might be old and drafty, but there was no one telling her how stupid or useless she was or screaming in the next room. The worst had been the late nights when her father stumbled in, followed by fights so loud the neighbors had called the police. But late at night in her dorm room, she could get lost in the silence and try to forget the past.

Leaving her parents' home had been nearly the greatest moment of her life. By that time, shells of the parents she'd remembered from her youth sat on the couch and recliner night after night, smoking cigarettes and speaking to her only long enough to remind her to pick up more beer and wine after school from the convenience store down the road, owned by her uncle.

One afternoon during senior year, she'd stopped on the way home and drunk one of the beers herself. She'd almost thrown up and spent the rest of the day in bed nauseous. She vowed never to drink again.

Dennis was so different from her parents. He never drank or smoked. He was young and intelligent and passionate about everything he did. He talked to her, not at her. He asked her questions and laughed at her jokes. When she was with him, she felt smart and beautiful.

The first kiss in his office had come at the end of a very long day. She'd walked in while he was on the phone. She started to back out, but he waved her in and motioned for her to close the door. After finishing the conversation, he'd told her he'd noticed her hard work and said if she needed a reference after the summer, he'd be glad to help. He'd stepped closer and admired her class ring and asked to see it closer. When she had held her hand out, he'd taken her hand in his and kissed it gently, then looked into her eyes.

"I've been watching you and I'd like to get to know you better."

Before she could say anything, he'd pulled her close to his body and kissed her lightly on the lips. A fog settled on her brain as she felt his arms go around her waist and pull her closer. The kiss seemed to last for hours. She finally pulled away and said she had to get back to her reports, but hours later, she stopped by his office before leaving. His tie was loosened and he smiled as she came in, shut the door behind her and closed the blinds.

At first, she had only been interested in Dennis as a lover. He'd told her he was married, but planned to leave his wife soon. His power and success were exhilarating to her. They ate fabulous dinners and stayed in the corporate apartment some weekends, making love until dawn and eating brunch in bed when they finally awoke. But after only two weeks, he was all she could think about.

Sitting at Henry's Grille tonight, she'd planned on that same chemistry, but found him tired and aloof. When she'd reached across the table to touch his hand, he pulled away, sat back in the booth and crossed his arms.

"Becky, you've got to realize this was a bad idea,"

Dennis had said, rubbing his temples and looking at her discouragingly. "You obviously still have feelings for me and I care for you, but I don't want to hurt you anymore than I already have."

"I thought since you agreed to see me, you wanted to—"

"Beck, those were great times, but they're in the past. You've got to move on and forget about us."

"I can't believe you've forgotten all the times we shared." Tears welled up in her eyes and her throat felt tight.

"Look, I think maybe this was a bad idea," he'd said, getting out his wallet and laying a ten-dollar bill on the table. "I hope you have a good life and enjoy college. It was nice knowing you."

He'd left the table, but after listening to her in the car, he'd come to his senses. She'd give him a little space. Maybe he just needed time to remember that it was Becky he loved, not his wife.

∾ ∾ ∾

Raindrops tapped on the skylight above the bar like a woman tapping her manicured nails on a desk. Dennis looked up and watched a lightning streak flash across the sky as he sipped his whiskey and felt the cool liquid coat his throat.

He realized now that tonight had been a huge mistake. He'd started the drive home, but the storm had gotten worse and he turned back to wait it out at Henry's Grille.

The combination of the whiskey and the driving rain outside the window took Dennis back to a stormy night during his senior year of high school.

∾ ∾ ∾

He had spent the evening at Zach's, and they'd been talking about colleges. Zach had been accepted at the University of Georgia. Dennis had applied to several colleges, but hadn't received any responses. He had just gotten home from Zach's and taken a shower. As he dried off, he heard a knock at the door and slipped on some shorts.

The two officers flashed their badges and asked if they could come in. Dennis stepped aside and the men walked into the living room, took off their raincoats and sat on the old brown couch with blocks under the legs. They asked him to sit down.

"Son, is anyone home with you?" asked the taller of the two men.

"No, sir. My mother just left to go to the grocery store. She should be back any time," Dennis lied.

"Son, I don't know how to tell you this," the shorter officer said, "but your mother was found murdered in the next town. Is there someone we can call for you? A relative? A family friend?"

Dennis sat stunned, digesting the news. His first thought was old man Namington.

He told the officers that Mr. Namington was his grandmother's friend and lived in the main house. The taller officer left and ten minutes later, George Namington entered the trailer.

"Son, are you okay? I heard the news about your mother."

"Yes, sir. I'm fine," Dennis said quietly, watching Namington look around the room in disgust.

"Thank you, officers, for coming to get me so quickly. The boy will stay in my house for now. Is that all right, son?"

Dennis nodded in disbelief. In all the years he had lived there with his mother, they had never been invited to the main house. He was curious what had happened to his mother, but that was all, just curiosity. He hadn't felt anything for Jane for years. She was just a woman who came and left groceries for him.

For the next few months, he made up for lost time. He enjoyed all that George's money could afford: swimming in the indoor pool, playing tennis with Zachary and having friends over for horseback riding.

After high school, he was accepted into Columbia University in New York. Namington had given him the letter personally. Dennis left Nevada behind and graduated at the top of his class with both a bachelor's and a law degree. He never looked back as he gained power and money and prestige. If he saw something he wanted, he worked until he got it. Business deals, cars, houses, women...Becky.

∾ ∾ ∾

With all the mistakes he had made in the past few months, knowing to keep his distance from Becky should have been instinctive. He knew he didn't want to be in a romantic relationship with her anymore. He thought they could just eat dinner together and be friends. He realized now the relationship had to be over completely.

"Hey, buddy, can I get you a ride home?" The bartender stood in front of Dennis, wiping a glass with a bar towel.

"No, I'm fine. But do you have an aspirin back there?"

Dennis rubbed his temples and took the aspirin offered him. A feeling of self-loathing settled in like a dark cloud. He didn't like the person he was at that moment. He'd committed more sins in the past year than most people commit in a lifetime and he wanted to do better.

He had to forgive himself for being with Becky tonight and make his way back to Claire. She was his wife, after all, and she deserved all his attention.

He slid off the barstool and steadied himself before heading to the door. Sure, he was drunk, but he deserved it after the bad decisions he'd made that day. As long as he made it home in one piece, the evening couldn't get any worse.

8

Annie knew she was driving recklessly. Between tears clouding her eyes and the rain hitting the windshield, she could barely make out the white lines on the highway. Images from the parking lot swirled through her mind. Dennis and that young girl parked under the tree in their own little world, messing up Claire's. How could he?

He was her best friend's soul mate, her life, and he had made a commitment to be faithful to her for the rest of his life. Slamming her hand on the steering wheel, she cursed him for being so insensitive to Claire's feelings. He wasn't thinking of her when he was giving himself to that girl in his front seat.

It made her almost physically ill when she thought about what this would do to Claire. Sure, Claire appeared strong on the outside and she worked at the college, but she clung to Dennis, allowing him to make decisions regarding their money and taking his criticisms to heart.

There was a day this past summer when Annie had walked into Claire's office and found her crying at her desk. After several minutes of questioning, she'd finally disclosed that Dennis had argued against her taking the department chair position because of her inability to organize her time.

Annie felt the need to tell her of what she'd seen in the parking lot, but at the same time, she wasn't sure how and if she could bring herself to hurt Claire that badly. As she turned onto the rural highway exit for the house, she wondered whether it would be better to let Claire find out on her own. She thought back on their years of friendship and hoped Claire knew Annie would never knowingly hurt her.

The rain was letting up as Annie pulled the truck in front of the house and shut off the motor and lights. Her hands were shaking and her stomach was turning flips. She felt faint as she stepped out of the truck. The red brick structure was dark except for the windows in the office downstairs. Annie remembered the first time she had come to the house earlier in the summer.

Claire had opened the door and run down the walk when she heard the truck pull in. They had talked for a moment in the driveway, then Claire pulled Annie into the house and gave her the grand tour. She remembered how Dennis had spent the evening in the office and had only come out when she first arrived, exchanging pleasantries as if he had no idea of her relationship with Claire or that they had been friends for years.

Now she walked toward the oak door with the beveled glass, feeling like an executioner with an ax in her hand. Annie realized Claire would probably be able to read the news on her face. She put thoughts of Dennis and his "friend" aside and smiled as she reached for the door knocker.

～ ～ ～

Sitting at her oak desk in her sweat suit, Claire finished paying the bills and closed the checkbook. Dennis left the bills on the kitchen counter once a week; these had today's date written on the envelope. She leaned back in the chair and stretched her arms and legs in front of her, feeling the weariness in her muscles. Yawning, she glanced at the pile of student requests for transfers and realized if she was going to tackle this next part of her night, she was going to need more coffee.

As she left the office, there was a knock at the door. Dennis had finally left a message, albeit short, that he was having dinner with clients, so she peered through the curtains. Seeing Annie, she opened the door.

"Is something wrong? What in the world are you doing here?" She grabbed Annie's hand and hugged her close.

"I was driving home to my empty apartment and a frozen entrée and realized I'd much rather spend a little time with my girlfriend, if that's okay." She stepped into the foyer. "I would have called, but my cell died and my charger's at home."

"Not a worry." Claire motioned for Annie to follow her to the kitchen. She dumped some grounds into the coffee machine and turned to her friend. "I'm so glad you stopped by. Dennis is having dinner with a client and this house makes so many creaks and moans. It's a little unnerving when I'm here by myself."

They walked into the living room and Claire sat Indian style on a large leather couch, facing Annie, who sat with her elbows on her knees. "So how are your classes going?" Annie was running a finger around the top of the coffee mug, staring at the fluid inside. "Is something wrong?" Claire asked.

Annie shook her head, then started to cry softly.

Claire moved closer to her, holding her hand. "Honey, what's the matter?"

Annie sat hunched over, crying uncontrollably. Claire took the coffee cup from her hands and set it on the coffee table.

After a few moments, Annie took a deep breath and sat back. Claire pulled a box of tissues from an end table and waited for her to speak, still rubbing Annie's hand.

"Claire, I have some really bad news to tell you and I don't know where to begin," Annie said.

"It can't be all that bad," Claire said, thinking the news must be about Annie and the loser she'd been dating recently, Tim. "If it's about Tim, maybe it's just time to let him go. You two seem so wrong for each other, I hope you don't mind me saying. Him being a hunter and you a vegetarian..."

Annie shook her head.

"Just tell me. I'm tough. I can take it," Claire said, pushing the hair back from Annie's face.

Annie took a deep breath. "It's about Dennis." She closed her eyes, then opened them and looked straight at Claire, putting her hand on top of Claire's.

"I know this will be hard to hear, but he's lying to you."

9

Luke squeezed the bridge of his nose and closed his eyes for a moment. He leaned back in the dining room chair and closed his laptop. The e-mails were piling up from students with questions about his first assignment. At his Ohio college, kids just walked into his office and asked him questions. Hell, that kid Owens used to corner him after class nearly every day. But here, they didn't have time to stop by or wait after class. Luke imagined fingers flying over the Blackberry keys as they left their seats and walked right past him after class.

He stood and stretched, then walked to the condo's kitchen, where boxes still sat in a corner. He grabbed a beer from the refrigerator and snapped off the top. There were plenty of cabinets, so finding spaces for his beer mug collection shouldn't be difficult. He wiped out the cabinet closest to him and was reaching for the box when his cell phone rang.

"This is Luke."

"Hi, Daddy."

"Hi, sweetheart! What are you doing up? Shouldn't you be getting ready for bed?"

"I'm in bed. I asked Mommy if I could call you and say good night."

Feelings of love and inadequacy battled in his head. How could he have left his daughter? Yes, his relationship with Patty was strained, but wasn't a father's responsibility to be there for his child?

"Daddy?"

"Sorry, honey. I'm here."

He listened as she told him about a boy in her grade who tried to kick sand at her on the playground. She told him about a new doll his mother had brought her, then he said her prayers with her. Then Patty's chilly voice filled the line.

"Hey."

"Hey. Thanks for letting her call me."

"She's been asking for you all night. I'm not going to keep her from you, Luke."

He heard her exhale and could imagine the cigarette poised between her fingers. He'd made her promise not to smoke near Elizabeth, but she couldn't be more than a few steps from her room.

"I didn't say you would do that. I know you wouldn't. That's not what this is about, Patty. This is about doing what's best for Elizabeth. It's about moving on with our lives and making the best life for her."

He took a long drink of beer. The last thing he needed was to get her upset. It had already been a long day.

"Oh, I'm moving on. I just chose not to leave my child in the process."

"Patty, we've been through this a thousand times already. The chance to work at a college this size doesn't come along very often. I wish it was closer to Elizabeth, but I took the job because it's an amazing opportunity for my career."

"I suppose it's just coincidence that your 'pal' Annie works at the same college, huh?"

He closed his eyes and leaned against the counter.

"She's been my best friend for the last fifteen years. This has nothing to do with her. She just helped me get the job. She's like a sister to me and if you'd taken the time to get to know her, you'd see that."

"Tell me, Luke, who would you rather spend time with: Annie or Elizabeth?"

"I would pick Elizabeth every time, and you know it. She's my daughter, for Christ's sake."

He heard her exhale and cough. "I've got to go tuck her in. I'll talk to you later."

The line went dead. He laid his phone down and took another swig of beer. As he stood in the kitchen, a feeling of relief came over him that he'd moved. That level of tension wasn't good for Elizabeth.

∾ ∾ ∾

Claire recoiled from Annie. She pulled her hands away and sat back abruptly against the couch cushions.

"What are you talking about? What would Dennis lie about and how would you know anyway? You don't even know him."

"Honey, I don't know how to say this. I saw something tonight that you need to know about, but it's going to hurt. It's going to hurt really bad," Annie said.

"You're confused," Claire said, as she stood and walked toward the kitchen, shaking her head. "You don't know Dennis the way I do. Like right now, he's probably in his office finishing paperwork so he can—"

"Claire." Annie stood and walked to her side. "He's cheating on you."

"No, you can't be right. He would never—"

"I was meeting a blind date at a restaurant in the next county and saw Dennis having drinks with a young woman," Annie said. "They left the restaurant and walked to his car."

"It was probably just a client or maybe a coworker and he was walking her to her car. Maybe she had heard of a new restaurant and wanted to try it out and she invited him. You're making too much of this."

Tears filled Annie's eyes. "Honey, I parked across from his car and I saw them having sex in the front seat."

Claire stepped back from Annie, shaking her head, as if trying to shake the image from her mind.

"Stop it! Why are you trying to ruin my life?" she screamed.

"I'm trying to save you from being hurt by this man who swears he loves you," Annie said. She grabbed Claire's arms, held her tight and looked her in the eyes. "For whatever reason, he's with this other woman. He may come home to you, but you don't have him completely anymore."

The sound of a car in the driveway startled both women.

"He's home," Claire said defiantly. "I'll show you how wrong you are. Dennis may be busy and distracted, but he still loves me."

"Claire, I don't mean to hurt you. I just want you to know the truth."

Dennis opened the front door and walked into the foyer. His tie was loosened and his shirtsleeves were rolled up to the elbow. He swayed slightly as he laid his keys on the desk, then turned to see Annie and Claire standing in the living room.

"Well, what a nice surprise. Annie, I didn't know you were coming for a visit. I didn't see your car."

"Mine's in the shop again. I'm driving my brother's truck."

"It was nice of you to come over. I'm glad Claire has such

a good friend," he said as he crossed the room and kissed his wife on the forehead. The smell of whiskey filled the room. He turned to look through the mail on the hall table.

"How was your day, Dennis?" Claire said.

"It was good, very productive." He poured some whiskey into a highball glass and turned to them. "Can I get you anything, ladies?"

"No, thank you," Claire said. Annie just shook her head, looking at the floor. Claire stepped toward Dennis.

"You haven't been working at the office this whole time, have you? You've been putting in some long hours this past week. Do the other partners know you have a family that you want to see from time to time?"

"Yes, Claire, I just came from the office. I'm tying up loose ends on the Miller case and we have to have all our paperwork to the judge first thing in the morning. Remember I told you I'd be working late tonight?"

"So you didn't stop anywhere on the way home?"

His brow furrowed. "No, I came straight home from work. Why do you ask?"

His gaze shifted to Annie, who was shaking her head, still looking at the floor.

"Am I being accused of something?" he asked Claire.

"What's her name?" Annie asked, finally meeting his eyes and stepping forward. "Was the piece of tail you got in the parking lot at Henry's worth tearing apart your marriage?"

No one moved. Claire stared at him as though she was looking at a stranger. Dennis stepped toward Annie, looking at her as if she was crazy.

"I don't know what's wrong with you, but I think you have a lot of nerve coming into my house and accusing me of being unfaithful to my wife. You're upsetting Claire for no reason at all. Do you think this is funny, Annie? Is this some kind of sick joke to you?" Dennis was only two steps from Claire and Annie and was screaming. "Why would you come over here and bother Claire with some bullshit you made up for kicks?"

Claire turned to Annie, silently praying it was a joke. But Annie didn't back down; she stepped toward Dennis until their shoes were touching and pointed her finger in his face.

"I came over here after I left Henry's tonight. I saw you with 'your friend' in your car not an hour ago. How old is she, Dennis? Is she eighteen? I think you're the sick joke."

He stepped back and looked down at his drink. Claire watched his lips begin to move, then stop. He rubbed his temples and looked around the room. Finally, he spoke.

"I didn't mean for it to happen, Claire. You have to believe me."

Claire threw herself at him, arms raised, screaming, "Get out of my house! Get out, you lying, perverted piece of trash. You son of a bitch!" Her right arm came back and her fist landed on his chin. He stumbled back a few steps.

Annie grabbed Claire by the waist and pulled her back. Claire's entire body was pulsing and she fought to reach him.

"I don't want to hear anything from you. Just get out!"

Dennis straightened up and wiped at blood dripping down his chin from the cut her ring had made.

"I don't know what to say. I'm so sorry, Claire."

"Get out! Get out! Get out!"

Annie held Claire back as she lunged for him again. Annie glared at him and motioned with her head toward the door. He moved toward the door, then stopped and turned towards them.

"I didn't mean to hurt you, Claire. It was a stupid mistake and it's over now."

"I don't care, you bastard. Get out of my house!"

Dennis walked out the door and closed it behind him.

It was as if someone pulled an electrical cord from the wall. Claire cried out and collapsed on the floor at Annie's feet. Annie sat down and held her, stroking her hair, wondering if she had done the right thing by telling Claire.

10

✌⟩🙰

The small black SUV made its way slowly down the interstate through the thunderstorm. Pouring rain and fifty-mile-per-hour winds battered the vehicle, making it nearly impossible for Patty Fields to stay on the road. Gripping the wheel and leaning forward toward the windshield to see the dimly-lit road through the downpour, she took a deep breath. Her exit was only a mile away; she was almost home.

Stopping at the light at the end of the ramp, she glanced at the clock on the dash. Nine-thirty. The last three miles before home were country roads and she knew these like the back of her hand. There was another entrance at the front of the subdivision that most of the residents used, but she preferred this route. Only a few drivers even knew it existed and it would cut a few minutes off her time. She normally enjoyed the view and serenity of the area, but tonight, getting home was the only thing on her mind.

Leaving the lights of the highway, she turned left onto the dark road and started to relax. She was in her element now and would soon be in her warm, dry house with her daughter. Her foot involuntarily pressed on the gas pedal as she imagined the tight hug she would receive once she arrived home.

In a second, the dark night sky was gone and in its place was a blinding light paired with a thundering crack, then darkness again. The oak tree landed in the road seconds later just twenty feet in front of her. She turned the wheel as hard as she could and slammed on the brakes to avoid the massive trunk, but it was too late.

The driver's door hit the tree with such force that the vehicle flipped over the tree and continued to hurl side over side four more times before landing on the passenger side in the middle of the road, smoking and hissing.

Broken glass from the windshield littered the road as gasoline poured out from the ruptured gas tank. Fifty feet from the wreckage in the gully, Patty Fields took her last breath.

∾ ∾ ∾

She was being followed, but couldn't see through the darkness. Claire tried to run, but tripped every few steps. She heard a small moan behind her and turned to see what was making the noise. At first, it sounded like a small animal that was hurt, but the noise turned into panting and whispering voices surrounded her.

The air smelled of warm bodies and she backed up against a wall and started moving along it toward a dim light several yards away. Suddenly, a hand wrapped around her throat and started squeezing and another grabbed her arm.

She coughed and tried to kick at her attacker, but her body was pinned to the wall by an invisible force. She grabbed the thick fingers on her neck, but the grip was like steel.

"Claire, wake up."

The voice seemed to be coming from a distant room.

She ran her hand up the arm of the attacker, dragging her nails through the flesh. It didn't release her, but it began to shake her.

"Claire, stop it. You're hurting me."

Consciousness flooded over her and she realized she was holding Annie's arm. There were red marks from her elbow to her palm.

"Oh, God, Annie." She pulled Annie onto the edge of the bed, looking at her arm. "Did I do that?"

"It's okay. You were having a bad dream."

Claire sat up and looked around the room. Sunlight and breezes flowed through the curtains and the "Today Show" was on, nearly muted.

Suddenly, images of the previous night attacked her mind like stabbing knives in flesh: Dennis coming in drunk, Dennis giving her a peck on the forehead, Annie asking her question. The lies—and then the truth. Warm tears rolled down her cheeks as she relived the betrayal. He was intimate with another woman and he had lied to her about it. Then she looked at the clock on the nightstand: nine-thirty.

"I missed my class." She moved to jump from bed, but Annie laid a hand on her shoulder.

"I called your secretary and told her you were sick and wouldn't be in today." Claire started to protest, but Annie glared at her. "You're in no shape to teach today. Your class is being covered and your secretary said she'd have the grad students e-mail you on what they covered with the kids." She took Claire's hand and rubbed it. "Why don't you lean back and relax? I brought you some tea."

Claire pulled the comforter up to her chest, leaned back into the pillows Annie propped up and took the mug Annie handed her. She sipped the steaming liquid and placed the mug on the nightstand. She glanced at the other side of the bed, then back to Annie. But it was as if Annie read her mind.

"I can't imagine what you're going through right now, but I do know that I'm here for you as long as you need me."

Claire looked into Annie's face and saw tired, red-lined eyes looking back at her.

"You didn't get any sleep either, and then I nearly attack you while I'm dreaming. Why would you want to stay with me?"

Annie smiled. "Because you're my best friend and this is where I need to be. Besides," she pulled her legs in, Indian style, "I got someone to cover my classes too. We'll take a day off together."

The images from the night before flooded Claire's brain again and she felt warm tears escape down her cheek.

"It's okay. At least you know now what kind of man you're married to," Annie said. "I see you made one big change already." Claire rubbed her empty ring finger and started to cry harder.

"I took it off. I threw it into a corner of the bathroom. Last night, I felt like I was watching a stranger enter my house. He and I have barely been talking lately and now I find out that he's been making love to another—" She choked on the last word.

"So this wasn't a surprise? Did you feel your marriage was over before this happened? I had no idea things were that bad between you two."

"Our marriage wasn't so bad. At least I didn't think so," she said, wiping her eyes on the comforter. "How am I going to get through this? I'm not that strong."

"You are that strong and you're going to take it one day at a time. Today is about recovery. We'll worry about tomorrow later. Do you want some more tea?"

∽ ∽ ∽

The apartment smelled of whiskey. Two bottles lay scattered around the floor next to the bed. A gym bag lay on the floor in front of the dresser and the light in the bathroom was on, even though it was nearly noon and the room was dark except for small slivers of light around the edges of the curtains. Zach carefully made his way across the room to the window and pulled the panels apart.

The body on the bed curled into a fetal position. Lying half under the blanket, Dennis still wore his dress shirt and slacks, and his tie lay on the floor at the foot of the bed. His hair was disheveled, his face in need of a shave, but he was in one piece.

Zach watched his friend as he woke, looking around the room like a patient coming out of a coma. Rubbing his eyes, he licked his lips and turned toward Zach. The two men stared at each other for several moments before Dennis sat up slowly in bed.

"How did you get here?" Dennis said, holding his head.

"I was just about to ask you the same thing," Zach said. "Do you want some coffee? It should be finished by now."

"Yeah. Thanks." Dennis swung his bare feet off the bed. "You must know what happened last night if you're here."

"Yeah, I know," Zach said, walking into the kitchen. "When you didn't show up at work by nine-thirty, I called the house and Claire answered the phone. She told me you'd moved out, she wasn't sure where you were and said she really didn't care. I figured you were here."

Dennis was silent. "She told me you've been having an affair and that Annie had caught you in the act at a restaurant," Zach said.

"That explains a lot," Dennis said, lying back on the bed.

The company apartment would need to be aired out and cleaned, but right now, Zach had to get Dennis cleaned up and sober. Looking at the broken man in front of him, the task seemed daunting. He walked across the room holding a mug of steaming coffee from the kitchen.

"I don't know the whole story, but I do know you can't hole up in this apartment forever. You've got clients that need you and court appearances scheduled. I'm sorry things are bad between you and Claire, but you've got to admit, you haven't treated her that well lately."

"Is this your idea of tough love?" Dennis said, squinting up at his friend.

"No, it's my idea of helping my friend realize that he's not the victim here," Zach said, sitting on the edge of the bed. Zach handed the mug to Dennis cautiously. "Claire deserves the best, man. Where have you been?"

Dennis stared out the window. It was a long time before he spoke.

"You're right. I've been an ass and she does deserve better. I realized that when I started my second bottle last night. But there's nothing I can do about it now. I've been making bad decisions for months and now I've got to pay the price. She'll never take me back. I don't deserve her."

"Look, Dennis, you're a good man. You've just made some bad decisions lately." He looked down at his hands. "Did this girl mean anything to you? Were you in love with her?"

"No, no, no, nothing like that. That's the worst part. It was just sex."

Dennis stood and crossed the room. He remembered standing in this room just a few weeks ago with Becky, undressing her, caressing her skin as he removed her clothing, feeling her light touch on his chest, followed by her kisses. He shook his head and focused on Zach.

"It was someone at the office. It lasted most of the summer, but I never fell in love with her. It was strictly sex, but Claire won't care about that. All she knows is that I lied to her and betrayed her. I realize now that I should have worked harder on my marriage, but that's not going to help me now."

"Well, I stopped by the house and picked up a few changes of clothes. You can stay here for now until you find a place, but we need to keep the apartment open for clients. Go get in the shower. I'll clean up the room and then we'll get out of here."

"Okay, Zach." Dennis walked up and punched him in the arm lightly. "Listen, I appreciate you being here. I don't know what I'm going to do about me and Claire, but I can't let this destroy me. I'll win her back."

"Let's just get into the office. We'll talk more in the car."

"Thanks for the coffee. I'll be out in a couple of minutes."

11

✍︎

Annie had to admit it was good to get back to class. Claire had woken up that morning determined to jump back into her life and leave Dennis and their problems for a while. She had insisted to Annie that two days off was enough. After spending two hours on the phone with her attorney the previous day, Claire seemed more herself when they passed on campus that morning.

"Aren't you ready to go yet?" Annie asked, stepping into Luke's office doorway. There were papers piled on the desk and he sat hunched over in front of the computer screen with a pencil behind his ear and a pen in his hand. He looked up at her with a furrowed brow.

"Ready to go? Are you insane, Gordon? Don't you see all these papers I have to grade for tonight's class? How in the world am I supposed to finish this and go to lunch with you?"

She walked across the room and took the pencil from behind his ear, setting it on the desk. She sat on his desk facing him with her feet on his chair, rested her elbows on her knees and shook her head.

"I'm going to tell you two things right now that I want you to remember for the rest of your life, okay?" Luke looked slightly startled at her delivery of the line, but nodded at his friend as she squinted at him to emphasize her message.

"Number one, regardless of whether you have a mountain of paperwork or one report to grade, you always have to make sure that you leave time for you. That was a hard lesson for me to learn. I don't know if you remember, but I also started working here after teaching at a small community college. I'd come back to my office with a stack of papers taller than me and stay up all night several times a week because I thought the students had to have their papers returned to them in minutes."

"Have you taken a look at some of these kids?" Luke chuckled. "I've walked past a couple that I thought were bouncers-in-training. I don't want to tell them I don't have their grades yet. They could lay me flat."

"My late-night escapades only lasted about a month," she continued as if she hadn't heard him. "I was coming to class blurry-eyed and one day, the dean called me in his office. He told me he had heard from several students that I wasn't covering the material very well. He reminded me that he hadn't hired a machine to grade papers. He'd hired me because he believed I connected with the students and I was going to lose that if I didn't work out a schedule."

"I see where you're going with this," Luke said, placing his hand on her knee. "I promise I won't push myself so hard. You're right. I do need to eat and I've been correcting papers for more than two hours. A trip to the cafeteria is just what I need."

"Well, then, let's go and don't even think about bringing any work with you." She stood and walked toward the door. "This is strictly a fun lunch."

"Yes, ma'am," he said, standing and following her to the door. He stopped suddenly. "Gordon, what was the second thing you were going to tell me?"

She turned and poked him in the chest. "Don't ever make me wait when it comes to food."

∾ ∾ ∾

The smell of roasted meat and potatoes wafting from the student union kitchen pulled Luke back to his childhood, coming home after an afternoon of wiffle ball with his brothers. He could picture his mother in her favorite red apron, stirring some great culinary creation at the stove.

He looked around the room as he and Annie walked in. There were only a few students left from the lunch crowd, and most of them were either deep in conversation with friends or had their noses in books, cramming for afternoon tests. Then he saw her.

Claire Bennett sat at the other end of the room by herself, eating a salad and reading a novel. He caught up with Annie, who was in the lunch line.

"Here you go, stud." Annie handed him a tray and a steaming plate of stew from the woman across the counter, then put a bowl of salad on her own tray.

"Thanks, darlin'. Hey, I couldn't help noticing your friend Claire is here. Why don't we sit with her?"

"I don't know. She's having a rough week. Why don't we leave it up to her?"

Annie led the way across the room.

"Hey, babe." Annie walked up to the table. Luke was only a few steps behind her. "Do you mind if we sit with you?"

"No, not at all. Please, sit." Luke looked at her and noticed there was something different about her. She looked tired and distant.

"You remember Luke?"

"Of course. Nice to see you again." When she looked at him, it was as if she didn't see him, a change from their first meeting and all its electricity.

The three sat and shared small talk for about ten minutes until Susan, the history department secretary, came to the table in a rush and reminded Annie of a meeting with one of her students. He was waiting in her office.

"Oh, my gosh, I totally forgot," she said, almost tripping as she got up from her chair. "Do you two think you'll get along without me for a while? I'm so sorry."

"Gordon, get out of here. Claire and I will fine, won't we?"

She nodded. "Go take care of your student, Annie. I'll see you later."

He watched her and Susan walk away, realizing he had been relying on Annie for the conversation.

"You must be glad to have such a good friend so close by to help you transition," Claire said in a soft voice. He glanced at her face and realized her eyes were bloodshot. "Are you okay?" he asked, searching her face for the answer. "You seem distant, like there's something pressing on you. Is there anything I can do?"

He watched her search the courtyard and saw tears stream down her cheeks. She quickly brushed them away with her fingertips.

"No, I'm fine. It's just been a rough morning, that's all," she said, drying her eyes on a napkin and taking a deep breath. "Too many students, not enough time, you know the drill."

"I'm sorry. I didn't mean to upset you. I just want to help if I can."

The room was silent as if everyone was waiting for her

answer. He looked at the students around them, expecting to see all faces turned their way, but no one was looking. He turned back to face her.

"My husband and I split up this weekend. Our marriage is over," she said in a pinched voice. "We talked on the phone this morning and it turned into a screaming match that no one could win."

"I'm so very sorry," he said. He understood the look now, the red-rimmed eyes, the tired expression. "Are you all right?"

"I don't know, really. I feel like a character in a movie and I'm moving slowly through the scenes while the rest of my world is in fast forward."

"You're in shock. You can't expect your life to return to normal immediately. That's unrealistic." He sipped his tea, his eyes never leaving hers. "Give yourself time to heal and surround yourself with people who care about you. They'll understand."

"I just can't believe how much I put up with. Dennis worked late so many nights, or so he said. And he won't tell me who she is or how long the affair went on, but I feel I have to know. She took my place."

Luke reached over and took her hand. "I'm sure he didn't love her, but that doesn't matter now. The important thing is that you're moving on."

He looked up as a student approached the table. The girl's long dark hair and expressive eyes caught Luke's attention.

"Professor Bennett, excuse me, I was wondering if I could talk to you about the assignment that your assistant gave in class yesterday when you were out? Can we meet in your office later?"

"Sure, Becky. How's three o'clock sound?"

"Great. Thanks." Becky moved on through the tables.

Claire smiled. "One of my freshman students, Becky Overton. Nice kid. I'm hoping to help her come out of her shell this year. I think someone hurt her heart recently. She wrote an essay for me that she swears was based on a friend's experience, but I think she lived it. Maybe we can help each other this year."

 handhand handhand handhand

Annie watched as Luke reached up and turned the blinds in her office. He had walked in a few minutes earlier, and now he half-lay, half-sat on her couch, holding his stomach and talking about eating way too much. He'd just announced that the light was too bright.

"Are you about done bellyaching? Quit your whining."

"I work better in dim light with pillows and leather surrounding me."

"Well, if I hear snoring, I'm leaning over and pinching you. Now, c'mon, we need to come up with some good questions for our first tests."

Susan suddenly appeared in the doorway, a worried expression in her eyes.

"Luke, your mother is on hold. Just dial pound one two three."

"My mother? What in the world?"

He moved quickly across the room, picked up the receiver and dialed the numbers.

"Mom? Mom? It's Luke. Is something wrong?"

Annie and Susan watched as he sat in the chair and, a moment later, put his hand to his forehead and closed his eyes.

"When did this happen? Oh, my God. How's Elizabeth? Who has Elizabeth?"

He sat straight up, his eyes bright.

"Good. Thanks, Mom. Does she know what's going

on? Don't tell her yet. I'm on my way. I love you, too."

Luke replaced the receiver and covered his mouth with his hands. Annie came to his side.

"What's wrong?"

"Patty was in a car accident last night. The sitter called my mother at two a.m. and said Patty wasn't home yet. The police found her car on a small country road near the subdivision. According to the police, she died at the scene. Mom has Elizabeth."

"Oh, my God, Luke, I'm so sorry," Annie said softly.

"I have to leave right away for Ohio. Susan, can you help me?"

"Sure, Luke. I'll help however I can."

Annie took Luke's hand as she sat next to him on the couch. "What can I do?"

He looked into her eyes and clenched her hand. "Cover my classes for the week, give my test tomorrow and tell me how in the world I'm going to handle this."

12

✺

Movement on campus always slowed once the sun went down. Other than spectators of a spontaneous fraternity basketball game and students leaving late evening classes in a daze, the streets were usually empty. Claire glanced up at the lights in the dorm rooms. In one room, girls were dancing to hip-hop music and in the next, a male student leaned over his desk reading a book with his hands over his ears. Somewhere in the distance, she heard a pizza delivery person yell for someone to open a door.

After her morning classes, she had locked herself in her office to catch up on some paperwork for students who had registered late, and she ended up working through dinner. Now, she breathed deep as she crossed the courtyard, the cold air filling her lungs, the full moon casting light into the darkest corners.

Looking around, she realized how little things had changed since her days as a student walking the same path. The college grounds were small but more than two dozen buildings filled the seven-block property. In the center of campus was a courtyard shadowed by oaks, some standing fifty feet tall. Wooden and cement park benches were placed around the grass and the original ivy-covered classroom buildings lined one side of the yard while the older dormitories lined the other side. The student union building stood at the end of the yard.

Claire pulled out her keys and headed for the parking lot. Approaching a bench near the middle of the yard, she suddenly felt uneasy. Something was lying on the park bench. She couldn't tell if it was a person or an animal, but either way, it was large and sprawled on the bench.

As she came closer, she realized the shape was a person covered by a black bomber jacket. A nearly-empty whiskey bottle sat in the grass next to the bench. Stepping closer, Claire saw the girl's face. She put her hand on the coat and shook her gently.

"Ms. Overton, Becky, wake up." A cold wind sliced through Claire's thin jacket and pushed the whiskey bottle onto its side. Becky moaned as Claire looked around for help.

"Becky, Becky, wake up."

The girl's eyes opened slightly, but they wouldn't focus on Claire. Her long brown hair fell to the ground over the edge of the wooden bench slat. There was no blood or apparent injuries that she could see, but Claire's anxiety increased as she took Becky's wrist and felt with her fingers for a pulse. It was very slow and light and her breathing was shallow and labored.

Berating herself for not buying a cell phone when she had the chance, Claire ran across the courtyard to the nearest dormitory, ran into the hallway and pounded on all the doors.

"I need help. Please open the door. I'm a professor. Please open up."

Several students came into the hall in their pajamas.

"Someone, please call 911. There's a student unconscious outside."

∿ ∿ ∿

Coming down the ramp toward the airport food court, Luke watched his daughter waving wildly at him. Luke could see right away that Elizabeth knew nothing of her mother's fate; her smile spread ear to ear. Even though it had only been a few weeks since he'd seen her, she looked more mature to him. Brown curls danced on her shoulders as she jumped up and down, pulling on her grandmother's arm.

Maria Rosentino looked up at her son and smiled. It was the tired smile of a woman with grief she couldn't share. Luke stooped to pick up Elizabeth as she ran to him with open arms.

"Daddy, Daddy," she squealed, squeezing his neck.

"Hey, pumpkin," he said, kissing her soft cheek. "How's my girl?"

"Good. I want to pull your suitcase. Can I? Can I?"

"Sure, sweetie. Hi, Mom." He hugged his mother close.

"We haven't told her anything, Luke," she whispered in his ear. "She thinks Patty is still away on business." He pulled back and saw tears well in his mother's eyes, but she wiped them away before turning to Elizabeth.

"Lizzie, give me your hand. It's crowded in here."

"Lizzie? Who is Lizzie?" Luke asked, looking back and forth between his mother and daughter.

"It's me, Daddy. I changed my name." She stood a little taller as she made the announcement.

"Her best friend in first grade is an Elizabeth who goes by Lizzie," Maria explained as they walked toward the exit. "They wanted to be alike. She informed her teacher last week. We're giving it a try."

"Mommy said it sounds like a big girl name and I want to keep it, Daddy," his daughter said, stopping in front of him. "Will you call me Lizzie?"

Scooping his daughter in his arms and hugging her tight, Luke held back tears as he thought of Patty.

"If Mommy said Lizzie is a big girl name, then that's what we'll call you."

∾ ∾ ∾

Claire pulled hard on the steering wheel, bringing the Audi to an abrupt stop in the parking space nearest the hospital's emergency entrance. She jumped out of the car and ran to the ambulance's back doors as the paramedics lifted Becky out on the stretcher. Her complexion was more ashen than it had been in the courtyard and her moaning filled the air. Claire held Becky's hand as the men hurried through the double doors.

The bright lights in the hospital hallways nearly blinded Claire as nurses rushed past her. As they approached a second set of swinging doors, a nurse stopped in front of her.

"Are you her mother?"

Claire blinked hard as she watched the stretcher roll around a corner. "No."

"You can't go in there. We need you to fill out some forms." The nurse pointed to the nurses' station across the hall.

Claire stared at the woman in disbelief.

"I don't have any information about her other than her name. I'm a professor at the college and she's one of my students."

"Then you'll have to sit in the waiting area if you're not family. They'll come out with news as soon as they know something."

Claire walked across the room and sat in a plastic chair. Images of the evening raced through her mind and she tried to concentrate on what to do next. She had called campus emergency services and tried to track down Becky's parents, but the girl hadn't listed any phone numbers for them.

A few chairs to the right, a mother sat with a little girl on her lap. The child looked like she was about two years old. Her tired eyes stared hard at Claire and she held tight to a tattered blanket with ducks on it. Her mom was brushing her hair out of her eyes. To Claire's left sat an elderly couple. The man sat stooped with an oxygen tank next to him and tubes running to his nose.

Claire could hear the second hand on the clock across the room and a baby crying down the hall. All around her sat families, waiting with loved ones for help, and Becky was behind those swinging doors, all alone. Claire was more and more convinced that she was meant to find Becky and help her.

Almost an hour later, the doors swung open and a doctor in green scrubs walked to the nurse's station. The nurse pointed to Claire, and he walked over and sat next to her.

"Hi. I'm Dr. Thomas. Did you come in with the student about an hour ago?"

"Yes, her name is Becky Overton. I'm a professor at the college. Is she all right?"

"Normally, I wouldn't be able to talk to anyone but her parents about her condition, but we found this." He held out a piece of folded paper to Claire. She took the paper, unfolded it and read the document.

"We found it when we looked through her purse for identification. The nurse noticed the raised seal. It is notarized written approval by Becky naming you as her emergency contact."

Claire read the words for a fourth time. It stated that Claire was the only person to be contacted in an emergency and listed only her office number. She had no idea what Becky's situation was at home, but she realized she couldn't leave until she helped her.

"I heard the paramedics found Becky with an empty bottle of whiskey." Dr. Thomas looked at Becky's chart, then glanced up at Claire.

"Yes, that's right."

"It appears that was only part of the problem, Mrs. Bennett."

"Call me Claire."

"Along with the alcohol, Becky swallowed a number of sleeping pills. We're referring her to the psychiatric department for evaluation, but we believe this was an attempted suicide."

13

ᴊᴏᴄᴠ

Luke drove to his mother's house, pulled into the driveway and they all went inside. Lizzie ran into the guest bedroom and Maria followed Luke into the kitchen where he was pulling leftovers from the fridge.

"How are you going to tell her?"

He grabbed a bottle of beer from the door and looked at his mother. "I don't know, but I know I have to be the one to do it." He closed the fridge. "She needs to know the truth."

"Who needs to know the truth?" They both turned to see Lizzie standing wide-eyed in the doorway, holding a small doll in a red dress close to her chest. Luke looked at his mother, feeling his heart race.

"I was just telling Grandma…" His mind went blank.

"Honey, Daddy was telling me that for the past few days, Annie's forgotten to zip the zipper on her pants and he was trying to decide whether to tell her."

Lizzie let out a huge laugh and doubled over.

"Is that true, Daddy? She forgot to zip her pants?"

Luke watched his daughter cover her mouth as she

laughed harder, and he silently blessed his mother for her quick response. "Yep. Do you think I should tell her?"

"Of course you should. Someone might see her underwear."

The next morning, they played with her dolls, then he suggested they go to the park. Twenty minutes later, he pulled into a parking space. He had to break the news to Lizzie, but there was no easy way to do it. Turning off the car, he turned to her and saw that she was watching him with her head cocked to the side.

"Daddy, what are you thinking about? Are you thinking about Mommy? She has to stay longer on her business trip. That's why I was at Grandma's."

"I was actually thinking maybe you and I could have a picnic together. What do you think?"

"Yay! Really, Daddy? Can we swing? I want to show you how high I can go."

"Sure, baby. Let's get some lunch first. I brought some sandwiches and chips."

They walked through the grass until he found a spot at the top of a hill overlooking a pond. Three teenagers were doing jumps on their skateboards on nearby steps. As he flung open the picnic blanket, he remembered Patty bringing her paints and canvas to this area soon after they met, saying she wanted to capture the morning light through the trees. He remembered how she brought the picture to life.

Now, he watched their daughter as she took her sandwich from the plastic bag and handed him her bottle of juice to open. In between bites, she told him about her teacher and about her friend, the other Lizzie, and how the girls had gone to the mall with their mothers and bought beaded necklaces in matching colors.

They finished their lunch, Luke pushed Lizzie on the

swings, they tossed a Frisbee, then they lay down on the blanket. Lizzie sighed.

"I'm tired."

"Honey, I need to talk to you."

"Silly Daddy, you are talking to me."

He tickled her and laughed at her giggles. "I need to talk to you about Mommy," he said, leaning up on one elbow.

"What about Mommy?" Lizzie wiped a leaf off Luke's arm.

"Honey, I want you to think about Mommy's favorite place to go, the place where she's the happiest."

"She loves the zoo." Lizzie sat up and watched the boys skateboard down the hill toward the parking lot. "She loves the butterfly building. There are butterflies flying everywhere. They even land on your nose." She pointed to her own nose and smiled.

"Okay." He felt the lump in his throat returning, but looked at Lizzie and kept his composure. "Did Mommy ever talk to you about heaven?"

Lizzie turned to him with a quizzical look. "Isn't your Daddy in heaven? You said he went to heaven when he got real sick and the doctors couldn't fix him."

"Yes, sweetheart, that's right. Heaven is a place where people go when they die and it's a beautiful place, the most beautiful place ever."

Lizzie watched him and his stomach turned. How could he hurt his child this way? How could he tell her that her world was turning upside down? He took a deep breath and looked into her eyes.

"Honey, Mommy's not on her business trip. She was coming home late at night and she had a very bad car accident. The ambulance took her to the hospital and the doctors tried to help her, but she was hurt too badly." He took her hands in his. "She's not coming back because she went to heaven."

Lizzie stood up quickly, released his hands and stared at him with enormous eyes.

"Mommy died? Mommy can't be dead! I just talked to her the other day! She was fine! She wasn't sick! Daddy, you're lying! Why would you tell me Mommy was dead? She's not!"

His eyes blurred and he looked down at the blanket for a moment. When he looked up, she was running down the hill and was almost to the lake. He stood and chased after her.

"Lizzie, come back. Lizzie!"

∞ ∞ ∞

Claire couldn't believe what she was hearing. "You must be mistaken. Becky—"

"Claire, we made the diagnosis after pumping her stomach. She's still unconscious, but when she wakes up, she's going to be very sick for a while. I'm taking it from this note that there won't be any parents showing up?"

She handed the note back. "I really don't know about her family situation. I only know that she and I have talked about her college goals several times and she's never mentioned any family. May I see her?"

"She probably won't come around until morning, but she'll be very groggy. You should go home and rest."

"Let me give you my home number. Please call me when she wakes up."

He took her number and walked back through the swinging doors. Claire was unable to move for a moment, letting the doctor's diagnosis register. She couldn't get the words of Becky's essay out of her mind. Wiping away a few tears that escaped, she sat down and wondered if Becky's ex-boyfriend would visit her if he knew she was here. Claire made a mental note to ask Becky for his name and number once she woke up. Maybe they could reconcile.

∽ ∽ ∽

The sound of the phone made Claire jump and it took several rings before she found it under the comforter.

"Hello?" Her voice came out much huskier than she expected.

"I'm looking for Claire Bennett."

"Speaking."

"It's Dr. Thomas. Becky's awake now. You asked me to call when she woke up."

"Thanks. I'll be there shortly."

Thirty minutes later, she followed a nurse down the hall to the last room on the right. Three of the beds were empty and a curtain was pulled around the bed nearest the window. Claire walked to the far side of the bed and slid the curtain back.

Becky's skin was ghostly white compared to the dark circles under her eyes. Her dark hair was spread out over the pillow and an IV bag hung next to the bed with a clear liquid dripping into the tube connected to her heavily bandaged arm.

Claire stepped next to the bed and lightly touched her hand. Her eyelids fluttered and she stared at the opposite curtain for a few moments before turning and seeing Claire.

"Becky, it's Professor Bennett. It's Claire. How are you? Do you need anything?"

"Where am I?" Her voice was a scratchy whisper.

"You're in the hospital. I found you last night on a bench in the courtyard. You drank half a bottle of whiskey and the doctors said you took some sleeping pills, too." Becky closed her eyes. "I called 911 and they brought you here and pumped your stomach, but they said you'll be fine now."

"I don't want to be fine." Becky looked the other way as tears rolled down her cheeks. "You should have just left me on the bench."

"Becky, don't talk like that. Nothing could be bad enough that you would want to end your life."

Becky stared out the window behind Claire. The room was completely silent for a moment.

"Nothing matters. I thought it did, but it really doesn't. Classes, grades, none of it matters because when it's all done, I'm all alone." She looked at a ring on her right hand. The band was gold with a small ruby stone in the middle.

"He told me he loved me. He told me he could see us together for a long time. He told me all these things and now it's over. It's over and I don't want to be without him."

Claire watched Becky twist the ring. She felt Becky's loneliness but suddenly realized why she was the one to find Becky.

"Honey, you don't need a man to be happy in life," she said, taking the girl's hand. "You are the only one that can make you happy. No one can do that for you."

Becky now looked at Claire like she was seeing her for the first time. "When he held me in bed at night, I felt completely safe. He told me I was his girl and when we made love, it seemed like the rest of the world disappeared. I don't want to live without him," she said, her eyes closing.

"Shhh, Becky, try to rest," Claire said, pushing the hair from her face.

Suddenly, Becky opened her eyes. "You're not mad that I put you down as my emergency contact, are you?" She tried to sit up in bed but lay back in pain.

Claire shook her head. "I'm flattered, but I'm also worried about you. Why didn't you put your parents' information on any school forms?"

Becky's expression hardened. "My parents aren't in my life anymore."

"Can you tell me—"

"I don't want to talk about it."

Claire took her hands. "Okay, if you promise to talk to me when you're hurting, I won't ask you about your past."

"I promise."

"Becky, that essay was real, wasn't it?" Becky didn't answer, but fresh tears left her eyes. "Tell me, Becky. What was his name?"

14

His mind was blank as Luke sprinted down the hill, never taking his eyes off Lizzie. Her foot caught the root of an oak at the edge of the lake and she screamed as she tripped, then fell face first off the bank into the water. A second later, Luke jumped off the bank into the thigh-deep brown water, reached into the water and pulled her into his arms.

"Lizzie! Lizzie!" He stepped onto the bank and fell to his knees, hitting her on the back. She coughed and spat out lake water for a few minutes. When she caught her breath, he picked her up and held her.

"Lizzie, baby, I'm so sorry." She laid her head on his shoulder and cried softly. "I'm so sorry. I'm so sorry." He held her shaking wet body against his, his hand on the back of her head.

"It's just you and me now. I'm so sorry, but Mommy's gone."

"Daddy, she can't be gone." Lizzie coughed hard several times, then said in a quiet voice, "Who's going to take care of me?"

Luke stopped instantly and looked at her. Her hair was

hanging wet in front of her face. Luke pushed her hair back and wiped her tears. "I am. I'm going to take care of you. You're my family, baby. I'm going to take care of you."

"You're moving back here?" She leaned back in his arms and wiped her face with the back of her hand. There was a light in her eyes for a moment.

"No, baby, I'm sorry. I live in South Carolina now. You're going to live with me there. We'll move all your toys and your bed to my house in about a week." She stared at him and fresh tears dripped down her cheeks.

"What about my school and my teachers and my friends, Daddy? I have to leave my school and my friends. I don't want to move."

Luke pulled her back to his shoulder and felt her body shake as she cried again.

"You'll go to the school near my house and live with me. I'll work it out, darling. You'll make lots of new friends. I promise. Everything will be fine. I promise."

ᘓ ᘓ ᘓ

Becky stared into Claire's eyes and saw kindness and concern. Why was Claire still here? It didn't make any sense. Why would someone like Claire, a college professor, want to spend time with a freshman student she barely knew? Surely she had papers to grade and classes to plan. Why was Claire sitting on the edge of her bed, so interested in her life?

Maybe she didn't have any family or children of her own. She dressed so classy. Becky couldn't imagine her lugging kids out of car seats and juggling sippy cups. She didn't look like the mom type. Of course, she couldn't use her own mother as a model for all mothers; she was more like the model for anti-moms. Maybe Claire had a baby when she was young and put it up for adoption. Maybe Becky was the same age as Claire's daughter.

These thoughts ran through her mind, bumping into each other as another wave of nausea rolled over her. She closed her eyes, held her stomach and scrunched her legs toward her body.

"I'm so sorry, Becky. Here I am questioning you and you're in terrible pain. Let me get the nurse."

Becky reached out toward Claire and touched her leg. "Please stay."

The words were barely a whisper, but she didn't want Claire to go. The last thing she wanted was to be alone. The wave passed and she opened her eyes. Claire was still sitting on the bed and she'd moved closer to Becky.

"Okay. Whatever you need." Claire brushed the hair away from Becky's eyes and then held her hand.

"Why are you being so nice to me?" The moment the words left her lips, she wondered why she said them, but knew she had to know the answer. Even her own mother had never treated her with this much tenderness. "You don't even know me."

"I can't explain it." She rubbed the back of Becky's hand, then looked over her head at the IV bag. "I feel bad that you don't have anyone in your life that you can rely on."

"This is all because I put your name on that stupid emergency letter." Becky stared down at the sheets. The nausea was nothing compared to thinking Claire felt responsible for her now. "I've dragged you into my pathetic life for no good reason."

Claire placed her fingers under Becky's chin and lifted her face until their eyes met and locked.

"I don't ever want you thinking that I'm being dragged anywhere with you. I found you in the park and I had them bring you to the hospital. I'm sitting here with you because I want to be here, not because you dragged me anywhere."

Becky searched Claire's eyes for the expression she was used to seeing. It was a mix of resentment and disgust and her mother had perfected it over the years. But Claire smiled and continued to rub the back of Becky's hand as if being here was part of her plan for the day.

"Look, I'm a big believer in fate. People meet people every day for a reason. They might not know what the reason is right away, but it's there and it's real. You see me as your professor and you expect that I should just see you as a seat number in one of my classes, but I think you and I are supposed to help each other."

"Help each other? How?"

"You're in a new town going to college classes for the first time and you don't have any family or friends to support you. I'd like to help you with that. Be there for you, answer questions, whatever you need." Becky started to question her, but Claire added, "Because I want to be there for you."

"But what could I do for you?"

"Stop by and see me from time to time and let me know how you're doing. Tell me about your classes and assignments. I know college can be overwhelming at first with all the reading and tests and assignments, but I know you have what it takes. Hearing your progress will make my day. It'll make me happy if I can help you be successful."

"But that sounds like it's helping me more than you. I don't understand."

"Becky, I've got a lot of challenges ahead of me this year at school and at home. Hearing from you will be a nice break from my workload."

Becky noticed then the small lines around Claire's mouth and the darkness under her eyes.

"Yeah, I could do that." She relaxed for the first time all day. "I'd like that."

15

∽∾

The sky over the cemetery was a steel gray, mirroring the mood of the crowd surrounding the grave. More than two hundred people attended Patty's Mass and more than half braved the misty cold wind to hear the final blessing at the gravesite.

The Rosentino family and Patty's mother, Judy Fields, stood close together at the head of the coffin. They surrounded Luke and Lizzie as the priest read a few prayers, then held out a single rose to Lizzie to place on the casket.

Dressed in a simple black dress and black patent leather shoes, Lizzie clung to Luke's leg and refused to look at the priest. Luke took the flower and lifted Lizzie into his arms. She put her head on her father's shoulder, her arms wrapped around his neck. He walked with her to the side of the casket, stopped and after a moment, he whispered in her ear. She turned and put the flower on the lid of the coffin, but suddenly began crying uncontrollably.

"No, no, no, don't put my Mommy in the ground! She's not dead! She has to come back to me! I miss her so much!"

Kicking and screaming, she wiggled from Luke's arms

and tried to open the box, crying for her mother. The crowd moved forward toward her, but Luke's brother Tom was the first to reach her. He picked her up and moved to the back of the crowd. Family and friends moved in procession, each placing a flower on the casket. Over Lizzie's sobs, the priest said the final blessing and thanked everyone for coming. The clouds and guests shed tears for Patty and Lizzie.

∾ ∾ ∾

"Your house is so beautiful, Maria." Judy Fields sipped her tea in the kitchen. "I see why Patty loved coming here with Lizzie. It has such a warm feel to it."

Maria slipped a napkin across the table to Judy. "Thank you. How are you holding up? Are you doing all right?"

Judy sighed and wrapped her hands around the small blue teacup. "As good as can be expected for a widow who just lost her only child."

The past few days seemed like an unending nightmare. First, the call from Maria in the pre-dawn hours, saying that Patty had been in a car accident and to come to the hospital immediately. She didn't remember driving, but she'd never forget sitting down with the emergency room doctor who told her Patty had died hours earlier. Then, talking with Luke the next evening, she realized he would be moving her granddaughter to live with him in South Carolina. Her only family gone in less than two days; she would be completely alone.

She envied Maria her seven children and ten grandchildren.

The Rosentino house was brimming with people. Conversations filled the rooms with children's high-pitched laughter adding to the harmony. Her own apartment seemed like a cave after a visit to Maria's house. Watching three of Maria's smallest grandchildren chasing each other under the oaks in the backyard, Judy felt the lump in her throat grow.

"I remember how it felt to lose Carl twenty years ago." She realized how small her voice sounded. "But this is a whole different pain. Patty and Lizzie were all I had. Maria, I don't know what I'm going to do without them." She covered her mouth as fresh tears streamed down her cheeks. She felt as if she would never stop crying. Maria reached across the table for Judy's hands and held them tight.

"Let me make this very clear. First of all, you are not alone. Your daughter gave birth to our granddaughter, a granddaughter you and I share. So you are my family, that's an indisputable fact."

Judy looked into Maria's eyes and realized how much Luke resembled his mother. All the Rosentino children had the same brown hair and green eyes.

"Secondly, Lizzie is only moving a few states away. Yes, Patty is gone, but Lizzie is only going to be a phone call away. Judy, she's going to need both her grandmothers in her life, especially now. I see some granny road trips to South Carolina in my future and I'd love to travel with you. What do you think?"

"I think you're a good friend and I appreciate you." Judy stood and hugged Maria tight.

"C'mon, let's go find that little beauty and get some hugs. Grab those chocolate chip cookies on the counter. I think I saw her out back." She looked back at Judy wiping her eyes. "Take a breath and watch that face when we walk up together. It's like a thousand twinkling stars."

Judy took a sip of tea, picked up the cookies and smiled at Maria.

"I think I saw her under the tree by the garage."

ৡ ৡ ৡ

Dark clouds surrounded the plane. Luke looked out the window across the aisle, hoping to see a glimmer of light, but saw only dreary gray. He felt as if he were in a submarine in a drab, lifeless sea. He turned on the overhead light and looked down at Lizzie. Right before takeoff, he had raised the armrest. She'd laid her head on his leg and fallen asleep almost instantly.

She looked peaceful for the first time in days. He realized that just a week ago, he had talked to Patty about setting up child support payments, and now this fragile young child was his complete responsibility. A month ago, he had been a man starting a new life in a new town with a new job. Now his life was turned upside down.

He had called the school near his condo to enroll her and packed her bedroom. Tom had offered to drive the U-Haul and help Luke transition Lizzie. Luke was quick to accept his help, thinking he would have to move the boxes out of his second bedroom to make it her bedroom, and there were so many other things to do. The list seemed endless.

Lizzie had been quiet since their picnic, except for crying at the cemetery. She stayed next to Luke day and night as friends and family stopped by to pay their respects. He remembered his father's death and tried to remember how he had behaved afterward, but it didn't matter. Lizzie's situation was different. She was just a child. He had been a teenager when his father, a relatively healthy man, had died from a massive heart attack. His mother had been a rock after his death, never showing any weakness.

"Do you want this extra pillow?"

Luke looked across the aisle. An older woman held out a small pillow. "My Henry asked for it when we got on the plane, but it doesn't look like he's going to need it." Luke looked past her at Henry, who was sleeping against the wall of the plane, his head tilted back, his mouth wide open. "It looks like your daughter could put it to better use." The woman reminded Luke of Maria, the way she tilted her head when she looked at him. He took the small pillow from her and carefully slid it under Lizzie's head. "Thank you. These planes aren't really made for sleeping. She's exhausted, though, so the bumpy ride isn't bothering her." He put his hand out to her. "I'm Luke and this is Lizzie."

"I'm Theresa," she said, taking his hand. "I noticed she hasn't moved since we took off. She must have had a long week at school."

"Her mother died earlier this week and she's coming to live with me in South Carolina." The words fell out of his mouth before he could stop them. He hated when people he didn't know told him their problems, but it seemed natural in this case.

"Were you and your wife married long?"

"We never married, but we were a family for a long time. Patty and I split up a few months ago and she had custody of Lizzie. Now Lizzie's going to have switch schools, move to a new state, make new friends. I'm feeling pretty overwhelmed right now."

It was quiet for a moment, then Theresa touched his arm and he looked up.

"Luke, that little girl has a lot of changes to handle, but she can't handle them alone and neither can you." She looked at him with a sudden seriousness. "You have two choices. You can let your family in to help you and Lizzie get through this time without too many battle scars or you can try to do everything on your own, suffer through this time alone and be miserable. Just remember, your decision on how to proceed is going to affect Lizzie and her family for the rest of her life."

"Everyone has been telling me that and I know it's true. But ultimately, her well-being is completely on my shoulders. I don't know where I'm going to get the strength."

Theresa reached under the seat and fumbled in her large black purse. She pulled out a small black pouch and handed it to Luke.

"Are you Catholic, honey?"

"Yes, ma'am."

"Then here's your answer." Luke opened the pouch and pulled out a black-beaded rosary with a detailed gold crucifix. Instinctively, he wrapped it around his hand as he had been taught in grade school.

"Saying the rosary helps me when my strength is drained. Just pull it out when you feel empty and you'll feel better right away."

Luke ran his fingers over the small beads, similar to the one Grandma had given him after his first Communion as a boy. He realized the beads were shining. Looking out the window, he noticed they had finally risen above the clouds into the blue sky. He smiled at Theresa and thought about the week after his father had died.

A vivid memory came to him of a full house of aunts and uncles taking care of him and his siblings while his mother met with visitors. He remembered wishing at the time they'd all leave, but now knew their strength had kept Maria on her feet. Turning off the overhead light and thinking of his family, he closed his eyes and prayed.

16

Dennis glanced at his Blackberry. There was an e-mail from Donna asking him to come to the front lobby. It must be urgent. He had told her he was not to be disturbed during the negotiations with Forte and Shelton. It had taken weeks to set up this meeting. Looking across the table at the attorneys from Forte and Shelton, he realized he had been daydreaming about Claire. He had left messages at the house several times this week. All he wanted to do was talk. Maybe she was busy at the college. That might explain why she hadn't returned his calls.

"Listen, I think we should all take a ten-minute break and get some fresh air, some coffee and clear our heads. We need to come to an agreement today and I think everyone could use a breather." He looked around the room at each lawyer. Chairs scooted back as everyone grabbed their handhelds and started dialing.

Dennis stepped out into the hall and walked toward the lobby. He heard Donna say he would be there in just a moment. He turned the corner to see a short heavyset man in an outdated suit standing at the front desk.

"Donna, did you need me for something?"

She tipped her head toward the man in the suit.

"Can I help you with something?" Dennis stepped up to him, hoping Donna hadn't interrupted his meeting for a sales pitch. She should know better.

"Dennis Kincaid?"

"Yes."

"Here." Dennis looked down at the man's hand. He was holding a folded blue paper.

"You've got to be kidding me." He mentally ran through his client list. He couldn't think of any of his cases worth contesting. He took the paper from the man's hand and unfolded it while the man quickly left the lobby.

"Donna, next time, please get Zach in a situation like this. I'm in the middle of negotiations and they have to be done..."

The rest of his thought was lost when he saw Claire's name on the paper. He was holding divorce papers. Claire was filing for divorce after only two weeks of separation.

"You've got to be fucking kidding me!"

She had filed under charges of adultery and irreconcilable differences. He flipped through the pages, feeling the veins in his forehead throbbing. She wanted the house, the car and a million-dollar settlement.

"That fucking bitch! She can't do this to me!"

"Mr. Kincaid? Are you all right?"

He couldn't think straight. He stared at the papers, not seeing the words. The idea was crazy. So he'd slept with Becky. That was the end of the marriage? Claire wasn't like that. They had been together for almost a decade. She loved him. This must be a mistake.

"Mr. Kincaid? Sir?" He felt slender fingers touch his arm and he jumped. Donna was looking at him with wide eyes. "Are you all right?"

"Donna, tell the group we're going to have to finish the rest of the meeting another day. There's something I have to take care of right now."

"But sir...should I get Mr. Grossbart to take over?"

"Yeah, fine. Just do it. I'll be back later." Dennis pushed on the glass door and ran down the stairs toward the street.

∾ ∾ ∾

It was crowded for a Monday afternoon. Students crammed the sidewalk in front of the library. Backpacks lay strewn in front of wooden benches covered with students, some lying on their backs reading while others sat poring over books, iPods blaring. After battling her way through the outdoor study hall, Claire came to the courtyard where she'd found Becky.

She shielded her eyes from the sun with her hand and saw Luke sitting on the bench. He sat next to a large stack of booklets, thumbing through one, making notes with a highlighter. His frown disappeared as she approached him.

"Ah, finally, a friendly face. That's the bad part of being the new guy in town. I only know about a dozen people by name so far and I think there are ten thousand people on campus at any given time. I've been feeling a little like a needle in the campus haystack, if you know what I mean. Please, sit down," he said, scooting to the side of the bench.

"Are you grading papers? I don't want to bother you if you are."

He stared at her blankly for a moment, then looked at the papers. "Oh, no, no—I'm trying to find the best school for my daughter."

"Your daughter? I didn't know you were married." Claire sat and picked up the booklet on the top of the stack. A girl in a plaid jumper smiled from the cover.

He stared across the courtyard at the dorms. "I'm not. I never was." He paused and sighed, glancing at her apologetically. "You really don't want to know all about me, do you?"

"I want to know whatever you want to tell me." She looked into his face and noticed the circles under his eyes. "I'd like to help you like you helped me."

He hesitated for a moment, then reached in his wallet and pulled out a picture of a young girl with curly brown hair and green eyes matching his own. He handed Claire the picture by the edges.

"This is my daughter, Lizzie. She's six years old and up until about a month ago, I lived with her and her mother Patty in Ohio. Patty and I lived together for seven years. We fought for the past year, so we separated a month ago. A few hours after you and I sat together in the cafeteria the last time, I got a call from my mother who told me that Patty had been in a fatal car accident the night before."

"Was Lizzie in the car with her?"

He quickly shook his head. "I flew to Ohio that afternoon and spent the next few days making funeral arrangements, packing Lizzie's things and getting her ready for the move down here. My brother rented a U-Haul and moved all her things here this weekend. He's with her now; they're setting up her room at my condo," he said. "I'm trying to be strong for her, but sometimes the enormity of the situation hits me like a boulder."

He picked up the stack of booklets. "Like how am I supposed to figure out which school is the best for her? Should I send her to public or private school? Should I drive her or let her take the bus, and what about after-school care? What am I going to do about after-school care?"

"First of all, I'm so sorry for your loss. Last week must have been one of the worst of your life. First, you lose this woman that you loved and then to see your child in pain. I'm sure you have thousands of questions, but I don't have any easy answers for you. What I do offer you is my friendship and an ear to listen."

He breathed deep and took Lizzie's picture from her. "I think my immediate problem is learning how to cook for a six-year-old. I've been told chicken nuggets and macaroni and cheese would be great every night, but that doesn't sound right to me. What do you think?"

Claire laughed. Even in such a painful situation, he still had a sense of humor. She inhaled deeply, catching the scent of his cologne in the air.

"I'll tell you what I'll do. Put away the chicken nugget bag and come to my house with Lizzie tomorrow night. I'll make the three of us a home-cooked dinner."

"I couldn't ask you to do that," Luke said, cocking his head at her. "No, that would be an imposition."

"It's only an imposition if you ask if you can come over. I invited you. Say yes. Please? I'd love to have company. It's been so quiet the past few days."

He started to answer, but she put her hand up and looked at him with wide eyes.

"Even better: I'll invite my neighbor Carley and her daughter, Sabrina. Carley's wanted to come over for weeks and that way Lizzie would have another girl to play with. What do you say? A relaxing evening that doesn't involve frozen food? Maybe even some adult conversation?"

Luke laughed and nodded. "You're on. I'm sure Lizzie's tired of playing Barbies with old Dad. Men don't understand the world of Barbies, did you know that?"

Claire nodded and laughed.

"We'll come over on one condition. I take all you ladies out for ice cream after dinner, my treat."

"Deal."

They shook on it. Claire searched the bottom of her purse and finally found a scrap of paper at the bottom. She wrote her address and phone number and handed it to him. She'd started to walk away when he called her name. She turned to see him walking toward her.

"Here." He was holding a piece of pink paper with Snow White's picture at the top. The words "I love you, Daddy!" were written in bright crayon colors and at the bottom was a phone number written in pen.

"Just in case you want to call and talk later."

Claire smiled, took the paper and waved to him, already thinking of ideas for dinner.

∾ ∾ ∾

The throng of students thinned as she approached the liberal arts building. The university's oldest oaks stood guard over the entrance of the two-story brick building at the edge of the campus. Approaching the entrance, Claire removed her sunglasses and slid them on top of her head. She stepped into the lobby and moved toward the stairs, allowing her eyes to adjust to the darker tiled space. A few students passed her, eyes scanning small screens, earbuds blaring what they called music. It was just noise to Claire.

Most of the time, she resented how easily the kids learned the latest technology, but for once, it didn't bother her. For the first time in weeks, she felt lighthearted. She had a dinner to plan, she had to call Carley and invite her and she'd have to straighten up the house tonight. She pulled open the second floor door and stepped directly into the path of a student. The girl glanced at Claire, muttered what sounded like "sorry" and ran down the stairs as Claire stepped out of the stairwell. The door slammed behind her and she breathed deep.

Her classes were over for the day and the department was empty – the secretaries had the afternoon off. Claire had practically the whole floor to herself. No students, no administrators, no faculty, no one asking her for her time; just peace and quiet to work on her lesson plans. She had to laugh at herself as she approached her office. She realized how stressed she'd been the past few weeks. Hearing Luke's situation, she realized he needed a friend. They could both use a friend.

She pushed open her office door, hearing the familiar squeak, and set her books and purse on her desk. Running her fingers through her hair, she walked to the window, smiling when she thought of Luke standing at the freezer door, searching for chicken nuggets. Her mind wandered, imagining what it would feel like to have his arms around her. She closed her eyes and pictured him in her office, leaning down to kiss her. She swore she could smell his cologne in the room.

"Hello, Claire."

She jumped and turned toward the voice. Dennis sat in an old brown chair behind the door. His black pants, jacket and starched white shirt stood out against the faded brown. She watched as he pushed the door closed and stared at her.

"What are you doing here?" She heard the tension in her voice, but hoped he hadn't. "You've never come here." He stood and reached into his inside suit pocket, pulling out a folded blue set of papers and shook them at her.

He took a step toward her. "What is this, Claire?" He held the paper by the top and let it flip open. She glanced at it and read "Petition for Dissolution of Marriage" near the top. "I'm sitting in a meeting at my law firm and I'm called to the lobby where a man I've never seen before hands me these papers informing me that you want to divorce me. Is that right, Claire?"

He was standing within inches of her, scowling at her. Suddenly, she realized he'd boxed her into the corner. She was inches from the wall and her desk and credenza were behind him, blocking her exit. She started to shake, looking at the phone on the opposite side of the desk and realizing he was still looking at her. But his expression had changed. The anger was gone and he ran his fingers down her arm with a light touch, laying the documents on her desk.

"We need to get back together. I know you still love me and we can work this out," he said. "She meant nothing." He ran his finger down her cheek and lifted her face to his. "Besides, you need me in your life. I'm your husband. You love me."

"You cheated on me with another woman, Dennis."

The air conditioning kicked on and out of the corner of her eye, she saw something flutter off her desk. Dennis reached down to the floor and picked up a pink sheet of paper and read it. He took a step back.

"Where did you get this? Are you seeing someone already?"

She felt her heart racing in her chest and tried to grab the paper from his grip, but in one move, he moved it out of her reach and shoved her against the wall, his hand around her throat. She tried to pry his fingers away, but it was no use.

"So you have a boyfriend? That's why you're in such a hurry to clean me out, huh? Thought you'd get the house, a car, and a million dollars? What about the firm I've sweated over for a decade and made into one of the most successful firms in the state? You think you're entitled to a part of it, too?"

"What were you thinking, Claire? You only kicked me out two weeks ago and now suddenly you're ready to pay me back by screwing some new guy with a kid?"

She looked into his eyes and saw nothing that resembled the Dennis she had married. She was getting lightheaded and without thinking, she brought her knee up into his slacks. He immediately dropped to the floor on his knees and then rolled onto his side in a fetal position, howling and cursing.

She jumped over him, ran out of the room and down the hall. She shoved the stairwell door open, took the steps two at a time, shoved the first floor door open and ran across the lobby toward the sunlight. Tears blurred her vision as she shoved open the front door, looked to her left and ran to the right directly into Luke.

"Whoa, what's going on? Are you okay?" He grabbed her by the arms and looked into her face. "Why are you crying?"

She whispered in a hoarse voice, "Dennis," and pointed toward the building. He set her down on the stone retaining wall behind her, swung the door open and ran through the lobby.

17

✶✶✶

Luke jumped the stairs two at a time. He braced himself as he opened the second floor door. No one was in the hall or at the reception desk. He stood quietly for a minute and heard a thud down the hall. He walked quickly toward the sound and listening closer, he heard heavy breathing. Prepared to fight, he stood in front of Claire's office door and looked in.

A man in a dark suit was on his knees on the floor next to Claire's desk. His head was down and he was holding on to the side of the desk with one hand, breathing heavily. Luke felt some of the tension in his body relax as he walked toward the doorway.

"Are you Dennis? What did you do to Claire?"

Dennis looked up and Luke felt bad for him for a moment; his face was flushed and angry and he was gasping for breath. "Who the fuck are you? It's none of your God damn business who I am."

Luke stood in the doorway and looked down at Dennis. "Actually, it is my business. Claire's my friend and she just came running out of this building, hysterical, saying you were in here. But it looks like she took care of things herself."

"So you're the asshole who's screwing her. You need to stay the hell away from her! She's still my wife and there's no way that I'm going to let the two of you take everything I've earned." Dennis sat on the edge of her desk, still bent over. "It's not going to happen, you son of a bitch!"

"I don't know what you're talking about, but I do know that you need to leave this building and not come back. Claire told me about your affair and the divorce and I intend to be there for her as a friend. She certainly needs one after the way you treated her. So why don't you leave this office and building, get in your car and leave Claire alone?"

As the last word left his lips, there was a crash down the hallway. It sounded like a large piece of equipment hitting the floor. Luke stepped into the hall and looked in the direction the sound had come from. An instant later, out of the corner of his eye, he watched Dennis spring from the desk and run toward him. Their bodies collided and Luke's back hit the wall across from Claire's office.

Dennis' fists fired into Luke's stomach and sides with a fierceness Luke didn't expect. He doubled over and tried to cover his face, but one punch connected with his jaw. The force took him to the floor. He tasted blood in his mouth.

"What happened between Claire and me is none of your fucking business. She is *my wife*."

Luke looked up as Dennis leaned over to catch his breath. Luke swung his foot into the back of Dennis' knees and Dennis hit the floor. Dennis screamed in pain as he pulled his hand out from under his back. At the same moment, the door at the end of the hall opened and two campus security officers ran down the hall toward them.

"Gentlemen, stand on your feet with your hands behind your head."

Luke looked toward the men and saw Claire behind them with her hands over her mouth. Dennis continued to cry out in pain and Luke stood against the wall.

"That's him. That's my husband. He attacked me." Claire pointed to Dennis and the men picked him up by the arms.

"He broke my God damn hand!" Dennis pointed at Luke. "Arrest him for assault."

The men looked at Luke as they held Dennis' arms behind him. "What's your name, sir?"

"Luke Rosentino. I'm a professor and I came up here because Professor Bennett came running out of the building, looking like she'd been attacked. I came up to her office and this man attacked me." He put his hand to his mouth and pulled back blood.

"Do you mind coming down to our offices to straighten this out, sir?"

"Not at all."

Claire came toward Luke and handed him tissues from her bag.

"So you're going to let him go but you're treating me like a criminal?" Dennis yelled. "I came to talk to my wife and he came in and attacked me for no reason." Luke watched as Dennis struggled against the officers, but they held him in place.

"We're going to sort this out in our office. Mr. Rosentino, this way, please."

"I'm right behind you."

Claire leaned against the windowsill next to Luke. "I'm so sorry that you had to get involved in my problems. He hurt you." She touched his chin lightly and he winced. "He had no right to do that."

Luke lifted her chin. "It was my decision to come up here. He was yelling that you and I are planning to take everything he owns. I told him to leave, then I took my eyes off him for a moment and he jumped me. But I tell you what—he won't come near you again." He started to follow after the officers.

"He won't come near either one of us again," he said over his shoulder. "You can count on that."

18

୵ଠଠ

Driving into the darkened parking garage of his office building, Dennis pulled the Mercedes into a space on the second floor and turned off the engine. He slammed his palms against the steering wheel. Curse words spewed into the air along with the name Luke Rosentino. Pounding on the steering wheel, he relived the past few hours and how the officers treated Luke with kid gloves while he was stuck in a small room with one of the officers, being questioned like a child. Luke had talked with the campus police director with Claire, free to go whenever he pleased. He'd caught the two of them looking through the window at him, watching him like a caged animal.

A police cruiser with sirens blaring sped past him as he walked out of the garage. He glanced at his watch and realized it was after five o'clock. He still had at least an hour or two worth of work to do. Rain started to fall and he ran the last hundred feet into the lobby, nearly running into employees leaving the building, pointing their umbrellas skyward.

A few moments later, the doors opened at the fourth floor and he stepped out. Compared to the noisy, pushing crowd in the lobby, the fourth floor was dark, deserted and silent. He unlocked the glass doors and stepped into the firm's lobby. He thought he heard a scratching noise from the hallway near his office as the sound of another police car siren bounced off the walls. He felt the urge to turn on some lights, but stopped himself.

You're just tired, he thought. You've been in this office for years and have never had a problem. Plus, Donna said she locked the office so you know no one else is here.

Still, he couldn't shake the feeling that someone was in the office. He walked down the hall past Zach's office on the way to his own and decided to put his cell phone in his pocket. He wouldn't admit he was scared, but there was no use taking a chance.

Dennis opened the door to his office and stepped inside. The blinds were down and closed, so the room was near pitch dark. Lightning lit the room for a few seconds, then the darkness returned. Dennis felt along the back of the client chairs, and searched for the pull cord of his desk lamp with his back to the door.

The sound of the door slamming made Dennis jump and turn at the same moment.

"Who's there?" he whispered. "Show yourself."

The only noise was from the traffic outside. He leaned backward over the desk and with a shaky hand, he pulled the light cord. The lamp bathed the room in light and Dennis saw Rodney Landis sitting across the room from him in an oversized easy chair. He was staring at Dennis with a smug expression on his face. He held his briefcase on his lap.

"Rodney, what in the hell are you doing in my office?"

Rodney didn't move. The smirk never left his face.

"What the hell are you doing here?" Dennis said. "How the fuck did you get in my office?"

He reached in his pocket for his cell phone. Rodney was on his feet and in Dennis' face before he pulled it out.

"What exactly are you going to say to the police when they answer? Please come help me! A man is trying to blackmail me and I can't get out of it? Give me your phone. This is between you and me."

Dennis stood toe to toe with Rodney, fists clenched. "You break into my office after hours, threaten me and you expect me to just take it?"

Rodney didn't blink. "Yeah, I do."

Dennis had never stood this close to Rodney. He never realized Rodney was at least four inches taller than him and the look in his eye made Dennis wonder what damage this man was capable of causing. If he had half the information he said he did, Dennis' professional reputation would be ruined forever. Not to mention legal action and possible jail time. He handed Rodney his phone.

After a moment, Rodney walked around the desk and sat in Dennis' leather chair, leaning back, putting his hands behind his head and smiling.

Dennis suddenly realized his silent alarm was under the desk directly in front of Rodney. He hadn't seen any weapon yet and he could just run from the office. But then Rodney would be alone in Dennis' office. He couldn't leave him here.

Dennis felt the walls closing in on him. His decisions from ten years ago seemed harmless and he considered the contacts he'd made those years crucial to starting his own firm and his current success. He had only remembered Rodney after he explained their past connection. He had racked his brain looking for the reason for the vengeance.

"Penny for your thoughts, counselor."

"Why me?"

"Excuse me?"

"What did I ever do to you that you're bringing up these allegations now, ten years later?"

"You think you're above the law, Kincaid?" Rodney sat forward in the chair and stared at Dennis. "You assumed that someone rich and powerful like you can't be brought down? That was a stupid assumption. I know what you did and no one else does. That puts me in the driver's seat and you under my shoe."

Dennis sat in the oversized chair and ran his hands through his hair. "What do you want?"

Rodney stood, gathered his belongings and walked toward the chair. He stood towering over Dennis.

"The cost of my silence is one million dollars. I'll give you one week to get it to me."

19

The sunset blazed in color. Pale yellows and oranges lined the horizon while darker oranges and hot pink streaks illuminated the full white clouds above. The view from his condo's balcony was the main reason Luke had bought the space. The apartment he had shared with Patty in Ohio backed up to woods. He felt claustrophobic most of the time he'd lived there. This balcony off his bedroom overlooked a lake with a city park beyond it. Leaning against the doorway, he watched the colors reflect off the ripples of the lake.

"You all right, bro?"

Luke turned to see Tom in the doorway. He was carrying his toolbox toward Lizzie's room. Tom's trip, originally scheduled to last only two days, had turned into a week. Luke smiled at his older brother, wondering how he would ever repay him for all the help he'd given.

"Yeah, I'm fine. I was just thinking about...never mind."

Tom walked in, laid down his toolbox and switched on a lamp.

"Don't give me that. What's her name?"

"Nothing. It's not important."

"Dude. You're staring at a sunset with a smile on your face. There has to be a woman involved."

Luke looked at him and grinned. "It's no big deal. Lizzie and I are invited to dinner at a friend's house tomorrow night. You're on your own for dinner."

"A friend, huh?" He walked to Luke. "So am I right? This friend is a woman?"

"Could you be any more nosy?"

Tom stared, waiting for an answer. Luke had to laugh.

"Yes, it's a woman. Her name is Claire Bennett and she's a professor at my college. Actually, she's a department chair. Anyway, she just felt sorry for me and invited us over for dinner. She's inviting her neighbor and her daughter so Lizzie will have a playmate while we're there."

"Sounds nice. And you want to be more than friends, I'm assuming?"

Luke remembered Claire's smile, the toss of her hair as she walked and the green specks of color in her blue eyes.

"You don't have to answer that. It's written all over your face."

"Goddammit, Tom, I don't know what to do. I can't stop thinking about her, but the timing is all wrong. She's going through a divorce, and with me just getting Lizzie and Patty gone, it couldn't be worse. I can't jump right into another relationship. What would that look like to Lizzie? I've got so much on my plate right now."

"So just let her be a friend and help each other. It doesn't have to be anything if you don't want it to be. Just enjoy each other's company and see what happens. There's a sports bar down the road I've been meaning to try anyway. Just make sure Lizzie has a good time."

Luke turned off the lamp and followed Tom out of the room. "I just hope I don't make a fool of myself."

❧ ❧ ❧

"A million dollars in a week? Are you out of your freaking mind? You expect me to pay you a million dollars to avoid the chance of you ruining my life?" Dennis looked up at Rodney and began to stand, but Rodney pushed him back into the chair.

"Do you understand what I'm saying, Dennis?" Rodney said quietly, as if he was talking to a small child. "I have proof that you stole thousands from our former employer and in order to keep that information to myself, I need cash and lots of it. See, my little announcement wouldn't hurt me at all. But you..." He paused and looked around the room. "All this would go away."

Dennis just glared at him, and Rodney added, "I suppose if the money is going to be a problem, I could always call my friends at the city newspaper and have them start an investigation, but you don't really want that, do you?"

The two stared at each other for what seemed like five minutes, then Dennis stood.

"I'm not giving you a single penny. I looked over your documents or 'proof' as you call it and there's not enough there to convict me of anything. It's your word against mine and I'm a respected member of this community. No one would believe you. You have no standing. You're nobody." Dennis began to walk around his desk. "I think you should leave now and take your so-called proof with you. I really don't want to see you ever again."

"The only way you're going to get rid of me is by making me a million dollars richer. And how to do that is not my problem, that would be yours," Rodney said calmly. He lifted his hand from his suit pocket and extended his arm straight and pointed a small revolver at Dennis' forehead.

"I guess up to this point I've been too easy on you, so let me clarify. I need one million dollars in one week or every media outlet in this country will have your name and picture plastered on the front of their paper, Web site and news program. But if you try anything smart and I don't get my money, I'll shoot you dead and then sell your story to the highest bidder. Either way, I get paid. You just have to decide how badly you want to live."

ॐ ॐ ॐ

Claire cracked the spaghetti in half and dropped it in the boiling water as the doorbell rang. She walked quickly from the kitchen to the front door, wiping her hands on a kitchen towel before she opened the door. Carley stood on the porch with Sabrina. The little girl held a large bagged Italian bread loaf in one hand and a bag of dolls in the other. Claire opened the door wide and they walked in.

"Hi, Carley, I'm so glad you could make it. Here, honey, let me take this."

"Say hi to Ms. Claire, Sabrina." Sabrina waved to Claire and walked into the living room, where she sat down with her dolls in the middle of the floor.

"How are you doing, honey?" Carley hugged Claire tight. "I didn't know what you needed so I brought some bread. Are they here yet?" she said, peeking into the living room.

"No, silly, it's just us right now. They're due in a few minutes." The two women walked into the kitchen and sat down.

"So, tell me all about Luke," Carley said with wide eyes. "How did you meet? Do you like him?"

"Of course I like him or I wouldn't have invited him to dinner," Claire said, laughing.

"That's not what I meant and you know it." Carley spun the kitchen chair around and straddled it, resting her chin on her hands on the back of the chair. "This could be just what you need: a nice romance, a friend, maybe with benefits?"

Claire turned from the stove and stared at her neighbor.

"Carley, you know Dennis only moved out a few weeks ago. I get the definite impression you're trying to fix me up already."

"You haven't answered my question, lady. I just wonder if there's chemistry."

The doorbell rang and Carley went to check on Sabrina. Claire gave the spaghetti another quick stir and walked to the door. She realized her heart was racing and took a deep breath before opening the door.

Luke smiled at her and her mind went blank. He wore a Georgia State University sweatshirt with blue jeans that fit in all the right places and allowed Claire to imagine things she hadn't thought of in weeks. Shaking her head slightly, she invited them both in and took the two-liter soda bottle from Luke.

"Who is this beautiful young lady?" she said, smiling at Lizzie, who stayed behind her father's leg despite his attempts to bring her out.

"This is Lizzie. Lizzie, this is Mrs. Bennett. She and Daddy work together."

Claire looked down and looked right into Lizzie's eyes. "Lizzie, don't listen to your daddy. You can call me Miss Claire. Come on inside. There's another little girl here I'd like you to meet."

Just then, Sabrina raced into the hall. "Is she here yet?" She stopped in her tracks, stared at Lizzie, then grabbed Lizzie's hand. "Do you like Barbies?"

Lizzie looked up at Luke, then nodded.

"Come on in here. I brought all my dolls and we can play together." The girls walked off hand in hand.

"Looks like you're off duty for a while," Claire said playfully. "It's good to see you. C'mon in the front room. I want you to meet Carley."

20

❦

Claire watched Lizzie from across the table as she giggled with Sabrina. The girls had been joined at the hip since they arrived. Her smile told Claire that leaving her new friend at the end of the night would be difficult.

"They seem to have hit it off," Carley said, turning to look in Claire's direction. "Isn't it funny how two people can connect so quickly?"

Claire felt the blood rise to her cheeks as she looked down at her plate. Carley might have meant the girls but Claire had a feeling she was matchmaking like she had been doing most of the evening. Claire stood and started to clear the table and was surprised to see Luke clearing his and Lizzie's places.

"You don't have to do that. I can clear the table. Please sit and relax."

"That's not how I was raised," Luke said, picking up Lizzie's cup. "Everyone spends time together and dinner is a time of sharing. Please let me help you in the kitchen. It's the least I can do after that delicious dinner."

They walked into the kitchen, leaving Carley and the girls talking about their favorite television shows. As Claire placed the dishes on the counter, she felt Luke's arm brush hers as he scraped the plates. She turned around to find herself only inches from him. Looking up, she wondered how it would feel with his arms around her and how tender his lips would feel on hers. The chemistry in the room was so powerful, she felt her legs become weak.

"Are you okay? You looked pale for a moment there. Let's sit down." Before she could respond, his hand was under her elbow and he led her to one of the kitchen chairs. He pulled a chair for himself and sat facing her, their legs touching. Her thoughts raced as she sat looking at her hands in her lap, feeling his leg resting against hers. It was comfortable and she wanted more, but reassured herself it was all in her mind. She looked up and realized he was staring at her.

"I'm sure I'm way out of line here, but I feel I need to say something. Ever since we met, I've felt a connection with you, a connection I hope you've felt too or else I've just put my foot and my ankle in my mouth." She started to open her mouth, but he held his hand up and leaned in closer. "Don't answer yet. If I'm going to look like a fool, I might as well go all the way."

"I can't believe I'm saying this and acting this way with the new directions our lives are taking, but I think we can help each other. He took her hand, his green eyes wide. "I want to be your friend, Claire, and maybe more if you'll let me."

She wondered if he could hear her heart beating. To her, it was deafening, making it difficult to think. She leaned toward him and kissed him softly. He touched her cheek and she felt the warmth of his skin.

He laid his forehead against hers and whispered, "I never expected this. I dreamed it, but I never expected it. You're so beautiful, Claire. I never planned to feel this way, but I need you. I can't get you out of my mind."

He pulled back and saw her eyes filled with tears.

"Oh, God, I didn't mean to upset you. I just—"

"Shhh," she whispered, putting her fingers on his lips. "You've just put into words all the thoughts that have been spinning in my head for weeks and I didn't have the courage to say." He pulled her hands to his lips and kissed them. "I've felt this connection since the day we bumped into each other. I don't know where this is going to lead, but I want to find out with you."

He shook his head in disbelief. "I expected you to leave the room when I started talking. You invited me into your home for a casual dinner with my child and here I am asking you to be my girlfriend."

"Do you know how many different outfits I tried on before you got here? I never dreamed you felt the same way."

She kissed him again, then they heard the girls coming and quickly scooted their chairs back. The girls and Carley came into the kitchen, telling stories of Barbies and toys and a game they'd played with Carley.

"Looks like you need more help with the dishes." Carley winked at Claire and walked to the sink as the phone rang.

Claire picked up the phone and stepped into the dining room.

"Hello?"

"It's me." The sound of Dennis' voice turned Claire's stomach.

"What do you want?"

"I'm meeting with my divorce attorney in the morning and she needs some financial documents relating to the firm. It's in one of the boxes in the garage. I need to come over tonight and get those papers."

"Tonight's not a good night for me." Claire heard Luke and Carley laughing in the next room with the girls. "You'll have to get them another night."

"I need those papers tonight, Claire. I don't want to intrude on your new life, but I need to come over."

"Listen, I have to go. We'll talk tomorrow."

Claire pushed the "End" button on the cordless phone and placed the receiver on the base. Looking at her hand, she realized she was trembling. Images of that afternoon filled her mind and she took a minute to calm down, then walked back into the kitchen.

"Everything okay?" She looked across the kitchen. Luke was looking over his shoulder at her with his hands in the dishwater.

"Hmmmm? Oh yeah, everything's fine." She turned to the others and tried to inject herself into their conversation about cartoons and which show was the funniest, but she could feel his eyes burning into the back of her neck. She wasn't about to let Dennis ruin the evening.

When the girls and Carley went into the living room to watch one of the shows, Claire picked up a dishtowel and started drying the plates and putting them away.

"That must have been some phone call," Luke said.

"Excuse me?"

He was looking at her with his head tilted to the side. His expression was so calming, she exhaled deeply.

"It was nothing. I'm sorry." He continued to look into her eyes with a slight smile on his face. There was such kindness in his eyes.

"You can tell me."

A thousand thoughts ran through her mind, but she said softly, "It was Dennis."

The moment the name left her lips, she wanted to pull it back. She watched as Luke went back to washing the glasses, but the smile was gone.

"He wanted to come over and dig through boxes in the garage for some papers he needs, but I told him no. He can't just barge in with no notice and assume it's fine. Anyway, I took care of it. I'm done talking about him. I'm not going to let him ruin this fantastic evening. I have some dessert for everyone. Will you help me?"

They brought a small cake with plates and forks to the dining room and the girls came running.

"We need to get going," Luke said ten minutes later, picking up his and Lizzie's plates.

"We should go, too. It's getting late and it is a school night," Carley said.

Both girls started to whine in protest, but Luke and Carley helped Claire wipe down the table, then corralled the girls toward the door. Carley and Sabrina walked across the grass and Luke put Lizzie in the booster seat, closed the car door, and walked back to Claire.

"Are you sure you're going to be okay? Maybe Lizzie and I should stick around and make sure Dennis doesn't come by. After what happened at your office, I don't think you should be alone."

She took his face in her hands and kissed him. "Thank you for worrying about me, but I can take care of myself. He won't come over. And you need to get Lizzie home." She waved at Lizzie, who yawned and waved back.

"If you're sure." He pulled her close and kissed her gently on the lips. "I'm looking forward to being able to do that from now on." He smiled. "A lot." He kissed her again and stepped backwards, their hands sliding apart, then fingers, then fingertips. He blew her a kiss, got in the car and drove off. Claire stood in the driveway watching the tail lights get smaller and smaller, then walked toward the house.

21

Dennis barely remembered driving to the house, but was careful to park far enough away so she wouldn't see his car—yet close enough to watch them all leave. He was probably too close, but the tinted windows would keep him hidden.

He hadn't planned to push the issue, but hearing Luke's voice changed that. Claire had hung up on him like he was some telemarketer interrupting her dinner. Luke was in his house, hitting on his wife when the divorce hadn't even begun. And Claire...this wasn't like her. She had always stood by him and now suddenly, she was tossing him out like yesterday's trash and had moved on to Luke.

Suddenly, two little girls ran to the cars giggling as the neighbor and Luke came out, hugged and laughed. It was like he had already moved in. What infuriated Dennis was how open Claire was being about her new relationship. The two of them held hands in the driveway like they were newlyweds, then they kissed. At first, he thought he was hallucinating. Was he really watching his wife kiss another man in their driveway?

It took everything he had not to drive across the lawn and run Luke over like roadkill. It was no longer about getting the papers for tomorrow's meeting. She was embarrassing him in front of the neighbors, making out with her new man.

Finally, Luke drove past Dennis and Claire went back in the house. A moment later, Dennis was in the driveway. He walked to the front door and knocked. The porch light switched on and she appeared at the door, saw him and for a moment, he thought he saw fear in her eyes.

"What are you doing here? I told you that tonight is not a good night for me."

"I need to talk to you. Can I come in?"

"After what you did today, you expect me to ever let you into my house again? You tried to choke me in my own office, and now you want to come over here at night and I'm just supposed to let you inside?" Her face was getting red and she stepped onto the porch.

"Let me explain this very clearly so there's no confusion. Don't come by here anymore, don't call me, don't come to my office." She was nearly screaming by this point. "If you have anything to say to me, call my lawyer."

"Claire, I just don't understand why after all the years we've been together, there's this sudden rush to end things so quickly." He stepped toward her and she took a step back, looking at the door. "Yes, I cheated on you, but it meant nothing. I'm sorry, but that can't be the reason you're ending our marriage."

Suddenly, the front of the house lit up and Dennis heard a car pull into the driveway and brake hard. He turned to see Luke jumping from the car and walking quickly toward him.

"Get the hell away from her!" Luke shouted. "Claire, get back in the house. Now!"

From the corner of his eye Dennis saw her go into the house and shut the door. The next second, Luke was standing over him. He had a good six inches on Dennis.

"You need to leave now and not come back." Dennis stood toe to toe with Luke and hatred filled every fiber of his body. Why was this man here? The urge to fight and kill raged in him.

"This isn't your business," Dennis said in a low voice. "You don't belong here." He clenched his fists, fighting the desire to lay Luke flat. "This is between me and my wife. You don't have a part to play in this."

Luke laughed. "Your wife? She's done with you, pal." He leaned in closer. "It's time for you to go now."

Every cell in Dennis' body wanted to drop Luke to the ground and kick him until he stopped moving. He pictured Luke lying in the grass, bloodied and still. But then there would be police called and neighbors watching and charges filed. They stood still, staring at each other for almost a minute, then a high-pitched voice came from the car.

"Daddy, let's go. Let's go home. Daddy!" Luke blinked, but only for a minute. The little girl started crying. Dennis realized he had an opportunity if Luke reacted, but another thought came to mind. He didn't have to solve this here.

"I'll go, but you need to stay out of my business. She's my wife."

Dennis slowly walked to his car. Luke didn't move as the Mercedes rolled down the driveway and sped away.

22

ตูว

Turning on the lights in his apartment, Dennis suddenly felt like a caged animal. Compared to the size of Claire's house, the four walls of the front room seemed to close in as he stepped into the room. He had only rented the apartment a few days earlier, but already hated it. It had one bedroom and a tiny alley kitchen. There were two hundred more just like it in his complex filled with people he had no interest in knowing.

He had bought a mattress and some bedding, but everything else was in boxes. Laying the newspaper on the counter, he walked into the bedroom and lay down on the mattress.

Thoughts and images raced through his mind like children darting around a playground. He felt the room spinning and tried to make sense of what just happened. Earlier that day, he thought getting back together with Claire was an option. He'd visualized them sitting together and talking out their differences. It would be a long night, but he was willing to be completely honest with her.

Instead, he arrived to find her with another man, Luke Rosentino. He felt sick to his stomach picturing the two of them kissing in his house and front yard. She turned against him and insulted him in front of her lover and he was banished from his own home by her new boyfriend.

Rolling on his side, he wondered why the name Rosentino sounded so familiar. It seemed he had just heard his name a day or two earlier. On the floor next to his bed were half a dozen magazines, including *Time* and *Newsweek*. He remembered flipping through them a few nights earlier and seeing a family portrait that suddenly seemed important. Picking up *Time*, he flipped the pages until he found the photograph.

The words "Real Estate Giant Expands West" jumped off the page along with a picture of well-dressed professionals in an office that reminded him of his own. He searched the faces, and it only took a few seconds to find what he was looking for. The tall man on the end of the back row had the same eyes and build as Claire's new lover.

The photo caption read "Rosentino family members (posed here in 1999) surround matriarch Maria Rosentino, including sons Bob, Tom, Tony, Alex and Luke in the back row." Scanning the story, Dennis learned Luke's mother was the president of Rosentino Development and most of her children were executives in the family business.

The story told of the company's growth in the thirty years since Maria's husband, Alex, started the company in a small town in Ohio. Most projects were on the East Coast, and a new casino in Nevada was the Rosentinos' first project west of the Mississippi.

Flipping the page, Dennis read that, of Maria's five sons and two daughters, six were involved in the company. The reporter noted the exception, writing that Luke had changed his major in his junior year from business administration to history and was currently teaching at a college in South Carolina.

Dennis felt his blood boil when he read Luke's quote on his professional decisions and the ensuing move south. "My love of history and the desire to help others understand the complexity of our past overwhelmed me in college. My father's business has seen amazing growth, but I see a clear future for myself in South Carolina and hope to work closely with my new colleagues."

Pages fluttered as the magazine flew across the room. Papers and clothing left their place on the dresser as wild hands cleared the surface. A ceramic lamp hit the wall, splintering into thousands of pieces. Dennis was filled with a rage that he'd never known before and he wanted to hurt Luke. His heart was racing as he relived being banished from his own home by his wife's new lover.

Then he remembered the little girl in the back seat crying out for Luke. She was obviously the apple of Luke's eye. In a split second, Dennis grabbed the magazine from the floor and turned back to the photograph. Then his cell phone rang in the kitchen. He walked down the hallway and picked it up off the counter.

"Dennis Kincaid."

"Dennis, it's me, Becky. Do you have a minute?"

A smile crept across his lips. "Honey, I've got nothing but time for you."

༄ ༄ ༄

Luke heard the roar of Dennis' Mercedes as he turned at the street corner and gunned the engine. Claire stared at the spot where the car had been and crossed her arms and shivered. The air was still and the only sounds now were the crickets in the bushes. Claire stood still as a statue and he watched a single tear flow down her cheek. She wiped the tear away, but otherwise didn't move. He felt guilty for leaving her by herself. He should have stayed; he'd had a feeling Dennis would try something stupid.

"Let me get Lizzie, then we'll go inside."

Claire turned, startled, as if she'd forgotten he was there. He ran to his car, pulled the keys from the ignition and lifted Lizzie from her booster seat. He moved quickly across the grass back toward Claire, with Lizzie running behind him.

"Come on, let's go inside." He took Claire's elbow and led her through the front door and to the sofa.

"Daddy, I want to go home. I'm tired."

He looked across the room at Lizzie, rubbing her eyes. He turned to Claire.

"I'll be right back."

He walked Lizzie into the kitchen, poured her a glass of milk, found cookies in the pantry and got her settled at the table.

"I want you to sit here and enjoy these cookies and milk. I've got to talk to Claire, then we'll go home." He kissed her forehead and stepped into the living room. Claire was sitting in the same spot, staring at the wall. Her expression was blank; her eyes distant. He sat next to her and took her hand.

"I think we should call the police."

She turned to him, shaking her head.

"No, I can't do that."

"Claire, he attacked both of us this afternoon and now he's coming to the house at night trying to talk to you? You're not safe here. If I hadn't turned around and come back," he paused as he imagined Dennis pushing his way into the house, "he might be in this house right now doing God knows what to you."

"What are you going to do? Move in here to protect me against my own husband?"

Luke leaned back against the sofa pillows. "I think I should stay here tonight." He watched as she started to protest, but held his hand up. "Lizzie can stay in the guest room and I'll sleep here on the sofa." He sat up and cupped her cheek in his hand. "I can't let you stay here alone. It's not safe."

She stood quickly and walked across the room, then turned to him, shaking her head.

"He's not some criminal. He's my husband and he wouldn't hurt me. He got served with our divorce papers today. Any man would be upset about that."

He moved to her side and looked down into her face. "He's a man and he already hurt you." He hugged her close to his chest and felt the tension in her body. "He's not acting rationally right now. Claire, I'm only trying to protect you."

"You think I need protecting from my own husband? I'm not a battered wife, Luke. I'll be fine. I didn't let him in the house. I didn't."

This stubbornness was a side of Claire he hadn't seen before. He couldn't believe she was defending Dennis. "Tell you what. I'll call Annie and see if you can stay with her. I'm sure she won't mind and she's got an extra bedroom."

"Luke, this wasn't a big deal. You're making too much out of this. Sometimes Dennis has trouble controlling his temper, but he would never hurt anyone."

"Give me just a second." He kissed her cheek and stepped into the next room. A minute later, he was back.

"Annie said she'll stay up until we get there." He saw the hesitation on her face, and kissed her again. "Please, let me take you to Annie's for a few days. I won't be able to relax if you stay here by yourself."

Her face softened. "You're sure Annie doesn't mind?

"I'm sure."

"Okay, but I need to pack a small bag. I still think you're making too much of this."

"That's okay. I'd rather be safe than sorry. Go ahead. I'll

wait in the kitchen with Lizzie."

He watched her walk upstairs, then went into the kitchen and sat at the table. Taking a cookie from the package, he looked at Lizzie's small cookie-covered lips and smiled.

"We're almost ready to go, honey. We just have to stop at Aunt Annie's on the way home. Finish your milk."

23

Shutting his laptop, he stretched his legs out straight and cracked his back and neck and looked at the clock on the wall. Only then did he realize he'd been grading papers for three hours straight. He rubbed his eyes and stood, stretching his arms over his head. Having no classes to teach on Fridays seemed great, but he had yet to enjoy a full Friday off.

Luke sat back down and leaned back in his leather chair. Looking around his home office, he was glad he'd taken the time to arrange this room first. Papers and tests needed to be graded whether he worked at school or home.

The condo was completely quiet and his mind drifted to Claire and the night they had dinner. Annie had met them at the door of her condo in her robe. Claire had insisted up to the last moment that she didn't want to put anyone out, but Annie had prepared her guest room and had welcomed them with a smile and a hug. Knowing Claire was safe from Dennis' temper was a huge relief for Luke.

The majority of the papers were graded and now he could relax with Lizzie for the afternoon. Her school was closed for the day and he hoped to take her to the zoo. He heard the front door open and little footsteps running down the hallway.

"Daddy, we're back," Lizzie called, rounding the corner. "Get ready, here I come." She jumped into his lap and wrapped her arms around his neck. The past three hours slipped away and he hugged his daughter tight. It doesn't get any better than this, he thought. A sweaty and tired Tom appeared in the doorway.

"What's wrong, Uncle Tom? Playing Frisbee with a six-year-old too much for you? How old are you, anyway?"

"Very funny. I'm only two years older than you, little brother." Tom laughed, turning to Lizzie. "We had a good time, didn't we, pumpkin?"

"Uncle Tom was talking to a pretty lady while I was on the swings. What was her name, Uncle Tom?"

Tom's face flushed and he glanced at Luke. "Paige. Now let's go get ready for lunch, little girl. Hit the bathroom and watch your hands."

Luke stood and followed Tom toward the kitchen. "Was she pretty, Uncle Tom?" Luke asked in a high-pitched voice. "She didn't interrupt your Frisbee catching, did she?" Then laughing, in his own voice he said, "I hope you got her number since you used your niece as bait."

"Yes, she's pretty and we're having dinner tomorrow night, smart-aleck. Now if you'll excuse me, I'm going to soak my old fat body in a hot bath." Luke stifled a laugh and started toward the kitchen.

Tom turned back to him. "Oh, and just to let you know, Lizzie might need an extra hug tonight. She was talking about Patty a lot today."

～～～

Dressed in a dark navy blue suit, Claire walked into her attorney's conference room. Susan Clarkson stepped in behind her and closed the door.

"Are you ready, Claire? This could get ugly."

"How much uglier can it get, Susan? My husband cheated on me God knows how many times and my marriage was a lie. The man I loved and was faithful to for ten years screwed another woman in public in his car, and an hour later, he wants to pick up his life where he left off. Then I start to pick up the pieces and he comes to my office and... never mind."

"What? Did something happen? He didn't hurt you, did he?" Susan leaned forward and tapped the paperwork in front of her. "If he touched you, we can bury him."

"No, no, no. Nothing like that. I just want this to be over."

"You'll get through this fine. It's tough, but so are you." Susan led Claire to a chair, then sat beside her.

Claire tried to concentrate on the calming words Annie had shared on the phone an hour earlier, but images of Dennis at the house the night before raced through her head. Then the nightmares flew through her mind. Dennis staring at her as he made love to women; every nightmare was someone different. She could never see their faces, but she always woke up remembering his cold hard stare.

"Claire?" Susan was touching her arm. "Are you all right? You don't look so hot." She handed Claire a glass of water.

Just then, the door across from her opened and Dennis walked in, followed by a tall woman wearing designer clothes and a killer smile. The sun moved behind the clouds, draining the room of its light and adding to Claire's uneasiness.

Dennis' companion stepped over to Susan and extended a hand.

"Veronica Coroso, legal counsel for Mr. Kincaid. Are we ready to begin?"

She and Dennis took their seats across from Claire and Susan. Claire could feel Dennis staring at her. She remembered how tightly he squeezed her throat the day in her office, and she thought for a moment that she should tell Susan about that day and the previous night at her house, but she closed her eyes. She just wanted the whole ordeal to be over. No one had witnessed the attack and dragging Luke into this battle wasn't fair to him.

Susan opened the file in front of her. "I think we're all aware of the circumstances leading to these proceedings. My client claims adultery and months and possibly years of deception led to the collapse of this marriage. We're petitioning for the residence, Ms. Bennett's Audi and an alimony settlement along with equitable distribution of any joint assets."

Claire was watching Susan but a sudden movement across the table caught her eye. Dennis dropped his head, shaking it, then looked up and glared at her.

"Do you want my blood too, Claire? How about my head on a silver platter? I admit I made one mistake, but it sounds like it worked in your favor. You get my house, my car, my money, and you have a new boyfriend! Lucky you! What do you want next? My firm?"

"Please control your client," Susan said to Veronica in a calm, professional voice. Veronica pulled Dennis back in his chair and whispered in his ear.

Claire searched Dennis' face for some similarity to the man she had loved, but she didn't see any. The veins in his forehead were throbbing and his face was blood red. She turned to Susan and listened as Veronica agreed to most of her requests.

☙ ☙ ☙

Dennis knew the lawyers were talking, but he couldn't make out what they were saying. It didn't matter; he knew they were fighting over his assets like dogs over a juicy bone. He closed his eyes and remembered Luke kissing Claire the night before in his yard. He shook his head, trying to lose the image. His life was falling apart: Claire had kicked him out and had a new boyfriend, Rodney demanded a million dollars to keep quiet, and now Claire was trying to take everything he had worked so hard for so she could start her new life with Luke. There was no way he would let her ruin his life over a few mistakes.

His plan could work, but every detail had to be perfect. It could work like clockwork and fix all his problems, but he worried about Becky. She was so young and sweet, but on the other hand, she was devoted to him. All she would need was reassurances that she was important to him and that they would be together. He could manage to pull that off.

It should only take a few days if things went according to plan, then he'd be free of her and bring the bastard to his knees at the same time. He pictured Luke in despair and almost chuckled out loud as he stared out the window.

24

Screams echoed off the trees as Luke ran through the dark woods, nearly tripping on gnarled roots and ducking under low branches. The sound seemed to be coming from up ahead and off to the right, but he couldn't be sure. The screams were muffled now and he struggled to pinpoint their location over the sound of rushing water ahead. His heart pounding in his chest, he ran into heavier brush, leaves and dead twigs pulling at the cuffs of his pants. He knew he had to continue, but he wasn't sure why. He just knew he had to find the screaming and stop it.

He came to the edge of the stream and looked to the other bank. The screaming was getting louder, but he couldn't see through the darkness. It wrapped around him as the screams got louder and louder.

Sitting up suddenly in bed, Luke felt a giant vice grip was clenching his chest. He struggled for breath, but the screaming continued. He tried to clear his mind, but the pain in his chest confused him. Patting the sheets and pillow, he became aware that it was a dream, but why didn't the screaming stop?

Jumping out of bed, he saw his clock read midnight as he ran toward the sound. The fog cleared as he heard the screaming coming from Lizzie's room. Pushing her door open, he saw his daughter on the bed in her pink nightgown. She was kicking her legs, trying to get loose from the blankets, muttering "Stop! Stop! No! Stop!"

"Lizzie, honey, wake up," he said, lifting her into a sitting position, then shaking her slightly and rubbing her cheek. "Baby, you're dreaming. Wake up." She struggled to open her eyes and slowly turned to Luke, then opened her eyes wide.

"Don't let them take her, Daddy. Please, stop them, Daddy," she pleaded.

"Honey, you're dreaming. It's just you and me. There's nothing to be scared of." He stared into the damp green eyes that slowly glanced around the room and came back to him.

"Daddy, it was terrible," she whimpered, hugging him tight before she sat up on her knees. "They had Mommy and wouldn't let her go."

The fear in Lizzie's eyes scared Luke. Her safety, both real and imagined, was his responsibility. Feeling her tremble in his arms, he forgot about his dream and rocked his baby.

"Shhh. It'll be fine. Mommy's in a safe place. She's with Grandpa Rosentino and other people who love her. Nothing and no one can hurt her," he said, stroking her hair. "And you know what else?" Lizzie shook her head. "She's watching you."

Lizzie looked around the room. "Where is she? Is she here?" She pulled herself from his arms. "I want to see her, too."

Luke scolded himself for not being clear and took her hands. "Honey, Mommy is in heaven, but she's always watching you. No matter where you are or what you're doing, Mommy is there with you. You have to believe that. She loves us forever, even if she can't be here to tell us."

She hugged him, then searched his face. "You're not going to leave me, are you, Daddy?

He held her tight and kissed the top of her head, running his fingers through her hair. "Baby, I will always be here for you. When you're sad or in trouble and I'm not there, just think of me and I'll be there as soon as I can."

"Promise?"

"Cross my heart," he said, crossing his fingers across his chest. Pulling the blanket up to her chin and kissing her forehead, he turned out the light and went back to his own bed, thankful that his daughter was safe.

25

◈

The pillows smelled funny. Lizzie felt a pain in her right leg that made her wince and close her eyes tight. She ran her hand down her leg and felt her ankle. There was a long scratch that she didn't remember. She rubbed her eyes and sat up quickly. This wasn't her room!

Was she dreaming? This room smelled bad, like the bathroom at school after gym class. She started breathing hard. Where was she?

She looked around the small room. The ceiling and floor were made of wood. The bed was old and squeaky and the headboard was rusty metal rails. The sheets smelled like they hadn't been washed in weeks. A bottle of water sat on top of a small wooden table next to the bed. There was a small window near the ceiling over the bed, but it had a lock on it and there were heavy bars outside the dirty glass. Boxes stood in the corner and her backpack was on top of one of the boxes.

She ran to open it and found shorts, t-shirts and underwear all wadded up along with Doodlebug, her stuffed panda bear. She pulled out the bear and walked toward the door, still wondering if she was dreaming. This was less frightening than the dream about Mommy being dragged away by men in dark capes, but this felt more real. Her head and stomach started hurting as she stood in the middle of the room and started to cry.

The doorknob turned and Lizzie jumped back onto the bed, pulling the sheets over her head. She peeked over the edge and watched the door creak open slowly. She couldn't see anyone, but then after a moment, a tall, thin woman walked in, wearing jeans and a black t-shirt. She had long brown hair with a barrette on the right side.

Lizzie slid back on the bed against the wall, pulled the covers to her chin and stared at the woman. She had never seen her before and wished Daddy would come wake her up because she was getting very scared. She wanted to be in her own room and wanted this woman to be gone.

"Good morning, sweetheart," the woman said in a kind voice. She sounded nice, but Lizzie closed her eyes and cried harder. Any minute now, she would wake up in her yellow bedroom with her soft pillows and Uncle Tom would kiss her awake.

"Don't be afraid," the tall woman whispered, walking lightly across the small tattered rug. Although she wasn't heavy, the wood boards creaked under her weight. Through her tears, Lizzie noticed several spider webs in the corner of the wood floor.

Where was Daddy? Where were her other stuffed animals? Why wouldn't this lady go away? Lizzie cried harder and hid her face under the blanket.

"I'm not going to hurt you, honey," the woman said, sitting on the edge of the bed. The springs in the bed groaned and dust particles flew into the air, making Lizzie cough and cry harder. "Lizzie, it's okay. I'm not going to hurt you. I just wanted to bring you something to eat. Don't be afraid."

She walked to the doorway, leaned over, picked up a tray and brought it to the bed. "I didn't know what you like, but maybe you can eat some of this."

Lizzie looked over the edge of the blanket at the tray. There was a spoon, a napkin and a chipped green bowl with something that looked like corn flakes. She looked up at the lady and put the blanket over her eyes. Maybe if she hid her eyes, the dream would end and she would wake up and Daddy would call her downstairs for breakfast. He never let her eat in bed. Closing her eyes tight, she tried to picture Daddy in his pajama pants coming in to tickle her awake.

She could almost smell his shaving cream and could remember how he would touch her leg under the covers and tickle it until she couldn't breathe. She felt a hand on her leg, but it was small and cold. Instead of lightly touching her, the hand grabbed her tight and wouldn't let go.

Lizzie felt a scream escape her lips and she pushed herself to standing in the bed, holding the blanket up to her face. She had to get away from this woman. Maybe if she screamed she would go away. But it made it worse. The woman stood on the bed in front of her and tried to pull the covers away.

"No, no, leave me alone. I want my daddy. I hate you! I hate you! Leave me alone," she screamed at the top of her lungs. She thought maybe if someone were walking outside, they would come and help her. "Help! No! Get off me!" she screamed toward the window.

"I didn't want to have to do this, but you need to calm down," the woman said in a low voice, turning Lizzie around and picking her up from behind. Lizzie felt a cloth go over her nose and mouth and she tried to scream, but the room lights dimmed and the last thing she remembered was hearing "I'm sorry" from the tall woman.

26

Gripping the feather pillow, Luke turned toward the window and squinted at the sunlight filtering through the blinds. For a moment, he thought it was a school day, then almost as quickly, he remembered watching the Friday night TV shows with Tom the night before. He laughed that he had to turn up the volume to drown out Tom's snoring. He rolled onto his stomach and closed his eyes.

At least he could sleep in this morning. Tom had mentioned a museum he wanted to take Lizzie to, and Luke was debating whether to call Claire and see if she wanted to come along. The truth was he hadn't seen her in several days and thoughts of her seeped into his brain at the strangest moments. He had been going over Civil War dates with his class the day before and suddenly he'd pictured her standing in the classroom doorway wearing a red hoop skirt and bonnet.

The intensity of his feelings surprised him. He had loved Patty for so long, he thought it would take months before another woman captured his mind so completely. He wanted to share stories of his students and their struggles with her. A knock on his bedroom door brought him back to reality. Tom leaned in.

"Sorry to bother you so early, bro, but do you know where Little Miss Sunshine snuck off to?"

Luke sat up in bed and stared at Tom. "What do you mean, where is she? She should be in her bed."

He quickly swung his legs from under the covers and stared at Tom as he made his way toward her room. As he opened her door, light streamed through the window. The blinds were up and the dresser drawers were pulled out. Her sheets were crumpled at the bottom of the bed and the stuffed bear she slept with was gone.

He turned to Tom. "Did you check across the hall? You've been letting her play with the little girl across the hall. Maybe she went over there."

Tom shook his head. "I've checked the whole condo, unless she has a hiding place you know about that I don't."

Luke looked back, looking at his daughter's bed. It couldn't be, he thought. Even Dennis wouldn't stoop this low. He felt Tom's hand on his shoulder.

"I'm going to call the police, Luke."

Twenty minutes later, the doorbell rang and Tom answered the door. A voice said "Mr. Rosentino? We had a report of a missing child. May we come in?"

Luke looked up from the pictures spread over the coffee table to see Tom walking in with two men. They wore slacks and dress shirts and both wore badges on their waistbands. Luke stopped flipping through pictures and stood.

"Gentlemen, this is my brother and Lizzie's father, Luke Rosentino." The taller and older of the two spoke first.

"I'm Detective Schultz and this is my partner, Detective Capriotti." They both shook hands with Luke and sat across from him. "We'll do the best we can, but we're going to need your help. Do you have a recent picture of your daughter, sir? The most recent would be best for our investigation."

Luke picked up a picture on top of the stack and handed it to Schultz, his hand trembling slightly. Lizzie was wearing a blue flowered dress and wore a matching hairband. "This was taken about a month ago at my mother's house," Luke said, searching through the other pictures. "That's the most recent. We haven't had time to take any new pictures since she moved here."

The men glanced at each other. "You recently moved here with your daughter, sir?" Schultz asked.

"Yes, I moved here a month ago to take a job at the university and my daughter was living with her mother in Ohio." Luke picked up a picture of Lizzie and Patty from the previous Christmas and handed it to Capriotti. It was taken in front of the tree at his mother's house and they were wearing matching red velvet dresses. "Lizzie's mother died in a car accident two weeks ago and she came to live with me right after the funeral."

He ran his hand through his hair and shook his head. "I need her back." He glanced at Tom. "I should be able to take care of her. Patty always took such good care of her. I have her two weeks and she's missing."

Capriotti laid the picture on the table. "Mr. Rosentino, I'm very sorry for what you're going through. This must be a difficult time for you. We're going to ask you some questions now. Any information you can share will be helpful."

Schultz pulled out his notebook. "Sir, can you think of anyone that would want to take Lizzie? Sometimes in cases like yours, family members don't want a child to leave the home they're used to. Some think they can be a better parent, even if they're not the child's real parent."

"No, no—everyone in my family and Patty's family knows my home is the only place for Lizzie," Luke said, picking up a picture of him and Lizzie from the summer before. He hadn't thought of family doing this, but Patty was an only child and Judy would never... "People would actually do that to a child?" he asked, looking up at Schultz. "Put their own happiness before that of a child?"

"You'd be amazed about what people will do when their lives get turned upside down," Schultz said, flipping through the pictures on the coffee table. "Is there anyone here in town that would want to hurt you or Lizzie? Anyone you've had a confrontation with—maybe a student or coworker? Have you noticed anyone suspicious around the condo or at the university?"

Luke thought of Dennis. He was the only person Luke had argued with since moving here, but was a kidnapping possible? Dennis' anger was with Claire and, besides, Dennis was a lawyer. He knew the ramifications of kidnapping. He wouldn't jeopardize his career and law firm because of Luke.

"Mr. Rosentino? Sir?" Capriotti leaned toward Luke. "Can you think of anyone that would want to hurt you or your child? We need to know for our investigation."

Luke slowly shook his head. "Please find my daughter. She's so little. Please find her."

Tom gave the men a few more pictures and their home and cell phone numbers.

Capriotti turned to Tom. "Can you think of anyone in your family or Lizzie's mother's family that you think would have taken Lizzie?"

"No, sir, I know that's not a possibility. I also know that's what scaring my brother so much. We have no idea where to begin looking for her."

27

Annie pulled up to the coffee shop and shut off the engine. Claire had left Annie's house before Annie woke up, but had left her a note to meet at the coffee shop at nine.

There was a chill to the air, even though the forecast said highs in the eighties for the afternoon. There were no clouds and the sky was a light baby blue. Annie loved the beginning of fall when the weather cooled a little. It reminded Annie of her childhood and her sister Karen.

They had ridden their bikes for hours on Saturday mornings down the trails behind the house. Their secret was the space in the fence that separated their yard from the park behind the house. One section of the chain link was lying on the ground and it was easy to jump if they got their bikes going fast enough down the hill.

Closing her car door and walking toward the coffeehouse, she could almost smell the fresh cut grass as the bike tires rustled through the tall blades. Being out of the yard was so exciting, yet both of them kept their ears tuned for their mother's voice calling them back. Their trips hadn't been discovered for almost six months.

"You look like you could use some coffee," Claire said, approaching Annie. "You look like you're a thousand miles away."

For a woman going through a nasty divorce, Annie thought, she looked happy and relaxed, wearing yoga pants and a tank top, as though she just jumped out of a catalog photo.

The women went in, ordered their coffee and sat at a small table by a plate glass window overlooking a lake at the back of the shop. There were tables at the front, but Annie wanted to talk to Claire privately. Now that Claire and Luke had started dating, she was determined to make sure Claire saw Luke's vulnerability. He'd been through enough and didn't need to add heartache to his list of problems.

"He's wonderful, you know?" Claire said to no one in particular as she watched some children feeding geese on the bank of the lake. One of the ducks waddled after a small dark-haired child. The girl went running to her mother, begging to be picked up and saved from the quacking bird.

"I assume we're talking about Luke?" Annie said, looking up from her steaming mug.

"I thought I was going to be married to Dennis for the rest of my life." Claire stared at her hands. She rubbed her left ring finger like an amputee patient rubs the stump of a leg or an arm. She held up her hand to show Annie. "It still amazes me that after only two weeks, my finger looks like the ring was never there."

Annie took a sip of her coffee and looked up, but her eyes were drawn to the overhead television behind Claire.

A picture flashed on the screen. The yellow flowers on the blue dress caught her eye, and then she realized she was looking at a picture of Lizzie. Above the picture were the words "Amber Alert." Scrolling across the bottom of the screen were Lizzie's name and several phone numbers. Annie heard the announcer say something about a missing six-year-old being abducted and turned to Claire, who was standing up, grabbing her purse.

"C'mon, Annie, we've got to get to Luke's. My God, how could this happen? Who would take such a beautiful child from her home?"

28

۶۸۲۵

Leaves crunched under his feet as Dennis followed the directions Becky had given him over the phone. Follow the main park road until he saw the sign for the hiking trail. Park and start down the main path, and there would be a large oak on the right side of the path whose branches hung low over the trail. Turn right off the path and follow the trail into the woods. After a few minutes, he would cross a creek and walk straight another one hundred yards to a clearing. At the other side of the clearing, he should see the cabin.

One hundred yards, my ass, he thought as he pushed his way through the branches and small bushes. I know I've walked two hundred yards already. A minute later, he stepped out into the clearing. He put his hand over his eyes to shade the sun. Across the grass field, he saw a small log cabin set up against the edge of the forest. He stood in what appeared to be a yard for the cabin. It looked as if someone had tried to clear the land several years ago, but never quite finished.

The building either needed repair or just needed to be torn down. The splintered wood structure sat on cement blocks, which were almost completely covered by the weeds surrounding the building. Wooden steps leading to the door, he noticed as he approached, were railroad ties stacked higher and higher to the bottom of the wooden door. There was no doorbell or knocker, nor any signs that anyone had been here in weeks or even months.

As he approached the front of the building, the door flew open and Becky jumped off the top step and ran to him.

"I'm so glad you're here," she nearly cried in his ear, putting her arms around his neck. "I heard strange noises all night. I don't think I slept for a minute." She started to rest her head on his chest, but he pushed her back.

"C'mon, let's get inside just in case someone sees us." He took her hand and half pulled her up the steps and into the building. His eyes had to adjust to the darkness of the room. The main room was the size of a small bedroom, with a doorway on the back wall and one small dingy window facing the field he'd just left. An orange cooler and a box of groceries sat on the floor at the opposite end of the room next to a small, round wooden table with one chair beside it. On the left side of the room was a ratty, dirty red cloth couch, half covered with a white sheet and a thin white pillow near the armrest. Across the room from the couch a large gym bag lay sprawled open on the floor with several pairs of jeans and t-shirts piled inside, and magazines and books were scattered across the floor.

He walked across the room, taking it all in. The headache he'd woken up with started to intensify and he put his fingers to his eyes to stop the pain.

"Are you all right?" Becky asked. "I cleaned up as much as I could."

"Where is she?" he asked, trying to steady his voice. His entire plan rested on her answer.

"She's in the back room. She's sleeping. Dennis, are you okay? You don't look well."

"How do you think I'd look? We've just kidnapped a child!" he growled at her as she backed toward the wall. "Do you think I would be all smiles and grins knowing that as we speak, the police are probably starting to search for the girl in the next room?" he whispered angrily as he walked toward her, watching fear spread across her face.

"I...I'm sorry. I'm so sorry, baby. I did everything you asked me to do. Nobody heard me, I swear. No neighbors saw my car. I double-checked before I left the street. No one was even outside."

His expression softened slightly. "I'm sorry." He took her in his arms and ran his hand through her hair. "We're going to get through this. This will all work out for everyone."

"Then we can be together, right?" She pulled back and looked up into his face with wide eyes. "I help you and then when they pay, we give the girl back and then we'll be together, right?"

"Yeah, that's right, Beck. When this is over, it'll just be us." He looked toward the door leading to the back room and wondered how in the world he would get out of this hole.

∽ ∽ ∽

A feeling of dread hung in the car as Annie and Claire drove the five miles to Luke's condo. Annie changed the radio station several times, but they didn't hear the Amber Alert again before pulling into the parking lot.

Half a dozen police cars were parked near the entrance to Luke's building and police tape surrounded his corner unit. It stretched from the back of the building, around the side, past some windows and around the front, ending just past the front door. A few neighbors stood in the hallway a few doors down, whispering to each other what was surely false information about the little girl they'd only seen a few times. A little girl about Lizzie's age hung onto her mother's leg.

"Can I help you?" an officer in the parking lot asked, as Annie and Claire approached.

"We're friends of Mr. Rosentino—" Annie began.

"She's fine. She can come in," they heard Luke call from the front door. Annie and Claire walked past the officer and followed Luke to the couch in the living room. An officer sat flipping through pages in a small notebook.

"You heard the news?" Luke asked as they both hugged him. He sat between them and held Claire's hand.

"We were having coffee and saw the Amber Alert." Annie said. "What happened? What do you know so far?"

"Tom woke me up around eight, worried because Lizzie wasn't in her bed. We searched the entire condo, we've talked to the neighbors, we've looked around the property and we can't find her."

"Mr. Rosentino, I have a few more questions for you." The officer looked up from his notes at Annie and Claire.

"Detective Capriotti, these are my friends, Annie Gordon and Claire Bennett."

"Hello," he said, nodding to them. "Mr. Rosentino, our men are starting to look around the property now. I'd like to go over my notes with you. I want to make sure we're not missing anything. Sometimes the tiniest detail can make the difference in our search."

"What can we do?" Annie asked. "Maybe a search party? Do we have flyers made up?"

Claire rubbed his hand. "We could speak with some of the professors. Maybe get the students involved."

"Detective Capriotti?" Luke said.

"Call me Nick."

"Nick, we need to start searching everywhere," Luke

said, watching crime scene officers come out of Lizzie's bedroom with a bag of clothes. "Would it be better to only have the adults help with the search or could our students help too?"

"Mr. Rosentino—"

"Call me Luke."

"Luke, our men are already out searching the area. As much as I understand your desire to be involved in the search, please let the police search for her. It may be good to have many people looking for her, but those people don't understand the best way to search without disrupting the scene and possibly damaging important evidence."

"I understand all of that," Luke said. He ran his hand over his hair in frustration. "I'm saying if we're going to find my daughter, shouldn't we have as many people looking as possible?"

"Think of the logistics for a minute. The clues we are looking for might be tiny and the untrained person might miss them or even destroy them. Please let my men do their job. Since we don't really have any idea where Lizzie might have been taken, my men are starting their search in this immediate area, the condominium property. We're hoping to find something right now that will give us a better idea of where to focus our search."

"I just feel so helpless."

"Luke, we're fighting a battle against time right now. We don't know when Lizzie was taken except that it was sometime between midnight when you woke her up from her nightmare and eight o'clock this morning when your brother discovered her missing. Our local sheriffs are working with members of the South Carolina Law Enforcement Division and the sheriff's bloodhound unit is on its way. We're setting up a command unit in the dining room and your phone has been tapped in case the abductors call."

"Are we sure she's been taken?" Annie asked Capriotti, as Luke stood and paced the room.

"Yes, ma'am."

Luke walked over to the doorway of Lizzie's room and pointed inside.

"These officers don't know my daughter, Nick. They don't understand how scared she must be right now. She was just here not ten hours ago and now someone," he pounded his fist on the wall, "someone's taken my girl and I need to go out and search for her. I'm her father. I need to find her. I need to find her and make sure she's safe."

"Detective?" A tall officer stepped out of Lizzie's room. "We need to see you in here for just a minute."

"I'll be right back in just a moment. Please stay here."

Luke walked back over to the couch and sank down next to Annie. He picked up one of the pictures and stared at Lizzie's face.

"How does that happen, Annie? I've only had her for a couple of weeks and now she could be anywhere. How am I going to find my baby girl if I don't know what kind of devil would have taken her away from me?"

Claire took his hand. "We're going to find her if we have to turn this city upside down."

Capriotti walked into the living room. "Luke, what we need most right now is for you to stay here and be available to answer questions. We're going to need all the help we can get." He was holding a folded piece of paper with a pair of tweezers.

29

Claire pulled into her driveway, put the parking brake on and stepped out of the car. She had volunteered to print flyers for Luke on her home computer, but more than that, she needed to escape the tension, despair and confusion of the condo. Sunlight peered from behind the clouds, trying to brighten what Claire thought was the gloomiest day she'd ever experienced.

Officers had swarmed Luke's front rooms, which became more and more crowded as the hours crawled along. Canine units searched the property beginning at noon, while members of the FBI went over the ransom note with a fine toothcomb, looking for the most minute clues.

Luke almost lost his composure at mid-morning. He had come to the doorway to see two officers in the front yard with "HOMICIDE" printed on their shirts. Luke didn't react at all at first, then he stepped to the refrigerator and took a colored picture that Lizzie had drawn out from under the magnet. Holding it and staring at it for a dozen seconds, he suddenly crumpled it in his hands and threw it across the room.

"How dare they?" he yelled. "How dare they assume she's already dead? She's only been missing for a couple of hours and now they're bringing in homicide detectives? It's not enough that I have no idea where my daughter is right now, but this early in the game, they're already making assumptions that she might be dead? This is bullshit!"

Capriotti came into the kitchen, looked at Luke, then turned and saw the homicide detectives outside the door.

"Luke, you need to stay calm. The homicide officers are here as standard procedure when a child is taken." He grabbed Luke by the shoulders and guided him into a nearby chair.

"I told you. The first few hours of a child's disappearance are critical. Anything can happen and the people we're dealing with are desperate. We're pulling in all available personnel for your daughter's search. I need you to be focused on helping us."

∾ ∾ ∾

Luke had calmed down, but remembering it now as she walked into her house, Claire wiped away tears.

Watching Luke go through this horrific ordeal broke her heart. She wanted to do whatever she could to help him, but he was so angry. He was going through so much in his own life, and then he had defended her from Dennis and gotten hurt in the process. Maybe she was causing more harm than good being in his life at this point. She had her own demons to work out. Although she didn't talk to Dennis, he was with her almost every night.

She couldn't do anything about the dreams. Going through an entire day without a thought of him and knowing throwing him out was the right decision, he'd be in her head the moment she fell asleep. Some nights, he was apologetic and pleaded for forgiveness. Other nights, the dreams were dark and he crept through the shadows, Claire only vaguely aware of his presence. Those nights, she woke up suddenly in a cold sweat, trembling, feeling as if she'd been chased.

She hadn't told anyone of these dreams. It was her problem to deal with and Luke would only worry about her. Dennis never hurt her in the dreams. He was just following her and watching her and there were voices. They were soft voices but Claire could never understand what they were saying.

She walked down the hall into the home office. She sat down at the computer to begin making the flyers and focused on getting them printed. She didn't have the energy to dwell on her failed marriage or the dreams and voices. Besides, Dennis wasn't a bad man. He'd just made some very bad choices lately.

෴ ෴ ෴

Rainwater dripped silently down the inside wall of the shack as Becky turned over under the thin sheet. A second later, a thunderbolt crashed right outside the window and she sat straight up on the couch cushions, the sound vibrating through her body.

Lizzie had been crying in the back room for at least an hour, but it was louder now. Jumping up from the couch, Becky hurried to the door, turned the knob and entered the room. The peanut butter sandwich and chips were on the table next to the bed where she had left them three hours earlier.

Walking to the bed, she found Lizzie curled in a fetal position under the sheet, trembling. Becky touched her shoulder and she pulled away, trembling and crying even harder. Becky remembered feeling that alone and scared as a young girl.

"Do you want to come out in the other room with me?" she asked softly. "I don't like storms either. We could sit together."

Lizzie's crying quieted slightly, but she wouldn't meet Becky's eyes.

"The rain's only going to get worse and I bet you'd rather sit on the couch out front with me than lie back here by yourself. What do you say?" Becky reached out to touch Lizzie's hair, but she pulled away.

A minute or two later, Lizzie slowly got up with her sheet and walked across the room toward the door. Gripping and turning the glass door handle, she opened the door and peered into the open space beyond. She walked across the wood floor, her sandaled feet sliding silently across the floor. She climbed onto the couch and curled up in the corner, in the same fetal position, and wrapped the sheet around her legs.

"Can I sit next to you?" Becky asked quietly as she approached the couch.

Lizzie said nothing. She just stared at Becky with wide eyes. Becky sat down a few inches from her. The rain poured on the shack roof and a lightening strike brightened the sky outside, but only for a moment. Another crack of thunder followed and Lizzie jumped at the sound, but she kept her distance from Becky.

Storm sounds reminded Becky of her family. Rainy days had always brought out the worst in her father. When she was Lizzie's age, the downstairs hall coat closet had seemed the safest place in the house during the storms. The sounds were muffled by the coats and boxes and the darkness was calming.

That was until he had found her hiding spot that Saturday afternoon when Mom was away. He brought the bottle with him. The smell…it seemed like it was coming out of his skin. A moment after he closed the door, she felt sick to her stomach, both from the smell and from his words.

"Maybe I could spend some time with you this afternoon? This could be our special place. No one needs to know."

The memories were as clear as if they happened yesterday.

Standing and walking to the cooler, she took a soda out, popped the top and took a quick drink while walking back to the room where Lizzie had been earlier.

"No one needs to know," she said softly. No one knew her. She never let people know the real Becky. They'd be shocked to know about her life. Keeping to herself was the only way she knew how to survive. The more people you meet, the more people you would miss when you moved. Her father told her that once while they were packing.

She had been to seven schools, had dozens of teachers and a couple of kids each year who had tried to buddy up with her, but the older she got, the easier it got. She'd tell them anything. She'd fallen, she was clumsy and they all believed it because they didn't know her. They were all the same, Becky thought, picking up Lizzie's pillow. Everyone except Claire Bennett.

Claire had seen through all the walls and somehow found her. The essay had been a nightmare to write, reliving all the emotions, but Claire saw something good in it and something good in Becky. It almost made the breakup worth it. Maybe she had some talent. The writing had come easy; it was the subject that had been difficult.

Stepping into the front room again, she felt it seemed brighter and quieter. The storm had finally passed.

"See, that wasn't that bad. I told you it was better out

here." Becky suddenly realized she was talking to herself. Lizzie wasn't in the room and the front door was open.

∾ ∾ ∾

The ransom note had been found with a dozen other papers, mostly pages from Lizzie's coloring books that she'd ripped out and thrown on the floor. All they had determined was that during the kidnapper's struggle with Lizzie, the note must have fallen to the floor and been kicked under the bed.

Luke thought he was going to be sick when he'd heard the detectives talk of a struggle with Lizzie. The image of a stranger even touching his daughter, much less possibly hurting her, made him want the intruder dead. He'd thought it was a burglary gone wrong until he saw the note with his own eyes.

"If you want to see your baby alive again, I need $1 million. You'll receive more information tomorrow."

Annie had taken Luke into the kitchen and gotten him a drink of water.

"Annie, where am I going to come up with a million dollars?" he asked as she filled her own glass. "Why is this happening? Why?" She jumped slightly, as he turned and punched the wall, leaving a mark in the drywall. He didn't pause or react to the pain and his eyes showed his fury.

"Who's targeting us? Why would they want to hurt Lizzie? She's just a kid, for God's sake."

Annie was quiet for a minute as she looked away.

"What?" Luke walked over to her. "Tell me what you're thinking."

"No, it's nothing."

"Annie, tell me."

"I'm just thinking about Dennis, but it can't be."

"Everything okay in here? What was that noise?" Nick

quickly entered the kitchen and followed Annie's glance to the hole in the wall. He stepped to the counter and faced Luke.

"I understand your frustration. We're doing everything we can to find your daughter, Luke, but we need you to focus and try to remember anyone that might have a grudge against you or Lizzie."

"I've only lived in South Carolina for a month at the most, and Lizzie only about a week. We haven't had time to make enemies," Luke said. He looked over at Annie, who held his glance for a few seconds. Maybe this idea of Dennis wasn't crazy after all if Annie had doubts.

Nick stepped between them.

"If there's even a thought in your mind, you have to tell me. Let me know even if it sounds ridiculous to you."

Luke shook his head.

"It's just that my girlfriend, Claire, had recently kicked her husband out for being unfaithful, and he and I fought a few days ago. He wants her back and thinks I'm the only reason she won't let him come home. But it couldn't be him. He's a lawyer and way too smart to do something this stupid."

"Okay, we'll check into it. What's his name?" Nick scribbled in his notebook. "Is there anyone where you lived before that had a grievance with you? A relative of Lizzie's mother who feels you're not a good enough parent to Lizzie? Did anyone react strangely to you at the funeral?"

"Everyone was grieving. Everyone was in shock," Luke said, standing up and walking to the kitchen window and staring into the backyard. "I mean, one minute, Patty was working and perfectly healthy and the next, she's gone and the whole family is watching me move my daughter hundreds of miles away, away from her friends and school and grandparents and everything she knows."

He ran his fingers through his hair. "All those people knew Lizzie was better off with her mother. They had such a strong connection."

Annie stepped forward and rubbed his back. "Lizzie loves you, Luke, just as much as she loved Patty. She had more flexibility with her job than you did. They spent more time together than you and Lizzie. It doesn't have anything to do with being more connected or her loving one of you more than the other. You have to believe that."

Nick looked up from his notebook. "Do you think any of Patty's relatives feel strongly enough that you're not a fit parent—"

"Stop saying that!" Luke growled. "I love my daughter more than my own life! I would do anything for that little girl. Anything! I'd give up my own life if I had to."

"Luke," Nick held his hands up as if to stop Luke's words in midair, "I believe you that you love your daughter completely. In situations like this where one parent suddenly dies, family members have been known to take matters into their own hands when they think the child is not getting the best care. I'm just asking you to talk to your family. Find out if anyone has mentioned any uncertainty about your ability to care for Lizzie. You told your family that she is missing, right?"

"No, not yet," he said, staring into the space. "Only Tom knows because he was here."

"You haven't called your family?" Annie asked. "Honey, you've got to call home. Think of all the help they could be in the search. You can't go through this alone. You need your family. They love you and they'll want to help however they can."

"You're right, but first, I have to tell them that Lizzie was taken from my house during the night and I didn't even notice until morning."

30

∽◠∾

Cool breezes flowed through the kitchen, circulating the aroma of lasagna throughout the first floor of the house. Maria Rosentino stood at the sink, finishing the last of the dishes. Her guests would be arriving soon and she still had so much to do. Set the table, a quick dusting of the living room and run a vacuum over the front hall carpet, then she'd feel more comfortable about people coming for dinner.

The Carters had been friends of the family forever. Cecile Carter had babysat for all the Rosentino children at one time or another and Peter had spent hundreds of weekends in the garage with Alex tinkering on cars and generally making a mess. Wiping down the counters, Maria remembered all the summers the families had spent together and felt a slice of pain as an image of Alex swept through her mind. It had been the middle of summer and she'd come out to the garage to discover Alex and all five boys with their heads under the hood of the old Buick. She'd quickly run back in the house, grabbed the family camera and ran back outside to snap the shot. Alex had been her life.

She'd known the night they'd met at the dance more

than fifty years ago that he was the man for her. The way he had glided across the dance floor watching her the entire time made her feel she was the only woman on the planet. Of course, there had been difficult years, but they were just blemishes on a complete partnership. When Alex had his heart attack and died, she thought she couldn't be alone, but she'd had to move on for the sake of the children, but at times like these, the pain was almost too much.

The phone ringing startled her from her thoughts and she wiped her hands on her apron as she crossed the kitchen.

"Good afternoon. Rosentino's."

"Mom?" Luke's voice sounded tired.

"Luke, what's wrong, honey?"

There was a long silence, then he spoke again in a much lower, weaker voice.

"Mom, she's gone."

"Who's gone, honey? Patty? I know, son. It can be difficult, but it will get better. I promise."

She heard him whisper something that sounded like "I know I have to tell her."

"Who's there with you, Luke?"

"Mom, it's about Lizzie."

"What's wrong? Is she sick?"

"No, Mom." There was a pause, then, "She's been taken."

"What do you mean 'taken'?" Maria said, feeling every nerve in her body stand on edge.

"She's been kidnapped. She was taken from her room last night and we don't know where she is or who has her."

Maria slumped into the kitchen chair nearest to her and clutched the phone tight to keep from dropping it.

"Tell me what happened." She tried to focus on his voice, but it was so soft and shaking.

"Mom, the police are here and they've already started to search, but I just don't know where she could be."

Her decision was instantaneous. The Carters would understand. She'd have to call the family and figure a strategy. Her strength came back as she started scribbling notes.

"You said she'd been kidnapped. Do you have a note?"

"Yes, the police have it."

"Do they have any leads?"

"Nothing." The background noise subsided and he was quiet for a moment. "Mom, they're demanding a million dollars."

Maria stopped writing and leaned back in the chair. God, help me, please, she prayed silently. I need your strength, please, Lord. She felt the clarity of mind to ask a question, but nothing more.

"Is there anything you're afraid to tell the police? Do you have any idea who might have taken her?" Suddenly, she realized her son might have hidden a part of his life from her. Who would take a man's small child?

"No, Mom. I don't know of anyone that hates me that much. I've just been trying to get to know Lizzie better and..." An overwhelming feeling of guilt took his breath away.

"What, Luke?"

"It's just...I don't know what to do. The police say I have to stay here in case the kidnappers call, but I should be out there searching for Lizzie. Can you imagine how scared she must be? God, I want to kill whoever has her."

Maria thought of Lizzie and listened to her son's voice and a sense of calm overcame her.

"Luke, I'm going to be there in just a few hours. We're going to find her, don't you worry. And don't you worry about the money. I'll gladly pay a million dollars to get your baby back."

"Mom...you can't just give these people that much

money. Who knows if they'll give Lizzie back? They could just ask for more."

"Honey, you just hang on. Your family is on its way. You just keep praying and this will all work out fine." She hung up and realized her family needed her like never before.

Dialing her oldest son's number, she heard Alex's voice and remembered what he'd said on the stretcher in the ambulance the day he died. "Family is everything, Maria. Whatever you do, keep our family together."

◊ ◊ ◊

The leaves and pebbles crunched under the tires as he pulled into the parking lot and turned off the car. Dennis started down the wooded trail. The canopy of pine and oak trees blocked the little sunlight peeking from behind the clouds. The recent thunderstorm left deep puddles on the trail. Stepping around them, Dennis ran into the branches that reached into the path from the forest. He wiped at his arms, feeling spider webs from the branches mix with the hairs on his arms.

Every slight breeze inspired the trees above to dump cold rainwater on his head, reminding him that his umbrella was in his car. He patted his pocket, reassuring himself that he had remembered his cell phone. He felt the lump in his pocket and moved forward, trying to stay to the center of the trail.

Approaching the clearing this time, he heard a woman yelling. It couldn't be possible. He'd just been here, not six hours earlier, and she was already losing her composure?

What could be going so wrong that she was outside screaming at the top of her lungs? A moment later, he was racing across the field toward the cabin, tall wet grass whipping against the bottom of his tailored dress slacks.

He came up quietly from behind her and wrapped his arms over hers from behind, covering her mouth with his hand at the same time.

"Are you out of your mind?" he whispered angrily in her ear. "What in the hell are you thinking? What if someone heard you?" He tightened his grip over her mouth and around her arms. "Now quietly, let's go back in the shack and figure this out before the girl wakes up."

He felt her body start to tremble and her slender frame went slightly limp, requiring him to hold her up.

"Okay," he asked wearily, once they were inside the building, "look me in the eye and tell me the truth. What could be so wrong?"

Tears were rolling down her cheeks. She was shaking uncontrollably from head to toe and her eyes were red and puffy. She looked at the ground at her feet.

"It's bad. I don't want to tell you," she whimpered. "You're going to hate me."

"Look, I know what we're doing is wrong, but pretty soon, it'll all be over. The girl will go home, we'll have our money and we'll be able to be together. We just need to work as a team." He put his fingers under her chin and raised her wet face to his. "Tell me what's wrong."

"She's gone."

For a moment, the words didn't make sense, then he dropped his hand and looked toward the ground, shaking his head. His mind raced as his plan unraveled. The girl was gone and Rodney was still going to require the million dollars.

All he'd asked her to do was to keep the girl in the shack and she had screwed it up. But the worst part was her crying and whining. She hadn't even tried to find the girl. This bitch had just screwed his whole plan. She stood in front of him, looking up with tears streaming down her cheeks.

"Dennis, I'm so sorry. I didn't mean to—"

The force of his hand on her cheek knocked her onto the dusty wooden floor of the shack. "You lost her? You lost the girl who was going to bring us a million dollars in just a matter of days?" His chest was tight and he couldn't breathe. He walked away from the crying, sobbing mess on the ground.

Rodney's threat rang in his ears from the phone call just a few hours earlier: *"It's only a million; it should be no problem for you."* Everything he worked for would be lost in one scandal, all because of this woman, this girl, this mess.

"How did you 'lose' her, Becky?" He walked back toward her. "How do you lose a child who's blindfolded and locked in a back room of a shack?"

"The storm was getting really bad and she was scared and crying." Becky sat up on the floor and held her cheek.

"That still doesn't answer my question," he snarled at her.

"I brought her out in the front room with me during the storm. She was back there all alone crying."

"So how was it that she escaped from you? She had a blindfold over her eyes." The realization hit him like a brick. "Did you take off the blindfold?" He stared at her as she stood and backed away from him.

"I couldn't help it. She's only six years old and the storm was really bad."

He walked right up to her and she shielded her cheek from another strike.

"Which way did she go? We've got to find her now," he said, inches from her face.

"I don't know. I turned away from her for a second and she was gone. I didn't see her leave." She turned and looked out the open doorway across the field, then back at Dennis, wiping her tears away. "She's only been gone for about ten minutes. We could look for her. She couldn't have gone far."

He glared at her. "You better hope we find her."

∾ ∾ ∾

Maria turned onto Luke's street. She'd been lucky; she was able to catch a flight an hour after his call. The sun was setting as she turned into the parking lot, but as she drove back to Building 14 and turned the corner, the light grew brighter. Nothing could have prepared Maria for the sight in front of her.

Six or seven police cars, two with police dogs in the back seat, were parked in front of the door, officers surrounded the front of the building and reporters walked to and from their satellite trucks, some speaking into cameras with lights shining on their faces, others talking to the officers, scribbling wildly in their notebooks.

She pulled into a parking space and stared at the crowd surrounding the entrance. Luke's in there dealing with all this by himself, but not for long. She gathered her purse and jacket and stepped out of the rental car. The humidity in the air made it feel like ninety degrees even though the sun was going down. Maria threw her jacket back into the car, closed the door and walked toward the crowd.

She approached the first officer she saw. He was leaning against his car, speaking into his cell phone as he read his notebook.

"Fuller and Richardson are in the woods behind the unit. Clayton, Williams and Hager are one mile north with FBI and canine units." The dispatcher said something in return that Maria couldn't understand. "No, there are no leads at this time on the child. Hold on."

"Can I help you, ma'am?"

"I'm Maria Rosentino. I'm 'the child's' grandmother," she said, eying him from top to bottom, emphasizing his words back to him. "Luke's mother."

The officer stood a little straighter. He looked toward the crime scene. "Any other questions, call Petts. He's here on site. I'm going to talk to the father."

He turned to Maria.

"Let me take you in to see your son, ma'am. He's handling the situation the best he knows how, but I'm sure he'd be glad to have family with him at this time." He put his hand on her elbow and started to walk toward the front door. She slipped her elbow from his hand and stood her ground.

"Are you the officer in charge of this operation?" He walked back toward her.

"Yes, ma'am, Detective Nick Capriotti."

She didn't say anything for several moments, then stepped toward him and looked him straight in the eye.

"Nick, is it?"

"Yes, ma'am."

"Nick, I am the mother of seven grown children and ten grandchildren. But I'd bet you'd be surprised to know that I own and operate a nationally recognized, nationally acclaimed contracting company with thousands of employees across several states. My company is responsible for some of this country's largest real estate ventures. Do you know my secret to success?"

"No, ma'am, I can't say I do."

"I look at the smallest pieces of information relating to every job my company takes on, and I know everything there is to know about my children's lives. I feel—no, I know— that details make the difference in every instance. And sometimes when you're looking too closely at the big picture, a small detail might be missed and change the outcome of the whole project."

Her voice was calm and steady to this point, but now she spoke more firmly and decisively.

"In this case, the 'project' is getting my granddaughter back from her captors. I've been told she was taken in the early hours of today. That means she's been gone about twelve hours. There's a million-dollar ransom note and I'll tell you I have the ability to get that amount in an hour."

She saw Nick's eyes sharpen as he listened. "What I need you to understand is that missing a single detail will sign my granddaughter's death certificate. That is unacceptable and there's no reason for it. Therefore, I need for you to tell me every single detail of what you know, what you think, what you're planning and what you're hoping will happen in this case before I go inside to see my son."

"Mrs. Rosentino, I—"

"Call me Maria. Nick, if you and I are going to work together to catch these bastards, we are going to have to work together closely and trust each other. I'll keep my son calm so he can help in the investigation and you supply me with every bit of information you have so we can get little Lizzie back."

31

Everything from his years as a police officer told Nick to turn this woman down, but something about this case was different. This family was much like his own and Maria reminded him of his own mother. Angelina Capriotti would do anything for her children and God help the child that disagreed with her or didn't follow her instructions. He knew from experience that Italian mothers don't take no for an answer. Nick looked over at the officers and reporters, wondering how much he should tell her.

She was right, details did make all the difference, but telling family members everything didn't help anyone. They begin thinking of their loved one being held against their will, and most people can't handle that type of stress. He looked at Maria and realized he didn't have a choice. Maria knew exactly what she needed and for some reason, he felt she would handle the information. He suddenly felt strongly about joining forces with her.

"I don't usually do this, Maria. There's so much speculation at this point. You need to understand that we don't have any leads at this time."

Her expression relaxed and she leaned against the car opposite him.

"Nick, we're going to find my son's baby, no matter what it takes. I made a promise to my late husband that I would take care of our family and I'm not about to stop just because some scum wants to threaten my son. Now, tell me everything you know so I can help Luke."

Ten minutes later, Nick took her elbow and this time she allowed herself to be led toward the condo.

∾ ∾ ∾

She said a short prayer as they walked through the front door. An officer leaving the building with a clipboard leaned in and whispered something to Nick. After a nod, the reporters all rushed toward the door as he started to speak to the group, and Nick closed the door behind them.

"I've told you more than they know, but we're trying to hand out Lizzie's picture to any news organization that doesn't have it already," Nick said quietly to her. "Please keep what I told you to yourself. I would rather no one knows you have that information." She nodded and they continued toward the kitchen.

"Detective Capriotti, we need you over here for a moment," an officer called from the next room where several men sat around Luke's oak dining room table.

"It'll have to wait a minute," Nick said without a look in their direction.

Maria approached a small table in the living room. Lizzie's face stared up at her grandmother from a silver frame. Maria stopped, picked up the photo and traced the girl's face with her finger, kissed her finger and touched Lizzie's lips, then returned the frame to its spot on the table and walked with Nick into the kitchen.

Luke was sitting at the kitchen table with his back to

them. His shoulders slumped forward and his hands were in his hair. Annie and a woman Maria didn't know sat across the table talking quietly. When Maria entered the room, Annie stood and ran to Maria and hugged her tight. Hearing the noise, Luke sat up in his chair and turned to face his mother. In the instant their eyes met, she knew she had to be there. He wore all his pain and worry on his face. Standing, he walked directly to her and bent down to hug her. There were no words for several moments, but she felt him breathe deep as he clung to her.

"I'm so glad you're here," he whispered. "We haven't heard anything from the kidnappers. They haven't called and we have no clues." They walked toward the table and the woman stood as Maria approached.

"Mom, this is my friend Claire Bennett. She works at the college with Annie and me." Maria noticed that Luke kept his hand on the small of Claire's back as the ladies shook hands.

"It's so nice to meet you, Mrs. Rosentino. I just wish it could be under better circumstances." There was a gentleness in Claire's face, and her smile was contagious. Maria glanced over Claire's head at Luke and saw the same smile.

"It's a pleasure to meet you too, Claire."

Maria then walked across the kitchen, opened the cabinets and found the coffee and the filters, dumped the small amount in the pot down the drain and quickly started another pot brewing. She turned around to the table, nodded for Annie to come to her and the two women whispered together for a moment, then Annie reached in the refrigerator and began pulling out lunch meat and condiments. Maria found the bread on the table and started removing slices.

"I'm sure," she said, looking at Nick, "that your men work better with some food in their stomachs."

"Yes, ma'am, but you don't have to—"

"Oh yes, I do, young man. Now, we're going to have some ham sandwiches and maybe some tuna salad sandwiches and I saw some two-liters of soda in the pantry. There should be enough for everyone."

"Mom, no one's very hungry. We've got—"

Before Annie was able to give him the "don't cross your mother" look, Maria spun to face her son.

"Listen to me and listen good. We all know this is a stressful situation, but if you don't eat during this investigation, you're going to get sick and then what good will you be to Lizzie? She needs you alert and ready to think on your feet. And these men," pointing to the officers in the next room, "need nourishment so they can find some clue to where Lizzie's been taken. Nick, please tell the men that there will be sandwiches, coffee and soda ready in about twenty minutes."

"Yes, ma'am." He glanced at Luke and he was immediately transported back to a night when he was fifteen and had tried to explain why he came home after curfew. Angelina had read him the riot act because she cared about him. He felt he had to defuse the tension. "I really appreciate you doing this. It's very kind of you."

"It's what I know to do, Nick," she said, tying on an apron that seemed to have materialized out of nowhere. "We have to eat. Annie, when that pot stops brewing, make another, please?"

"Yes, ma'am."

True to her word, twenty minutes later, several platters of sandwiches sat ready on the counter. FBI agents and officers made their way in, grabbing drinks on their way out. Maria brought four sandwiches over, gave one each to Luke, Annie and Claire and sat down with her own.

She held out her hands to Annie and Claire and watched Annie take Luke's hand. "We'll eat in a minute, but right now, we're all going to pray for Lizzie's safety."

32

উ৯৫

Stepping out onto Luke's backyard patio, Annie ran her hands through her hair and leaned against the brick wall of the building. The air was still and humid, even though it was nearly midnight. The yard was silent except for the occasional car engine from the front parking lot. The clouds had blown away, revealing the full moon. Its light shown on the grass, giving the yard the appearance of twilight. The pines along the back of the yard stood as straight and still as soldiers in a morning formation. Even with the moonlight, though, she couldn't see between the dark trunks.

Thinking of Lizzie alone in the dark sent a cold chill down her spine. She crouched down against the wall. The worst part is we have no idea where she is or who has her or why, she thought as tears finally welled in her eyes. She had tried everything she could to keep steady in front of Luke, but now she felt her resolve begin to collapse.

She put her face in her hands and tears streamed down her cheeks. She sobbed for the helpless little girl and her father, and for the first time that day, a sense of hopelessness draped over her. She almost felt its weight on her back and neck as the tears rolled freely and she took deep gulps of air as she cried.

"We're going to find her. You know that, right?"

The sound of a human voice hit her ears and shook her to the core.

Trembling, she wiped her eyes and looked up to see Nick standing next to her with his hand outstretched.

She took his hand and he pulled her up while holding her elbow for extra support. He had a kind face, she noticed as she wiped her cheeks with the back of her hand. He pulled a white folded handkerchief from his back pocket and handed it to her.

"I'm sorry to barge into your personal space. It just looked like you could use a friend."

"I don't feel like I'm being one right now," she said, scrunching her face when she saw her mascara smeared on his handkerchief. "Luke is my best friend and there's nothing I can do for him. I feel so useless just sitting here while Lizzie could be anywhere. God, she's just a baby."

Annie felt fresh, hot tears hit her cheeks. Nick took the handkerchief from her, folded it inside out, handed it back to her and rubbed her arm.

"You're being a great friend to Luke. What he needs right now is to stay calm and be ready in case we need information. It seems to me that you're a calming force in his life."

"Actually, I think having Claire here has helped more than anything I could do," she said, raising her eyebrows and looking through the sliding glass door. Claire was sitting at the kitchen table, holding Luke's hand, rubbing his fingers, and appeared to be talking softly to him. "They recently started seeing each other."

"She seems like a nice woman. He's a lucky man that she's here for him."

"I don't think anything or anyone could pull her away from his side right now. I don't know if you noticed, but she organized a truckload of students from our college to pass out flyers with Lizzie's picture in the area."

"I did notice. Those kids must really respect her. They all grabbed piles of paper and practically ran out the door when she told them what was happening." He looked into the condo and they both watched as Luke looked toward the living room and jumped out of his chair, nearly knocking it over on his way to the phone.

"We're on," Nick said, moving through the sliding door.

∾ ∾ ∾

After so many hours of silent prayer, research of dead-end leads and feelings of helplessness, Nick fed off the energy of the room. The phone was on a folding table next to a bank of digital recording machines. He raced across the room and got to the phone at the same time Luke did and grabbed Luke's hand before he could pick up the receiver. Luke's eyes were wide and he looked half-crazed.

"This is your daughter's life," Nick said, staring into Luke's eyes. "Get as much information as possible, but play it calm. You don't want to anger these people. We're listening and recording. Are you ready?"

They looked across the table at Schultz, who was wearing headphones, connected to the machines. Nick had put on a pair of headphones, also connected to the machines, and stood next to Luke. Schultz nodded at Luke. Luke took a deep breath and picked up the receiver.

"Hello."

"I'm looking for Luke Rosentino," said a deep electronic voice. Nick realized at that moment they were dealing with a pro.

"This is he." Luke glanced at Schultz, who moved his hand in a circular motion, as if to say "continue."

"I'm going to make this short and sweet. I have your kid." Nick watched as Luke closed his eyes and pinched the bridge of his nose with his eyes closed. He wondered if Luke would make it through the call.

"What do you want me to do?"

"I want one million dollars for her return. I want it by Tuesday night at six. That gives you a little less than three days," the voice said. Nick looked at his partner and saw the frustration on Schultz's face that he himself was feeling. The kidnapper had a voice-changing machine. They could be bought at dozens of stores around the city.

"I have it now. I'll deliver it whenever you say," Luke said calmly.

There was a short pause, then the voice spoke louder.

"You'll deliver it when I tell you. You're not calling the shots here; I am. But if you want to speed things up, it will cost you more. That sounds like a good idea. Let's raise the stakes. The price is now two million and you can have little Lizzie back tomorrow night. You'll receive directions where to drop off the money and pick up your darling daughter tomorrow. But you bring one cop with you and I slit her throat."

Nick scribbled a note and shoved it in front of Luke. It said, "Repeat stakes. Keep talking."

"You say if I pay you two million dollars, I can have Lizzie back tomorrow night?"

Nick looked past the men and saw Maria nodding to Luke from the kitchen doorway. Nick quickly scribbled "hear her voice" and shoved it in front of Luke.

"Yes," the voice said.

"I need to hear her. I need to know she's okay."

Nick listened intently for any background noise or voices, but there was nothing. This guy must not be near Lizzie.

There was a long pause, then the voice said, "You're really pushing your luck, Rosentino. I have your daughter, but you think you can order me around. I'm giving her back two days earlier than planned. Be happy with that or I might rescind the offer."

Schultz was motioning to continue the call.

"Let me hear her now," Luke demanded. "I need to know that she's okay. I need to know you haven't hurt her. Let me hear her."

Nick pressed the headphones to his ears tighter, listening for any sound that might help locate Lizzie. They needed a break in this case, but there was no sound at all. If they could only hear Lizzie...

"You don't need to hear her. You just need to do what I tell you—"

"Let me hear my daughter," Luke screamed into the phone.

"I'll let you hear her scream for mercy," the voice said, and the line went dead.

∽ ∽ ∽

Blinding rage built up inside Dennis as he disconnected the voice changer from the cell phone and walked to his car. He'd had the whole conversation planned out in his head, word for word. He was going to be in charge, not that asshole Rosentino. He was going to put the bastard in his place. Dennis wanted to hear Luke beg for his daughter's life. He started the car and turned onto the highway, pounding his hand against the steering wheel.

Who did Luke think he was? For him to make demands of Dennis was ludicrous.

Did Luke really think he could tell Dennis what to do or when to do it? He remembered seeing Luke's hand on the small of Claire's back at the house and the fury grew. Thinking back, he wondered if she knew he'd seen them kissing at the door. He was sure she had enjoyed the sweet revenge of him seeing her with another man. He pulled into the parking lot of the state park and jumped out of the car, unable to release the images from his mind.

Then there was Becky. He couldn't believe how close they'd gotten to losing everything. It had taken twenty minutes to find the kid. They found her fifty yards from the shack, hiding in a wooded area. They only found her because she coughed. Becky had almost blown their whole plan. Walking the trail, he tried to remember that he'd have his money in less than twenty-four hours. He could pay Rodney, put the blame where it belonged and get back to his life.

Ten minutes later, he walked through the brush next to the shack. He tripped over a small tree stump and the voice-changer dropped out of his hand.

"Damn!" He felt around in the dark for it.

"Who's out there?" he heard Becky call from the door.

"Get your ass back in that cabin! I'll come in when I'm damn good and ready!" he screamed in her direction. He heard the door close.

Walking around the front of the shack, he tried to calm down. After all, he was going to make a profit off this mess and he'd be able to ditch the kid three days early. He just hoped he didn't have to see her anymore tonight. Opening the door, he couldn't believe his eyes.

∽ ∽ ∽

The silence in the room only lasted seconds. Then officers and FBI agents moved quickly to the recording device in the dining room to listen to the conversation for clues. Across the room, Nick leaned over a map of the area with the U.S. marshals to determine the location of the call.

"What have I done?" Luke sank onto the couch next to Claire and covered his face with his hands. "What was I thinking, Claire? All I did was raise the price and I still don't have any idea where she is or who has her."

"Luke, they haven't won—not by a long shot. They want the money. They don't want to hurt her. Otherwise, they would have already. She's alive and this is going to work. We'll get her back."

Luke sat back into the couch. "How can you be so sure?" His stomach turned every time he remembered what he'd said over the phone. Lizzie needed him to protect her and save her, but he might have just killed her.

"I feel like I just signed her death certificate. Nick's sitting here telling me not to upset the kidnappers, then what do I do?" He stood up and crossed the room toward Maria. "I scream at them, insisting they do what I say? I say I love my daughter, but then I put her life in jeopardy by telling them what I need? What's wrong with me?"

Nick approached and stood in front of him.

"There's nothing wrong with you, Luke. But I want you to understand something. Claire's right. In most cases, what the kidnapper does or doesn't do in the first three or four hours decides the fate of the child. She's scared, but she's alive, Luke. He said you're getting her back tomorrow. We've just to work with what we've got and pray that he's going to stick to his word and not hurt her. He'll get his money, then we'll get him."

Luke felt his mother's warm touch on his arm. He

looked down expecting to see tears or fear in her face. Instead, he saw determination and confidence.

"Nick's right," she said. "There's nothing you can do at this point that you haven't done already. You told the kidnappers we have the money and you kept him on the phone as long as you could and you stayed calm. Now all we have to do is pray and wait for the next phone call."

There was a shuffle of movement from Schultz's side of the room. He walked to Nick as two marshals left the condo. "We got a location on that call. It was from a cell phone. We traced it to a cell tower just off I-77 a few exits north of here. The marshals and I are going to take some men and head to the area. We'll keep you informed over the radio."

Maria cocked her head at Nick as Schultz left the room.

"Isn't there something else you want to tell my son, Nick?"

"Well, there is one lead we're looking into," he said quietly, "but I didn't want to upset you until I knew more." He glared at Maria.

"Something new?" Luke walked across to Nick. "You have a possible lead? You think it's real?"

"I don't know. When our men did the initial search around the building late this morning, they found a boot print in the grass next to the patio door. The FBI matched the print to a brand of boot called Wolverine. They make work boots, the heavy style for construction workers. Carolyn Raymond, your building supervisor, said they issue Wolverine boots to their maintenance employees."

"Why are you just now telling me this?" Luke asked.

"Because at first, it didn't seem to matter. Ms. Raymond checked their records and no work had been done on your unit since before you moved in."

"I don't see how this is a lead," Claire said, coming up behind Luke. "What's the connection?"

"It didn't seem significant until I overheard one of your neighbors talking outside this evening."

"You need to get to the point, Nick," Luke said. "What did you hear?"

"She was telling another neighbor that she noticed one of the maintenance workers fixing the patio door around dinnertime the night before Lizzie was taken. She didn't think anything of it until she heard Lizzie had been taken just hours later."

"But you said they had no record of repairs to my unit," Luke said impatiently.

"They don't have any record of it. And the employee they described asked for vacation that afternoon and hasn't been seen since."

33

Driving down the exit ramp from I-77, Ray Campbell turned the radio up and cracked the windows of his '70 Mustang. The Doobie Brothers filled the car along with the cool morning air. Beams of sunlight were just breaking through the trees to the east as he pressed the gas and turned west onto Celanese Road.

The drive north from Columbia that morning had been uneventful, except for the drowsy semi driver who had almost drove Ray off the road on I-20. Being barely awake as Ray was, he'd swerved into the next lane, barely missing an old lady driving a new Cadillac. That was all he needed. A full day of fishin' and drinkin', a couple hours of sleep, then drive for twenty minutes and get pulled out of his crashed 'Stang in the dark because some old fart couldn't handle his rig.

He started to gun the motor but thought twice after glancing to his right and seeing a police car in the gas station parking lot. He had to be at the condos to start repairs on unit 1265 by seven-thirty this morning. Carolyn had approved his vacation time, but reminded him the new owners would be closing on the property Tuesday and he still needed to fix the leaky faucet in the bathroom, the locks had to be changed and new kitchen cabinets installed.

Pulling up to a red light, he glanced at the telephone pole on the corner and saw two sheets of paper stapled to the wood. Under the word "LOST" on both sheets were pictures of the little girl he'd seen on TV last night. The Amber Alert had crossed the screen, saying she'd been abducted from this area. She had a smile so bright, he wondered who in the world would be heartless enough to kidnap her. I wonder where her parents live, he thought, hitting the gas when the light turned green. The newspaper and television reports didn't say specifically. They must be going through hell right now.

The blue flashing lights in his mirror startled him and made him shade his eyes. What in the world? Why was he being stopped? He pulled over onto the shoulder, mentally scanning his car for any reason for the stop. His taillights and brakes worked as far as he knew and he'd just renewed his tags two months ago. He knew he hadn't been speeding, for Christ's sake.

The officer sat in his car, talking on the radio for almost a minute before opening the driver's door. He walked slowly toward Ray's door, speaking into his shoulder radio as he walked.

"Morning, sir," Ray said. "Is there a problem?"

"License and registration, please?" asked the officer in a monotone voice.

Ray leaned across and pulled the registration from the glove box, pulled his license from his wallet and handed them both to the officer.

"Please turn your car off, sir."

Ray watched as the officer walked back to his cruiser and sat typing on his laptop computer. He occasionally glanced up at Ray's car. Still not understanding what he had done, Ray suddenly remembered the small revolver in the trunk that he and Paul had used for target practice in the woods over the weekend. It can't have anything to do with that, he reasoned. He'd had it all weekend and it was registered legally.

Looking at his watch, he realized now he'd have to drive straight to the condos. There was no time to go home and get a shower before work. He looked in his outside mirror. What was taking this guy so long?

Suddenly, a sedan pulled up behind the cop's car and a man in slacks, shirt and tie walked up to the cop and leaned in the window. He wasn't very tall, but you could tell he worked out. Ray noticed a revolver in a holster on his hip and a badge on his other hip. There was a short discussion, then both men approached Ray's door.

"Mr. Campbell, would you mind stepping out of the car, please?"

Ray felt his pulse quicken as he opened the door and stood to his full six feet. He closed the car door behind him. What was an undercover cop doing on a routine traffic stop?

"Is there something wrong, officers?"

The plainclothes officer spoke in a deep voice. "How you doing? I'm Detective Nick Capriotti. You do maintenance work for Brookville Condos, Mr. Campbell?"

"Yes, sir," Ray answered hesitantly.

"I don't know if you've seen the Amber Alerts on television, but a young girl has been abducted from this area. Her name is Lizzie Rosentino."

"Yeah, I've seen the alerts. What's that got to do with me?"

Capriotti shaded his eyes and peered into the back seat of Ray's car. He turned and leaned on Ray's car. "Her father lives in the Brookville Condos. She was taken from his place yesterday morning. We were wondering if you'd mind coming down to the station and answering some questions for us."

Ray pulled his cell phone from his pocket and glanced at the screen. "I've got to be at the condos in about twenty minutes. I've got a bunch of work to do today on one of the units. I don't want any trouble with my boss and I didn't have anything to do with that girl missing." He ran his fingers through his hair and reached for the door handle.

"Take a minute. Think of her dad," Capriotti said, crossing his arms. " He's spent the past twenty-four hours working with us to find his only child, a girl that could literally be anywhere with anyone. You work at the condos and might have seen something, something small, that could give us a break in the case and give this man a shred of hope in finding his daughter. Now, you wouldn't want to take that from him, would you?"

Ray looked up at the traffic cop, then turned, only to find himself staring into Capriotti's face.

"I guess I could come with you, but I'm telling you, I don't know anything about the girl's disappearance."

"Good. Thanks. You know where the station is?" Capriotti asked over his shoulder as he walked to his car.

"Yes, sir."

"Great. We'll see you there shortly." Capriotti slid into his sedan and did a u-turn and drove off in the direction of the station.

The officer handed Ray's license and registration back to him. "We really appreciate you helping Lizzie's father. Any information you can give will be greatly appreciated."

"I'll answer your questions, but can one of you guys call my boss and let her know I'm going to be late? It's a good job and I don't want any trouble with my supervisor."

෴ ෴ ෴

Becky jumped as Dennis slammed the door quickly.

"Lock her ass in the back room where she belongs. She's worth two million dollars now," he bellowed through the thin wood.

She grabbed Lizzie's hand and pulled her toward the back room. Lizzie resisted and pulled against Becky, but it was the only way to keep Lizzie safe from his anger. She was just a child; someone had to protect her.

Becky pushed her into the room, closed the door, took the key from her pocket and locked the door. She turned when she heard the front door slam. Dennis stood just inside the door glancing around the room with a look of disgust. She hurried over to pick up the mess. A blue cotton blanket was crumpled on the couch. On the floor lay the remnants of two chocolate chip cookies and a smashed apple juice box next to an unraveled strip of duct tape. Dennis walked to the couch and threw back the blanket, picking up a ragged stuffed animal.

"What's this?" he asked, shaking the toy right in Becky's face.

She took a step back. "It's Lizzie's teddy bear."

"Do you think this is some kind of sleepover?" he boomed at her. He threw the bear across the room at the back wall. "What's next? Are you going to invite some of her friends over for a tea party?"

"But I—"

"You don't get it, Becky," he screamed as she backed away from him. "We stole this girl from her house so we could make her father pay millions of dollars. She doesn't need to be comfortable or happy. She just needs to be alive."

"Dennis, she's just a little girl." Becky stepped back from him and clutched the blanket. "She was scared of the storm and hungry. I wanted—"

In an instant, he was in her face. He pushed her against the wall and wrapped his thumbs and forefingers around the sides of her neck and tightened his grip. She dropped the blanket and tried to pull his hands from her neck, but she couldn't loosen his fingers.

"I just realized the problem here," he whispered softly in her ear. "You think this is about you and what you want. How stupid of me! I thought you wanted to be with me and help me and all you really want is to play kindergarten teacher with the girl."

He pushed his body against hers and his breathing was heavy. She felt his body trembling and he lifted her onto her toes while he kept his grip on her neck.

"You let her escape from this building and it took us twenty minutes to scour these woods in the dark before we found her. She escaped because you let her loose because she was scared of the big bad storm. You know what, Becky?"

She tried to shake her head, but couldn't move. He leaned back and looked into her face. Tears blurred her vision as the room started to go black and white.

"I don't give a damn if a lighting bolt comes right through the roof and strikes the floor right next to her bed. She's worth nothing but a bag of money to me. I need you to grow the hell up real damn fast, Becky. You need to understand that this is my operation. I'm going to make that Rosentino bastard pay if it's the last thing I do in my life." He whispered in her ear.

"You really don't think I care if the kid lives or dies, do you?"

Seconds away from passing out, Becky said a prayer for mercy in her head.

"Bitch."

Dennis loosened his grip and shoved her across the room onto the couch. She hit her hip on the cushions and rolled to the floor, landing on her stomach. After a moment, she arched her back, frantically trying to catch her breath. Coughing and wheezing, she rolled onto her side against the couch and watched as he approached.

"I never should have trusted you. Sure, you're good in the sack, but you're just a kid. I thought you and I could be together once we got this business taken care of, but you don't have the maturity to handle what needs to be done." He stood in front of her as she continued to cough and gasp for air.

"I need someone that can handle the situation when I leave the building." He looked down at her. "This ends tomorrow night. We're getting two million dollars for the kid now. Once we get the money, we're gone. But the way things are going, you'll probably walk her home and hand her to her fucking father yourself. Is that your plan, Becky?"

"No," she wheezed. "I'm sorry. She seemed hungry. I didn't think. I want to be with you. I want us to be together." She was trembling, but at least Dennis seemed to have calmed down some. This was just a rough point in their relationship and he was stressed about the plan. She realized she had to prove to him that she was on his side.

"I don't see it. I'm not seeing it," he said, walking away from her. "I need to see it. You say you love me, but then you snuggle up to the girl like you're her fucking mother or something." He crouched in front of her and caressed her hair and looked into her eyes.

She sat up and leaned against the couch. She had to prove she loved him. They only had one day left before all their problems would be over.

"What do you want me to do?" She looked up at him, rubbing her neck.

He reached into a gym bag next to the couch and pulled out a plain white t-shirt. Tearing it down the middle, he handed it to her.

"Gag the kid, then blindfold her and make it tight."

She stared at the cloth for a moment. It wasn't like it would hurt Lizzie. She was just going to make sure she stayed quiet. She thought about her and Dennis being together. The two of them talking and laughing and making love like they used to. She knew what she had to do. She stood and took a deep breath.

"I'll do what you want, as long as we can be together. I know this isn't the real you and things will calm down once we get the money. I love you."

She could feel his eyes on her as she walked toward the back of the shack, winding the strip of cloth around her hand. He was a good man normally, she thought, reaching for the doorknob. If we can just get through tomorrow, he'll give Lizzie back and we can finally be together and happy. I know that's what he wants too.

34

⠀⠀⠀⠀ᥑᕦᥱ

Claire stood in her classroom, watching the students as they pulled their books and pens from bags. Suddenly, the room became foggy, the lights dimmed and the temperature dropped. She walked toward the light switch on the wall; maybe a fuse had blown.

A moment later, every corner of the room filled with the high-pitched sound of a girl screaming. It penetrated every inch of Claire's body and she watched as two shadowy figures entered the room and started moving up the stairs to the back row. She found she couldn't move to protect the students.

Claire knew the figures were evil and so did the students. They reacted in anger, throwing the books and backpacks at the figures. Just as quickly as it had begun, the child's screaming stopped.

The larger of the two shapes stood on the back row and pointed in Claire's direction, bellowing in a deep voice words she could not understand. She moved toward the shapes, trying to understand what was being yelled, but when she didn't immediately respond, the figure grew larger and louder until the bellowing was deafening. Covering her ears, Claire noticed the smaller figure shrink in size, start to tremble and move behind the larger figure. Claire closed her eyes to shut out the sight.

When she opened them, the larger figure was floating inches from her face. The power of the shadowy entity pulled Claire's energy from her body and she felt herself starting to faint as it closed in on her.

"Claire. Claire."

The voice was softer than before, almost a whisper. She tried to strike at the phantom but her hands moved right through the shadows, although the figure continued to drain her energy. She felt something touch her arm and jumped.

Maria stood next to her with a mug of hot coffee, smiling. Claire looked around and realized she was in Luke's recliner. A blue handmade afghan covered her from neck to toe.

Maria handed her the mug. "You fell asleep around two a.m. right here in this chair. No one had the heart to wake you. Are you all right?"

Claire looked into the kind face and allowed the image of the spirit to leave her mind.

"Yes, I'm fine, thank you. Just had a really bad dream I couldn't escape," she said softly, running her fingers through her hair to straighten it.

"This is a hard time for everyone, but having you here has made all the difference for Luke. Now, when you're ready, bring your coffee in the kitchen and have some of my muffins. They just came out of the oven." She smiled warmly at Claire and walked back into the kitchen.

Claire set the coffee down and stretched, then pushed in the footrest, bringing the chair straight up. She picked up and sipped the coffee, and looked into the dining room where Luke stood with Detective Schultz. A map hung on an easel with pushpins showing where authorities had searched leads from the public. She noticed the search area had doubled overnight.

Walking into the dining room, she stood behind Luke as he listened to Schultz report on dead-end leads. She reached for Luke's hand, but her touch startled him and he spun on her in surprise. His face was ashen and his eyes, although focused, showed his exhaustion. He wore the same wrinkled t-shirt and shorts from the day before. She handed her coffee mug to him.

"You need this more than me."

"Thanks." He took the mug and turned back to the map.

"Your mom made muffins. You should eat something. Do you want one?" she asked, walking toward the kitchen.

He gave her a confused look as if she was speaking Chinese. "What? Yeah, that's fine."

She went to the kitchen and put two blueberry muffins from the stove on a plate and brought them back to Schultz and Luke, setting them on the table. They didn't stop talking and pointing long enough to notice.

"You really should eat something. You're running on empty, Luke. Lizzie needs you at your best."

He spun around and glared at her. "What do you know about what my daughter needs? You've only met Lizzie once. I'm her father. Don't you think I know better than anyone what she needs?"

"Of course you do. I just want to help."

"Well, while you were sleeping," he added emphasis on the last word, "the marshals went to the area where the kidnappers made the ransom call, but it was in the middle of nowhere. There are no houses around, all the area businesses were closed and no witnesses have come forward that might have seen him. A couple calls came in overnight, but they were useless. No one has seen my daughter or her kidnapper. It's as if she vanished." He shook his head in disbelief and continued in a louder voice.

"Then you wake up and you want me to eat muffins and

drink coffee like it's a normal day? I don't even know if my daughter is still alive. Eating is the last thing on my mind right now. The only thing that matters to me is finding Lizzie."

Claire backed into the kitchen and walked through the house to the front door. Stepping outside, she felt the warm tears roll down her cheeks and the cool morning air hit her bare arms. She caught her breath and felt a hand on her lower back. She turned to find Maria with a travel mug of coffee in each hand and a lightweight jacket over her arm.

"You're going to get sick being outside on such a cool morning with no jacket. Here. Let's walk, huh?"

For the first few minutes, no words were spoken. Claire fought hard to keep the tears from falling and wiped away the ones that leaked out. Maria stayed in step with her, not leading or following or pressuring in any way.

"I really was only trying to help." Fresh tears escaped.

"I know you were, honey. Luke knows that, too. This is a difficult time for all of us." She looped her arm through Claire's. "You have to know how much it means to him that you're here."

Claire sighed and glanced at Maria for a moment. "I can't imagine what he's going through. My husband and I don't have any children, but I met Lizzie once and she's such a sweet girl. And Luke loves her so much."

Maria didn't answer right away. Claire glanced at her. "What?"

"I thought Luke told me you're divorced."

"Well, I found out Dennis was cheating on me and I threw him out about three weeks ago. I've filed for divorce." She looked straight ahead and sipped her coffee, imagining Maria's eyes burning into her. How can she still like me, Claire thought, when I'm dragging her son into this mess of a life I have right now? He's got enough problems of his own. But she heard only compassion in Maria's voice.

"Men who cheat on their wives usually get what they deserve. The ones I've known are assholes, if you'll excuse my language." Maria chuckled to herself when Claire laughed at the word. "I mean it, honey. They don't have any regard for the women in their life and are only out for either power, money or adventure."

They arrived at the playground for the condos. Claire sat on a wooden bench next to Maria.

"I didn't see it coming," Claire said softly. "Annie saw him with the woman in a restaurant and told me she followed him outside. She passed his car and they were...together." Maria placed her hand on Claire's. "When he came home, I confronted him and he couldn't deny it. I threw him out that night."

"Good for you. You're a better woman for it."

"The strange part is he thought I'd just forgive him and welcome him back. I knew I couldn't; he'd broken my trust in him beyond repair."

"I'd worry about your sanity if you took him back, honey."

"I think he finally realized I wasn't taking him back when he met Luke."

"I don't remember Luke telling me about that."

"It was very awkward. Luke came over for dinner with Lizzie and my neighbor and her daughter. Dennis called and asked me if he could come over."

"You chewed him out, I hope?"

"I told him he couldn't just show up whenever he wanted."

"Good girl." Maria said. "I'm liking you more and more every minute."

Claire thought for a moment about whether or not to tell Maria about the fight on campus. She decided not to say anything. Even Dennis couldn't be that evil.

Maria stood up, seeming suddenly energized. "Why don't we get back and check on the men? I'll make sure Luke gets something to eat and drink. I'll have him rest too. He's going to need his strength."

∾ ∾ ∾

The tapping, the sobbing and the ringing were too much all at once. Opening one eye, Dennis realized he was still in the cabin, but sunlight was now streaming through the window across the room. Empty beer bottles from the night before cluttered the floor. Suddenly, all the noises stopped. He rolled over into the couch and closed his eyes again. He remembered Becky said she was going to the grocery.

After a moment of silence, the sounds all returned one by one. A woodpecker chipped away at the tree just outside the window, then Lizzie whined and cried just enough to be heard through the door. Finally, Dennis' cell phone started to ring. He rolled onto his stomach and reached around the floor trying to find it. Reaching under the edge of the couch, he grabbed it and pushed the talk button.

"Dennis Kincaid." The words left his lips as a grunt.

"I just wanted to remind you of the money you owe me and the consequences if you don't pay it," Rodney said calmly.

"You called me at..." Dennis lay back as he squinted at his watch for several seconds, "God-damn seven o'clock in the morning on a Sunday to remind me that I owe you money? Are you out of your fuckin' mind? You pop up one day with papers saying I stole money from my former employer and you want a million dollars for my silence or you'll release your information to the media." He was screaming now. "You don't think that would be something I'd remember?"

"Hey, man, no need to get upset. You just need to do what you're told and pay me by the deadline and everything will happen just the way you want it."

"How do I know you won't give this information to the media after I pay you? What guarantee do I have that won't happen?"

"You just have to trust me." The line went quiet for a moment. "Unless..."

"Unless what?"

"Now that you mention it, one million dollars isn't really going to be enough. I mean, it's nice and all, but... tell you what. We'll make it two million and I give you all evidence I have and you'll never hear from me again."

Dennis sat straight up on the couch. "You've got to be fucking kidding me."

"Yeah, that sounds good. We'll make it two million, same deadline."

"But I still have no guarantee that you'll keep quiet!"

"Dennis, I don't think you have any room to negotiate. You got yourself into this mess when you stole funds from our boss. Did you really think no one would ever find out? Well, now you pay the price or I blow your reputation to bits in the media. Can't you see the headlines? I can. 'Dennis Kincaid indicted for embezzling millions.'"

"Millions? What do you mean millions? I only took half a million."

"Well, yeah, that's true. You only took half a million from your first employer, but who's really going to be counting? People just read headlines. You're done. It's two million now. I'll be in touch."

The line went dead and Dennis dropped his phone on the couch. He was just going to make enough on the ransom to pay Rodney. All this bullshit he was going through just to pay some asshole off and go back to his life. He kicked at the bottles on the floor, sliding them into the wall where they shattered. The phone rang again. He looked at the caller ID and sighed as he answered.

"Dennis Kincaid."

"Hey, man, where are you?" Zach's voice was full of concern, but Dennis heard anger as well. "You haven't been in the office for days. No one's been able to reach you. What's going on?"

"Sorry. I've been out of town taking care of some personal business," Dennis muttered. "It came up suddenly and I've been busy every minute." He stepped outside the shack.

There was silence on the line, then Zach's voice lowered. "This doesn't have anything to do with that girl you were doing, does it? The one Claire knows about? Man, this little 'trip' of yours better not be about getting more tail."

"No," he inhaled deeply, "it's nothing like that. I just got to take care of this. I should be back to the office Tuesday morning."

"You sure you're okay? Can I do anything to help?" Dennis could picture his childhood friend and partner leaning back in his chair with a look of compassion on his face.

"I'm fine, really. Thanks for calling, Zach. Do me a favor. Tell Donna to clear my schedule for tomorrow and apologize to her for me for rushing out."

"Can't you call her in the morning?"

"Just do this for me buddy, okay?" Dennis clicked the phone closed. Then the woodpecker started again. The bird was twenty feet up in the tree next to the cabin, fiercely tapping at the bark. Then the sobbing seeped through the cracks in the door like a noxious gas.

Dennis walked into the cabin, reaching the back room in seconds. He turned the handle and stomped into the room.

She was lying on the bed on her back. Her bright blue t-shirt and shorts shone like a neon light compared to the dirty brown of the cabin wall or the dingy white sheet under her. The white strip of t-shirt bound around her mouth was soaking wet. Another one was around her eyes and her hands were bound together and tied to the iron bars above her head. Her hair lay plastered on her forehead with sweat and her jaw quivered as her whining filled the room.

"Why don't you just shut up for once?" he yelled at her, nearly tripping over her backpack. He kicked it across the room. "Why do you always have to make so much God-damn noise?" She continued to sob. He walked over and untied the gag around her mouth.

"You better not scream. I have a knife."

"You're a very bad man," she whimpered. "You shouldn't have stolen me from my daddy. I want my daddy. I want my daddy."

"You'll see him tonight, but only if you lie there and be quiet for the rest of the damn day."

"You're a very bad man," she said louder. "My daddy's going to find me and save me and he's going to hurt you for taking me away from him."

"Your daddy," Dennis laughed. "Your daddy will get you back if and when he pays me what he owes me. He doesn't pay me," he laughed to himself, "then you'll pay. It's his decision."

Suddenly, the front door of the cabin creaked opened and slammed shut, followed by complete silence.

35

The halls of the police station were dim and smelled of stale coffee. Ray followed Capriotti up the stairs to the third floor and they turned right. In contrast to the newly-painted lobby, the walls on this floor looked like they hadn't been painted for decades. Avocado green paint peeled away at the ceiling and the doorways.

Capriotti turned the knob of the last door on the right and Ray walked into the small interview room. The same faded avocado color continued. There was only an old oak table in the center with three wooden chairs.

"Have a seat, Ray." Capriotti pulled out the chair at the end of the table and gestured for Ray to sit. "You don't mind if I call you Ray, do you?"

"No, I don't mind." He sat down and pulled his chair in, resting his arms on the wood table.

"I've got to get some paperwork together, so I'll be back in just a few minutes, okay? Hope you don't mind. Can I get you something to drink? Some water? A soda?"

Ray realized he was a little thirsty. "A Coke would be great."

Capriotti stepped out. Ray sat back in the chair and looked around. This wasn't like the interview rooms he'd seen on TV cop shows like "Law and Order." It just had four walls, no mirrors or windows, just a door. The room was silent except for an occasional clicking sound coming from the vent above his head. It sounded as if a small piece of paper was stuck between the blades of a fan. A silvery cobweb hung in the corner above the door.

He put his head in his hands. He couldn't stop thinking about the girl from Friday. Everyone plays pranks and it sounded harmless. It was Friday as he was leaving the complex. A tall dark-haired girl had approached him by his car and asked him for a favor. It would only take a minute and she waved all that money in his face.

But that couldn't have anything to do with the girl missing. The girl said she was from the college and he was her professor. Why would that have anything to do with his kid getting kidnapped? No, no, he was good. He didn't have anything to do with the kidnapping. He just helped a student get one up on a professor that everyone probably hated anyway.

The door opened suddenly and Capriotti walked in with another detective, a taller, older man. He wore the same type of clothes that Capriotti was wearing, but he had at least ten years on Capriotti and a good forty pounds of gut on him.

"Ray, this is my partner, Detective Schultz."

"How you doing?" He stood for a minute and reached out a hand to Schultz, who shook his hand and motioned for him to sit.

"We really appreciate you coming down here to talk to us."

Capriotti handed Ray a can of Coke and sat to his left. Schultz took a seat across from Ray. Capriotti signed and dated the bottom lines of a form on a clipboard and Ray popped the tab of the can and swallowed hard.

"Before we get started, I need to get some paperwork signed." Capriotti leaned back in his chair. "Even though we're just talking here, federal law requires that we read you your Miranda rights and that you sign this form saying these have been read to you. Okay?"

"Yeah, no problem." Capriotti read him his rights, then Ray took the clipboard and signed his name below the officer's.

"So what do you guys what to know?" Ray leaned forward on the table on his folded arms as Schultz opened a file folder. He handed Capriotti a sheet of paper from the folder.

"First, let's verify some information. Your name is Ray Campbell and you're the maintenance worker at the Brookville Condominiums, correct?"

"That's right." Capriotti scribbled a note on the paper.

"How long have you worked there?"

"Almost two years." Another scribble on the paper.

"And what do they have you do on a normal day?"

"I do whatever they need me to do." He took another deep swallow of soda and leaned back in the chair, glancing at Schultz, then back to Capriotti. "It can be anything from replacing kitchen cabinets to plumbing to installing tile. Every condo is different, but I do it all."

"Have you ever met Luke Rosentino in unit 1240?"

He could answer this truthfully.

"No. Up until two weeks ago, I only worked the units in the front of the complex. Paul worked the back half, but management had to let him go. It had something to do with stealing, I heard."

"Was he a good guy other than that?"

"He was all right. He never did me wrong, but

management said they didn't have a choice. So I got all the units until they bring on somebody new. I hope it's soon; these hours are killing me."

Capriotti leaned back in his chair. "That's a raw deal, man. You work twice as hard, but you still get the same deadlines and the same pay? That's not right. A man's got to make a living."

"I know. But I've been making it." Ray shifted in his chair, nodded, and took another sip of Coke. "I couldn't believe how much crap they were piling on me, but at least I've got a job. I'm bustin' my ass, but I get it done."

"I hear you." Capriotti leaned forward. "Sounds like the management trusts you. Sound like they know you're squared away; they let you do what you need to do. That's cool. How long you been doing it? Construction work? Building maintenance and that type of thing?"

"As long as I can remember. My old man's in construction. I was on his crew at eighteen. He taught me everything I know."

How do you get your assignments?" Capriotti asked. "Do they come from the property manager or do tenants call you themselves with problems?"

"No, I only get assignments from Carolyn in the office. The tenants call them in to the office, then I get them from Carolyn. I have to keep a log of everything I do. I turn it in every Friday to Carolyn."

Suddenly, Schultz slid the file folder across the table to Capriotti. He opened it and pulled a sheet of paper off the top.

"Is this your log for last week, Ray?" He slid the paper in front of Ray.

He checked the dates and skimmed the handwritten notes he'd made. "Yeah, this is it." He tried to slide it back.

"No, you hold onto that for me. I've got my own copy."

Nick held up identical sheets. Ray took the sheets back and watched the detectives.

"You know, this is sounding more and more like you're accusing me of something."

Capriotti shook his head and looked straight at Ray.

"We're just trying to get our facts straight, Ray. A child is missing and we need to talk to anyone that might have information about her. Okay? This isn't about you. We're just trying to find this little girl and if you have any information, you would be the hero. Think of that, Ray. You'd be helping Mr. Rosentino find his little girl. There's a reward, too. Isn't that right, Schultz?"

Schultz nodded.

"I wish I could help, but I don't know anything." Ray sat back in the chair and crossed his arms.

"Ray, it says here in Carolyn's notes that you asked for the weekend off. Did you go out of town?"

Ray relaxed a little. "Yeah, I went down to Columbia to see my friend Bobby. We spent the weekend fishin' and watching some football."

"When'd you leave here? Friday afternoon?"

"Yeah, I got on the highway around four o'clock Friday."

"Are you sure about that time, Ray?"

"Yeah, because I remember talking to the secretary in the office right as she was leaving and she had to pick up her kid from the sitter by four."

"Do me a favor. Read your last entry."

Ray picked up the sheet and noticed his hands were trembling. He laid the paper back on the table.

"Tightened kitchen sink pipes in 610. Leak seemed to be fixed; told owner to call if more problems. Carolyn signed off at three-fifty. That's her signature." He turned the paper around for Capriotti to see. Capriotti looked at his own printout and nodded.

"So, Ray, if you were on the highway at four o'clock, tell me how you were seen working on Luke Rosentino's patio door lock at four-forty-five that day?"

∞ ∞ ∞

A gust of wind slammed the door shut behind Becky as she stepped into the shack. She set down the two coffees and the bag of doughnuts on the table and held the front page in front of her. She grimaced as she looked again at Lizzie's picture. The happy girl in the picture looked nothing like the gagged child locked in the back room wearing the blindfold, her hands tied to the headboard spindles. There was also a picture of Luke and one of a student nailing a picture of Lizzie to a wooden telephone pole.

Lizzie's grandmother and father were quoted in the story as saying they would do anything to get her back safely, even paying a ransom. Becky knew what she and Dennis were doing was wrong, but in the end, Lizzie would be back with her father and Becky would finally be with the man she loved. She just had to tough it out with Dennis for one more day and then he'd believe that she loved him.

The building was silent and smelled of stale beer. She stepped over a dozen empty bottles and set the paper on the couch. She grabbed the trash can and started picking up the bottles, one by one, and putting them in the trash.

The back door creaked opened and after a moment, Dennis stepped into the room. He wore his dress slacks and socks and a white t-shirt. His face was covered in stubble and his hair was tousled. He slowly stepped toward her and they watched each other as she picked up the last of the bottles.

"What are you doing?" He picked up one of the gas station coffee cups and took a long drink.

"Just straightening up, that's all. I brought some danish

for breakfast." She pointed at the white bag on top of the newspaper. He took another long drink of coffee.

"We've got a long day ahead of us," he murmured, as if he hadn't heard her. "The kid's been whining. Why don't you give her a bottled water from the cooler and one of those doughnuts?"

"Her name is Lizzie."

"What? Yeah, Lizzie."

Dennis stepped to the couch and picked up the paper.

"Why do you hate him so much?" She looked at Luke's picture as Dennis held the paper open. "It says here he teaches at the college."

"He ruined my life and now I'm ruining his." Lizzie's low whine came through the walls. "Please give that kid something to eat, but leave her eyes covered this time. She needs to forget what we look like."

"It's all going to work out, you know. I just feel it." She picked up the bag and walked toward the back door.

"Beck, wait."

He walked to her and touched her cheek. The bruise wasn't as dark this morning, but it still hurt when he touched it.

"I didn't mean to hurt you last night."

"I know." She put the last of the bottles in the trash and reached for the doughnut bag.

"You just don't understand that if tonight doesn't work out, my career is done. My law firm will be ruined, I'll go to jail and," he picked up the front page and looked at the picture of Luke, "he will have won everything."

36

Luke glanced up from pouring his mug of coffee to see Maria and Claire walk through the front door. Claire pushed her windblown hair away from her face and handed her empty coffee mug to Maria, who walked into the kitchen. She set the mugs down and walked over to kiss him on the cheek.

"Have we heard anything new?"

"No." He glanced into the dining room at Claire. "I shouldn't have yelled at her."

"No, you shouldn't have. She cares about you and Lizzie more than I thought. She even felt bad that she fell asleep in the recliner."

"She said that?" He felt his stomach lurch as Maria nodded.

"Listen, I know it's only been a few weeks since Patty died, and I have to admit I was a little skeptical at first when you told me on the phone about Claire, but if I'm reading you and her right, there's a real connection between the two of you."

"She's an amazing woman, Mom." Luke stirred, then sipped his coffee. "I didn't expect to fall like this. She's smart, intelligent, caring, but strong enough to leave a bad situation and look for something better."

He watched Claire as she looked at the map in the dining room. He realized she'd been in his house, reassuring him and being available to him for almost twenty-four hours. "I was tired this morning. I didn't know what I was saying. She's never going to forgive me for speaking to her like that."

Maria took the mug from his hand, put it on the counter and brought him a muffin, motioning for him to eat. "I think you're wrong. If this connection is what I think it is, she will forgive you, but she needs to hear what you just told me."

"She doesn't want to hear me babble. I practically cussed her out just an hour ago. I should keep my distance for a while and let things cool down."

Maria took his chin in her hand and turned his face to hers.

"Listen, go to her. Apologize and hug the girl. You two need each other and I've got to make more coffee for the men." She kissed him on the cheek and then moved to the coffeemaker, put in a new filter, then looked back at him in the doorway. "Go!"

Luke hesitated only for a moment, then walked up behind Claire. He tapped her on her shoulder. She turned and her eyes were puffy from crying.

"I'm so sorry," they both said at the same moment, then laughed. He placed his muffin on the table, pulled her to his chest and held her close. He ran his fingers through the back of her hair, kissing the top of her head and letting out a sigh of relief.

"I thought I was a goner," he whispered in her ear. "I watched you walk out the front door and thought I'd never see you again."

"You're not getting rid of me that easily." She gently kissed his lips. "I'm sorry I didn't stay up with you last night. I just couldn't keep my eyes open."

"You're here and that's all that matters," he said as he watched one of the officers walk toward them.

☙ ☙ ☙

Nick sat back in the wooden chair and watched Ray's expression evolve from calm to confused to frustrated. Decades on the force had made Nick a near expert at reading people and Ray Campbell was a cheap paperback at best. He wanted to laugh at Ray's transparency, but kept his face expressionless.

"I don't know what you're talking about." Ray sat back in his own chair and crossed his arms across his chest. Then taking the Coke can from the table, he took a long drink and set it quietly back on the table.

"Look, Ray, we know you know about the kidnapping. We know everything." Capriotti glanced at Schultz, who nodded in agreement. "We just need you to tell us in your own words what happened."

"Why do you think I would kidnap some kid I don't even know?" he said, leaning forward in his seat, his hands on the table. "You think I'm some kind of criminal or something, don't you? I'm just a carpenter, for God's sake."

"Then how do you explain the difference between these dated assignment sheets which are signed by you and the testimony of residents in the building where you work? You say you've been working there for years so everyone recognizes you. Now you're the only maintenance worker there, so there's no way you could be confused for anyone else."

These explanations seemed to quiet Ray for a moment, then his resolve of innocence returned with a vengeance.

"So why are you taking these residents' word over mine?

How do you know they don't have a grudge against me or something? Hell, I dated a couple of women in the complex. Maybe it was one of them and they just never got over me or something. You never know with women." He sat back in the chair, appearing to challenge Capriotti, like an overconfident chess player, having just made his best move of the match.

Capriotti waited. The human mind was an amazing organ. Ray's brain was working hard to explain his situation, but the mental anguish was easy to read in his body language. He was having trouble sitting still, he was fidgeting with his hands, and his forehead was covered in small beads of sweat. Capriotti was almost looking forward to taking him down.

"Look, we can do this easy or we can do it the hard way. There's a six-year-old girl that's been taken," he leaned on the table, looked into Ray's eyes and emphasized the last word, "from her father's home and we have no idea who took her or why. All we know is that she was taken from her room Saturday morning through the sliding glass door in the living room. This is the same sliding glass door residents saw you working on Friday late afternoon and there's no maintenance record of the work and the resident, the father, never requested for work to be done on that door. I have to say all that information tells me that you are involved." His eyes stayed on Ray's, never faltering.

He saw a short flicker of fear in Ray's eyes. "It doesn't matter what Luke did or said to you, Ray. We just need to find this little girl and fast. So why not be straight with us and quit wasting all of our time? She might already be dead, for all we know. And if that's true, you'd be looking at criminal charges."

Schultz slid an eight-by-ten copy of Lizzie's photo from the Amber Alert in front of Ray.

Several minutes passed. The detectives never took their eyes off Ray, whose stare never left the picture.

"He didn't do anything to me. I've never even met the guy," Ray muttered, his eyes still focused on the picture. Capriotti kept his silence. Ray's breathing was quick and shallow.

"She paid me." He nearly whispered the words, then was silent for another minute. He finally peeled his eyes from the picture and looked at Capriotti.

"This girl came up to me in the parking lot Friday and offered me a thousand dollars to loosen the lock before I left the property. She said she and her friends were from the university and wanted to play a trick on their professor. It was a lot of money and seemed harmless at the time. I'd heard some of the office staff say that he taught there, so I didn't see any harm in it."

"Had you ever seen her before?"

"No, no, never before. At first, I thought she was a girl I knew from Buddy's, you know, the bar down on Main. That's why I walked over when she called. But then she showed me the cash and started talking about this trick she was planning to play on him." He looked at Capriotti. "I saw the money and just stopped thinking. It was a lot of money!"

Capriotti looked at him and saw the same expression he saw every time a suspect confessed: relief; even if it meant they might be in bigger trouble than before.

"Has she called you since that night?"

"No. She met me in the parking lot, told me what she wanted, handed me the money and left."

"Do you remember what kind of car she was driving?"

"It was a tan Honda," he paused, closing his eyes. "It was an Accord. A tan Accord. I remember it had a bumper sticker. It said 'If you can read this, you're too close.' "

"We're going to need you to give a description of this girl to our sketch artist."

"Yeah, I'll give you whatever you need. God, I can't believe I fell for her story. I'm such an asshole. I'll never forgive myself if something happens to that little girl."

"I know several people that feel that way." Capriotti left Ray in the room and met his supervisor in the hall. "I'm going to call the sketch artist. I think we may have found our kidnapper."

37

An officer told Luke that Nick had just left the police station and would be arriving shortly. Claire looked around the condo at the volunteers of all ages. A dozen students from the college had showed up eager to help. These were the same lumps in the chairs of her classes that she couldn't dredge an ounce of interest from, but they gathered around the table like kids waiting for popsicles being handed out by a neighbor's mom. Nick's officers sent them out with brochures to cover every bare telephone pole.

Maria had contacted the local Catholic church the previous day. She had spoken to the monsignor and explained the problem, and now a dozen parishioners were offering their assistance. Another group introduced themselves to Maria and after she hugged them, she pointed them to a detective who showed them which areas still needed flyers.

When Nick returned from police headquarters, everyone in the condo seemed to move faster and with greater purpose. He hadn't stopped to talk to Luke, but Claire heard Nick tell his detectives to question Luke's neighbors about a tan Honda.

He and Schultz sat at the computer, Maria was in the kitchen making sandwiches for everyone, and Claire suddenly realized she didn't see Luke.

"Maria, where's Luke?"

"I don't know, dear. Check the bedroom. I told him he needs to rest or he's not going to be much good to anyone."

Claire left the kitchen and walked up the beige-carpeted stairs. Pushing open the door at the far end of the hall, she stepped into a small bedroom. The only furniture was a small daybed straight ahead and an antique oak trunk chest under the window to the right. Luke sat cross-legged on the floor with his back to the chest.

Dozens of pictures of Lizzie in all sizes were spread out on the floor in front of him. As she approached him, she noticed he was holding a portrait of himself and another woman holding an infant Lizzie.

She watched his eyes as he traced his finger over the baby's face, then stared at the woman in the picture. There was a sadness that she'd never seen before. He looked lost and shaken to the core.

She stood in front of him for almost a minute before he looked up. He looked back at the photo, shaking his head.

"I can't imagine what Patty thinks of me." Claire wasn't sure if he was speaking to her or himself, his voice was so soft.

"I remember right after Lizzie was born, Patty and I were so scared to hold her. The nurses showed us how to hold her neck steady as we cradled her. I was terrified I'd do it wrong. You'd think coming from a family the size of mine that I'd know how to hold a baby, but when it's your own... and she was so tiny."

"Was she premature?" Claire sat on the floor next to him and placed her hand on his arm. He nodded.

"She was about two weeks early. Plus, Patty and her

family tend to be smaller built. I'd just never seen such a helpless creature before." He traced baby Lizzie's face again.

"Patty was great. From the first day, she ran the show. It was like she'd done it all before. I stood back watching her feed and bathe Lizzie in the evenings. She was perfectly natural with her. I don't know what I'm doing."

He dropped the picture and put his face in his hands.

"You haven't slept at all since this started, have you?" He shook his head.

She stood up, turned and took his hand. She pulled him up and quickly moved the extra pictures off the daybed. She sat on the bed near the pillows under a blanket and patted the bed next to her. He crawled under the covers, then Claire lay on her side and he spooned up against her back, his arm lying across her waist.

"I'll lie with you. We could both use the rest."

"Thank you." His breathing seemed to slow and his muscles relaxed as her eyes grew heavy.

The noises on the first floor quieted to a whisper as he pulled her closer and sleep overtook them both.

ᔕ ᔕ ᔕ

Walking through the tall grass, Dennis felt the dew on his socks and small sticks poking at his ankles. It was almost over. One more day and he'd be done with all this bullshit. It seemed like months since his last full night's sleep. Just a few more hours and he'd have two million dollars and be able to pay Rodney his money. Once he got his hands on the ransom, he'd have Becky take care of the girl and then he'd take care of Becky. She'd become a liability in a very short time.

Just letting the girl see them both had made him realize how little she understood of the plan. He'd tell Becky to take the pillow into the back room and hold it tight on Lizzie's face for a minute and ... problem solved. His handgun was under the Mercedes' front seat. Becky would never see it coming.

He reached the creek and just beyond was the street at the end of the park. He was a good half-mile from the shack. If he timed it right, all the police would find was two bodies. He'd be long gone and there was nothing to tie him to the girl. He'd been extra careful not to leave fingerprints in the shack and now, using Becky's phone, he fit in the final piece of the puzzle.

Out of sight from the road, he leaned against a tree and snapped the voice-changer onto Becky's cell phone. He dialed Luke's number and waited.

It rang five times, then Luke answered in a groggy voice, "Hello?"

"You're falling asleep on me, Luke? I thought you'd be sucking down the coffee. Hell, I thought you'd be out here chasing me down."

"This has been the longest twenty-four hours of my life and I only just shut my eyes, you bastard! Let me hear Lizzie!"

Dennis could hear Luke breathing hard. This is perfect, he thought. He's right where I want him.

"I can't do that, Luke. Just do what I say and you'll have her back tonight."

There was a long silent pause. Dennis kicked the tree... God-damn mother-fucker!

"Did you hear me?"

"Yes, go ahead."

Dennis didn't hesitate. "I have directions for you to drop off the two million dollars. If you bring any authorities with you, I will shoot your daughter between the eyes. There is to be no police involvement whatsoever. Do you understand me?"

"Yes. Give me the directions."

"Travel on I-77 north to the Hill Valley exit. At the bottom of the exit, take a right and travel two-point-four miles. There is an abandoned restaurant on the left. The sign says Granny D's Diner. Park in the grass in front and come around the left side of the building. There's a wooden back porch with a wooden trellis. There are some broken slats on the right side.

"Place the money in two briefcases and slide them under the porch. Then leave the property and go back to your home. Once the money's been counted, I'll call you back with directions on how to get your daughter back. But I see one cop and your daughter pays for your mistake. Do I make myself clear?"

He only waited for Luke to say yes before he ended the call.

38

‿∽⌒∾

Nick heard the click of the phone and looked to his partner. Schultz whispered with his detectives, then poked his head up.

"The call came from a cell phone; the service is with Verizon. We're on the phone with them now. We should have the account and address within thirty minutes."

"Thirty minutes?" Luke spun around after setting the phone down and glared at Schultz. "I kept him on the phone for a full minute like you asked and now we have to wait another thirty minutes before we can even find where he is?" Luke banged his open hand on the wooden table, shaking glasses and coffee cups on the surface. Everyone stopped talking.

"What's the use of having this God-damn equipment if it's going to take hours to find who has Lizzie and where she could possibly be?"

"We're doing the best we can."

Nick watched Luke come off the couch and head toward Schultz. Nick signaled two officers and they each grabbed Luke by an arm and restrained him against a wall just before he knocked over the audio tracking device. Maria and Claire came in from the kitchen, as the officers pushed Luke into an armchair and stood next to him.

Nick walked in front of the chair. As the officers stepped to the side, Nick bent over and laid his hands on the armrests, staring Luke in the face.

"We're not going to be able to find her at all if you destroy my equipment." He could see that Luke was coming undone, but Nick couldn't have him losing his cool at his point in the game. He had to get control.

"It's been more than twenty-four hours," Luke screamed, "since my daughter was taken from her room by a total stranger and now we have to wait thirty more minutes to find out where the call came from? And you think I'm just supposed to sit here and pace the floors? You think that's somehow going to help my kid?" His face was contorted and his breathing was coming in spasms.

Nick pushed him back into the chair, one hand on either shoulder. "Man, you've got to get hold of yourself. We need you and Lizzie needs you. We're working on this as a team and I can't have you losing your mind every time we hit a snag. This person is obviously trying to get to you, Luke. Don't let that happen!"

Luke's eyes were desperate. "You've got to find her, Nick. You've got to find her. I still haven't heard her voice."

Two hours later, Nick and Schultz approached the door of a double-wide trailer about a mile from the state route. Nick had seen dozens of trailers in different levels of decay, but this one was one of the worst. Two rusted Chevy frames sat on cement blocks next to three metal, dented garbage cans toward the back of the dirty white building. A neighbor's Doberman strained at his collar across the dirt path, barking and growling, kicking up dirt.

Schultz climbed onto the metal step and knocked on

the door three times. The Doberman was now desperate to get loose, snarling and baring his teeth. The door slowly opened. After several moments, a woman stepped out from behind it, shading her eyes against the sun. Her gray hair hung thinly over her shoulders and barely covered the cigarette stuck behind her ear. Her cheeks were hollow and freckled, her eyes sunken and distant.

"What ya want? Did them damn neighbors call us in again? I swear," she shook her fist toward the neighbor's trailer and raising her voice, "people should mind their own damn business."

"No, ma'am, no one called us. I'm Detective Schultz and this is Detective Capriotti. Can we come in for just a moment?" Nick watched the woman's face, but her disinterest continued as she waved them in.

The men stepped into the wood paneled living room to the right. Two tan armchairs faced a television sitting on a tall shelving unit that nearly blocked all sunlight from the window behind. To the left was a galley kitchen and a small bedroom stood open toward the back of the trailer.

"So what'd y'all want?" She turned to Schultz, took the cigarette from behind her ear, lit it and took a drag.

"We're looking for a Becky Overton." Schultz stepped into the main room to put some distance between him and the woman. "Does she live here, Ms...?"

There was a flicker of interest in her eyes at the mention of Becky, but then, just as quick, it was gone. "I'm Sharon Overton." She took a long drag and blew it out the side of her mouth. "Yeah, she's my kid, but I ain't seen her in a while. She goes to the college; she lives down there. Why? What's she done?"

"We'd like to talk to Becky as soon as possible. Do you have her address on campus, ma'am?"

"I don't know where she lives." The woman walked

into the kitchen and poured a mug of coffee, then reached on top of the refrigerator for a small flask. Pouring some of the clear liquid into the mug, she looked at Schultz. "She was always trouble. She left home for days at a time and skipped school. Her daddy and I didn't know what to do with her."

Nick picked up a small framed picture from the end table. She didn't look like the troubled teens he'd seen brought into the precinct in the middle of the night. She looked normal and healthy and definitely not like a kidnapper.

"Is this Becky?" Nick gazed over at Ms. Overton, who was sucking down the last of the coffee.

"Yeah, that's her."

"Ms. Overton, do you and your husband pay for a cell phone account for your daughter?"

"Do we look like the Rockefellers?" She spread her arms and looked around the tiny kitchen. "I don't know anything about a cell phone. We can't barely afford a regular phone—we just got our damn service turned back on last month."

"Well, Becky has a cell phone and this is the address on the account."

"Well, she just started at the college last month. She probably hasn't changed everything over." For just a moment, her face softened. "Is she okay?"

Schultz put the frame down.

"We don't know. We're trying to contact her to find out."

She walked toward the front door. "Well, when you find her, tell her to come home." She opened the door and held it open while the men walked out. "She owes me two hundred dollars for them college books. What a waste of my money."

Nick heard the door slam behind him and ran his hand through his crew cut. He realized how short they were on leads. Most of the calls coming over the Amber Alert hotline were dead ends or duplicate calls from people who thought they saw someone that looked like Lizzie, but none of them had led to anything solid.

He hated this part of the job. Keeping a confident outlook when you have nothing new to tell a family member and keeping them from crumbling wasn't taught at the police academy. The phone company had called back with this address pretty quickly and he'd pulled her driver's license picture and put out a Be On the Lookout alert to the officers in the area, but they still didn't know where she was hiding Lizzie or if she was even the one who made the call.

And what was the connection? Why would a college freshman want to harm Luke's daughter? He had a detective on his way to the college to gather information on her. It couldn't be revenge for bad grades; the semester had only started a month ago. He didn't see Luke as the type to fool around with a student. He'd just moved here, the mother of his child had died and he'd just gotten custody of his daughter, plus just starting a teaching gig at a new college in a new state. There was no way it was a relationship gone bad.

Nick realized he'd done all he could for the moment and needed to update Luke and Maria.

രുരുരു

Luke and Maria were sitting at the kitchen table talking quietly while Annie and Claire were washing and drying the dishes when Nick walked in the kitchen.

"I've got some news."

They all turned to him and seemed to come to life.

"We've traced that last call to a cell phone. We're still waiting for Verizon to call us back with the location of the call, but we know whose phone was used. She's a student at the college. Her name is Becky Overton."

Claire felt the plate slip from her fingers. It broke into three large pieces and dozens of smaller slivers.

"Honey," Maria was on her feet and at Claire's side in a second. Claire stood as still as a statue, her hands at her side and she stared at Nick as if he was speaking another language.

"Say that name again." She turned her face slightly as if she would hear it better this time. Luke quickly moved to Claire. Annie took Claire's hand.

"Becky Overton. Do you know her?"

"Yes." Claire felt like the room was spinning. "She's one of my students." The idea wouldn't compute. "Are you saying you think she took Lizzie?"

"We're still not sure of anything, but we do know that the last ransom call came from Becky's cell phone."

Luke put his arm around Claire's shoulders. He walked her to the patio doors, where a cool breeze seemed to revive her. Her eyes focused on Luke and tears welled in the corners. Nick came out with a glass of water and made her sit in one of the patio chairs. He and Luke sat on either side of her.

"It can't be her, Luke. It just can't."

"Tell me about her."

She took a sip of water.

"She's the girl I told you about that tried to commit suicide right after classes started. It was about a month ago."

Nick pulled out his memo pad and a pen. "You say she attempted suicide? How do you know about that?" He scooted his chair closer to hers.

Images from that night ran through Claire's mind so clearly. The vacant look in Becky's eyes in the hospital still haunted her.

"I was the one who found her. We talked the second day of class. She'd written this heartfelt letter as an assignment and I thought I could help her. You know," she turned to Luke, "help her through the first few weeks of college. Then a few nights later, I was leaving campus after dark and I found her on a park bench. I thought she was just passed out from drinking, but I found out later she'd taken pills as well."

"Has she dropped your class?" Luke leaned forward, leaning his elbows on his knees.

"No, she missed a week, but then got with me after classes to catch up on the work and notes. She hasn't missed a class..."

"What is it?"

Claire shook her head, as if trying to capture an image in her mind.

"It might be nothing, but the other day, we were having a heated discussion on that day's topic in lab. Becky was making her point to the class when her cell phone rang. She stepped outside to take it, then rushed back in, grabbed her books and left the class. It was unusual because she's usually not one to make a scene."

"It might be something." Nick made a note. "Anything else you remember?"

"She wasn't there Friday." Luke put his head in his hands.

"How do you know?"

"She and I have talked every Friday since classes started—five Fridays—you know, talked about plans for the weekend and that sort of thing. She usually sits right in the front of the auditorium." She shook her head with eyes closed, like she was there in her mind. "No, she wasn't in class Friday. God, it can't be her. Why would it be her?"

"Detective Capriotti," a detective called from inside the condo, "Verizon called back with the location of the call."

∾ ∾ ∾

Feeling the first hint of hope that day, Luke nearly flipped the patio chair as he stood and ran into the condo. He reached the table at the same moment Nick did.

"Well?" said Nick, just as Luke said, "Where?"

"They said the call came from a wooded area east of I-77 between State Route 32 and Collins Road."

Luke stared at the officer, waiting for him to continue, but he stopped talking.

"That's the best you can do?" He pounded on the table and stared at Nick. "But that's almost two miles. You said they would be able to narrow it down to a specific place."

"They're still working on narrowing it down, but that's what we've got for now. The kidnapper was walking as he was talking, so there's not a static point. We'll send some officers down to the area to question residents."

"Question residents? We know where the call came from. Let's get this guy. We have all these officers—form a circle and trap him!"

"It's a big area, Luke. Let's listen to the tape again. Maybe there's something we're missing. We're trying to narrow the search area as small as possible."

They all gathered around the machine and Schultz hit "Play." The tape began playing and Luke heard the electronic voice fill the room. It didn't have the same menacing tone that he'd heard only two hours earlier. Luke heard the wind blowing and twigs snapping in the background. How could he have missed these details before? They were so clear.

Suddenly, Annie reached out and grabbed Schultz's shoulder.

"Stop, rewind that."

Schultz hit the stop button, then the rewind button,

then play. The voice filled the room again. Annie leaned over the speaker, waiting. Nick leaned down as well. Luke heard the wind and twigs, then another noise. It was a church bell deep in the background.

"Right there. Stop."

Annie turned to Nick.

"I'd know that sound anywhere. Those are the church bells at Woodland Baptist. It's just north of Collins. They play the bells on Sundays. The bells have been out of tune for almost forty years. Listen."

Schultz rewound the tape and turned some dials. When he hit play again, the bells replaced the kidnapper's voice. Luke cringed as the sound hit his ears.

Nick straightened and turned to Annie.

"How did you know that?"

"I lived a block away from the church when I was in grade school. We lived in that house for almost ten years. I've spent almost twenty years trying to forget that sound." She turned to Luke. "That's just what it sounded like from my bedroom window."

39

Nick pulled his department-issued Chevy Impala to the curb of Collins Road and watched three other unmarked cars pull behind him. The homes along Collins were built around the 1950s with big porches and big yards. Nick thought of his home and the ten acres surrounding it and realized how lucky he was to have found it three years earlier. His mind drifted to his back deck. Those mornings overlooking his lake with a hot cup of coffee at dawn were the most peaceful moments in his life.

Sometimes, the solitude was too much, but his work was his life and no woman would understand the hours these creeps made him work just to catch them. Besides, the bar scene and blind dates offered by his friends at the precinct depressed him. If there was a woman for him, she'd find him.

He walked past the first two cruisers and the men gathered around him.

"Listen up, guys, our latest information is that the second ransom call came from this area about two hours ago. We're going to check with every resident on this street and the next to see if anyone saw someone on a cell phone at that time, who may have seemed out of place or acting unusual. The cell phone belongs to a Becky Overton, eighteen, white, five foot nine, long brown hair. We don't know for sure that Becky is the one that made the call, only that it was her phone."

He looked at the faces around him and saw determination and intensity. These guys were the best in the business, but only one was a father. He needed them to understand the odds they were up against.

"Six-year-old Lizzie Rosentino has been missing for more than twenty-four hours. We have almost no information on where she is or who's taken her. We need to find her as soon as possible." He looked from one face to the next. "Any information you receive from these citizens, you report to me immediately. Let's find this girl."

He watched as the men moved toward the houses. Two officers started toward the nearest homes as the other two got back in their cars and headed to the next street. We've got to find Lizzie, Nick thought as he approached the front door of a house. Time's running out.

∾ ∾ ∾

Claire stepped onto the back patio and sat on one of the patio chairs. She inhaled deeply and tried to clear her mind. She couldn't stop thinking about Becky. During the days and nights following her suicide attempt, Becky had confided in Claire. They had talked long into the night about life and love and how important it was not to lose yourself in a relationship.

Becky had cried for hours about this man who had left her to return to his wife. She never said his name or what he did, only how he made her feel.

But when Becky returned to school, Claire thought she had a real chance of succeeding. She seemed determined and focused. How could Becky possibly be involved with Lizzie's kidnapping?

"Mind a little company?"

Claire looked up to see Annie in the doorway. "No, please, sit."

"Where were you just now?" Annie sat in the chair next to Claire.

Claire watched as three large crows circled over the pines. "I just can't understand how Becky could be involved in this mess."

"There is a chance that the kidnappers stole her phone and she doesn't have anything to do with Lizzie." Claire watched Annie's face and saw the doubt. "I know it doesn't sound plausible, but anything's possible."

"Annie, this girl is so young. She had a fling with someone over the summer and she fell hard. When he broke it off, she was destroyed; so much so that she tried to take her own life. She's got no family to speak of, not very many friends and this man, who swore he'd be with her for the duration, dumped her."

"I'm glad you were there for her."

"I am too. It's been a month since the night I found her on the bench. We talked a lot while she was in hospital and a dozen times in my classroom. She was in my class the past two weeks and she was back, better than ever."

"What did you tell her?"

Claire shrugged. "I just tried to tell her that she has to be her own person. She can't rely on a man to make her happy. It just doesn't work that way." A breeze blew through the pines and a pair of squirrels chased each other down one tree and up another. "I really don't know how I can tell anyone that, though, when you look at how I let Dennis rule my life."

"Rule your life? Was it really that bad?"

"I'm sure he didn't realize it, but I set my schedule by him. I tried to have dinner ready when he said he'd be home. I arranged my schedule at work so I could be home when he got home. There were so many decisions I made during the day to try and make his life better." She felt her eyes starting to tear up and shook her head. "And what did I get for it? My husband, the man I doted on, was sleeping around and didn't give a shit about me."

"But you discovered the truth. You're moving on. You're one of the bravest women I know." Claire looked quizzically at Annie.

"Bravest?"

"Hell, yes. You find out he's been lying to you and you kicked his ass out. That took a lot of guts."

Annie turned around and watched the men surround the fax machine.

"Let's go in and see what's happening."

They stepped into the dining room and watched as Nick pulled a few papers off the fax. He looked down the sheet, then put it on the table and pointed to several places on the page.

Annie turned to Maria. "What's going on?"

"Verizon just faxed over the last two months of calls from Becky's phone."

Claire walked toward Nick and watched as he pointed to line after line on the bill. She was standing behind Nick when she heard him say a familiar number.

She felt as if someone had kicked her in the stomach with a steel-toed boot.

"What was that number?"

Nick turned, surprised to see her and worried when the color left her face.

"Schultz just noticed that Becky's called this same number dozens of times in the past few days. I was just about to call Verizon and get the account information on the number."

"You don't have to call. I can tell you. That's my husband's cell phone number."

The dining room began to fade and all the feeling left Claire's legs. The voices in the room joined together in a loud hum as the room went dark.

40

✧

After days of wading through the tall grass and weeds surrounding the shack, there was a flattened path, but Dennis was still getting eaten alive. The bugs were everywhere. Smacking a mosquito on his forearm, he flicked it off with his fingers and wiped the spot of blood away.

The call had gone well and then he'd gone to get dinner. Thoughts raced through his mind so fast, he could barely recognize them. But one thing was certain: Luke Rosentino was on the edge. Dennis had heard it in his voice. The bastard was starting to crack. He was sitting in his condo waiting for Dennis to tell him what to do, powerless and scared.

Just a few more hours and this whole mess would be blamed on Becky. He'd tell her to stay with the kid and he'd pick up the money, then he'd come back for her. His original plan was to make Becky smother the girl, then he'd shoot Becky, but he realized now that Becky wasn't strong enough to kill anyone, so he decided he'd have to kill them both himself. He didn't want to kill Becky, but he had no choice. Becky would tell the truth if the cops found her.

She had the power to destroy him, his business and his reputation. Opening the door of the shack, he realized he needed to play along just a little longer.

She wasn't in the front room, so he quietly stepped across to the couch. He slipped her phone back into her purse on the floor. As he zipped the purse, the doorknob of the back room opened slowly and Becky backed out quietly. She was wearing jean shorts and a blue tank top. Her long hair was pulled back in a ponytail with strands of hair hanging by her face. She turned and jumped when she saw him.

"Oh, I didn't know you were back. Lizzie just fell asleep." She looked at the bag in his hand and her eyes brightened. "You brought dinner." She walked toward him and took the bag.

Her eyes were tired, he noticed. There were dark circles underneath and her eyelids were heavy. He saw she was wearing the same clothes from the day before. She bent over and pushed the magazines from two of the three couch cushions.

"Do you want to eat now?" He suddenly knew what he needed and it wasn't the burgers in the bag.

He walked to her and set the bag on the cooler in front of the couch. Touching her face with his fingertips, he leaned forward, lightly brushing her lips with his. He ran his finger down the side of her neck and followed it with his lips as he placed the other hand on her lower back and pulled her closer. She ground against him. He heard her catch her breath as he moved back to her lips.

"Sit down," he whispered. He sat next to her and leaned her back, sliding his hand under the tank top and bra, then cupping her skin in his hand. He'd always liked her firm breasts and they reacted so nicely to his touch. He pulled her top over her head and unhooked and removed her bra. Squeezing one breast, he flicked his tongue over her other nipple, then nibbled around it.

He could feel blood rushing in his head as he wrapped one of his arms around her back, bringing her body closer to his. His mind raced as he felt himself growing harder with every movement she made. Her body writhed under his touch. Her eyes were closed and her breaths came out in gasps.

"Make love to me," she whispered, taking his face in her hands. "Tell me you love me."

He ran his hands over her flat stomach and wrestled with the button and zipper of her shorts. Somewhere in the back of his mind, he remembered a night at the firm's apartment where she'd asked him to be rough with her. He remembered tearing her clothes off and pushing her onto the bed. She'd followed his commands and the sex was angry and almost dangerous that night. She had the same look in her eyes now.

The memories now sped him toward his destination. He quickly unzipped and pulled her shorts off, then undid his own button and zipper while holding his hand over her mouth. He spread her legs and wrapped them around him; her moaning and wild eyes drove him on. He had her pinned against the couch. She was really moving now. It was just as hot as he remembered. She couldn't move and he was in control. His pants were off and he put his hand between her legs when she suddenly bucked her hips and he landed on the floor on his back.

"What the hell is wrong with you?" He stared at her as she sat up on the couch in just her panties and breathing hard. "What the fuck did you do that for?"

She pulled her legs close to her chest and wrapped her arms around them.

"I don't want to just fuck and then put our clothes

back on." She was openly crying now and trembling. "I want you to love me, Dennis." She looked down at him with tears rolling down her face. "I want you to tell me you love me. I know you love me."

"Jesus Christ, Becky." He felt like hitting something. He felt like backhanding her. Every nerve in his body was on edge and now he was sitting in front of her in his underwear. "I don't love you right now, that's for God damn sure."

He watched as her body shook as she began to sob. He tried to focus. He had to get back in control. Sex was not going to happen. She was too emotional right now. He read it wrong. He had to fix this and fix it quick. He swallowed hard, stood up, put his pants on, and sat next to her on the couch, putting his arm around her waist.

"I'm sorry, okay? I'm sorry. I got carried away. I'm sorry. I just want to be with you." He whispered the words in her ear while leaning her against his chest. "I love you, Beck. You know that." She sobbed harder and let herself rest against him, shaking a little less. "These last few days have been difficult for both of us. I just wanted to be with you. You looked so beautiful just now. I just had to have you."

"You love me?" She sniffled as she asked.

"Of course." He pulled a handkerchief from his pants pocket and handed it to her. "Shhhh. Just calm down and dry your eyes. Just a few more hours and this will all be over."

∾ ∾ ∾

The voices drifted in and out of her head, but Claire couldn't hear what they were saying. A gray fog filled her head and she couldn't move. A moment later, a horrible acrid smell attacked her senses and she opened her eyes. Maria was leaning over her, waving a small bottle. Annie, Nick, Schultz and two other officers stood in the background, watching with shocked expressions.

"I think she's coming around," Maria said softly as she placed a cool washcloth on Claire's forehead. Claire suddenly realized she was on her back on the floor and the back of her head was pounding.

"What happened?" she asked, sitting up slowly with Annie's help. As soon as she said the words, she remembered the phone number. "Oh my God, it can't be." She began to sob. It couldn't be possible. Dennis was responsible for this entire kidnapping.

"Shhhhhh, you took a nasty fall." Maria took a sandwich bag filled with ice from one of the officers, wrapped a washcloth around it and held it to the back of Claire's head. The cold was worse than the headache, but Maria held it in place.

Becky had called Dennis a dozen times the past few days.

Suddenly, pieces of the puzzle came racing at Claire. Dennis' late nights and weekends at the office, Becky's broken heart, the man she'd fallen in love with during the summer, the fact that Dennis wouldn't tell Claire the name of his lover and the fact that Becky had raced from Claire's classroom three days earlier after receiving a cell phone call. The composition Becky wrote; it was a love letter to Dennis from Becky.

Claire's stomach churned. She was going to be sick.

"It's all my fault. Oh, my God, my husband and my student kidnapped Lizzie. Oh, my God." Tears streamed down her cheeks as more pieces fit together.

She remembered the night she confronted Dennis at the house. He said he'd been working at the office, but he'd been with Becky. That's who Annie saw him with in the Mercedes. Then the night Dennis came to get his papers from the house, and Luke had confronted him. That had been after Dennis had attacked Luke in her office.

"Where's Luke?" She looked around the room, but didn't see him.

"He's on the patio with Nick, honey. You just sit here for a few minutes and catch your breath."

She grabbed Maria's hands.

"I've got to talk to him. Dennis took Lizzie and I'm the reason."

41

∽∩∾

Looking out the patio doors, Maria watched Luke and Nick speak at the far end of the patio. Luke stood with his shoulders hunched over as they looked over the phone records.

Maria lowered her head and said softly, "Dear Lord, please help us find my granddaughter. There's so much pain in this house right now. Please show me how to help my son. Please give me a sign of what I'm to do. Amen." On the last word, she turned to see Annie.

"Maria, will you come with me, please?

Twenty minutes later, Annie and Maria pulled into Woodland Baptist's parking lot. The white wooden clapboard church stood back from the road on a small hill. Tall stained glass windows covered the sides of the building and rosebushes stood in rows against the stone foundation. The bell tower stood tall near the back of the church on the right. Two robins flew out from between the wooden slats just below the bell.

"It's beautiful." Maria got out of the car and turned to Annie, who was locking her door. "Did your parents go here?"

"They went every Sunday when I was little. My sister and I would always go to Sunday school in a room near the back while they went to services."

They opened the heavy wooden doors and walked into the cool open space. Maria allowed her eyes to adjust to the dark. The church was small with only ten double rows of wooden pews with red seat cushions. The middle aisle had shiny white marble leading to the wooden pulpit and a yellow marble altar. A statue of Jesus stood on either side of the altar, each with one arm outreached. The women stood at the back of the church.

Annie looked around. "I feel like there's a reason I should be here, but I don't know what it is. I just felt so drawn to this place today."

Maria bowed her head. Thank you, God, for answering my prayers.

"Been a while since you've been here?"

"Years and years, but it doesn't look any different from when I was little."

She followed Maria into the last row and sat beside her. They sat quietly for a few moments, then Annie spoke softly.

"Have you ever gone back to your past and suddenly remembered a moment you haven't thought of in years?"

"Of course."

"My sister and I would ride our bikes in the park instead of going to services."

"The park?"

"My parents' house is about a quarter mile from here. We lived on about twenty acres. We would tell our mom we were riding our bikes to church, then ride out the back of the property and over the broken fence into the state park behind our house."

Annie's expression crumbled and the furrowed brow returned.

"Honey, what's the matter?"

"I was remembering one Sunday morning. God, how could I have forgotten?" She put her hands over her mouth and her head down.

"What is it, baby?" Maria put her arm around Annie and pulled her hair back from her face.

"Those boys. Those horrible boys." She turned to Maria with moist eyes. "One Sunday, Paula and I rode our bikes over the fence into the park. We were riding through the grass and we noticed some older boys following us on their bikes. I recognized two of them from the high school; they'd just graduated. I didn't know the third boy." Annie looked at the altar and a tear rolled down her face.

"I had ridden up ahead around a bend and a minute later, I realized Paula wasn't behind me. I rode back and saw her bike on the ground and two of them were holding her arms and they were pulling her toward the third one. He was undoing his belt."

Maria felt Annie shaking.

"What did you do?"

"I rode as fast as I could up to them, dropped my bike and ran toward them, screaming at the top of my lungs. They let go of Paula and started running away. I grabbed her and we ran back toward our house as fast as we could. She said they were trying to get her into the cabin."

"Cabin?"

"They were standing next to an old cabin where the maintenance crew kept the lawn equipment and tools."

Maria and Annie turned to each other, then both stood and ran for the door.

"Call Nick on his cell phone," Maria said. "Tell him how to get to your parents' house and to bring all the men he has available."

രാ രാരാ

Becky walked back into the shack pulling Lizzie by the hand. Her blindfold was loose, but when Becky tightened it, it pulled Lizzie's hair. She hoped Dennis didn't notice. The last thing she wanted was to upset him again. It would be fine once she tied Lizzie back to the bedpost. He was pacing the room and looked up as they came in.

"Did you all go out for ice cream?" His voice was low and thick with sarcasm.

"No." Becky moved Lizzie behind her and stared into his face. "She needed to go to the bathroom and since you didn't want the shack to smell, I took her to the training potty you put outside." She looked back at Lizzie, who had her head down. She could feel the little girl shaking.

"You need to get her things together. This is all coming together tonight." He started to pace again, then said in a lower voice, "Only a few more hours."

"Then I'm going to see my daddy?" Lizzie said breathlessly, trying to take the blindfold off with her free hand. Dennis reached out and held it tight against her face.

"Take her back in the room." He glared at Becky and spoke the words through clenched teeth. "And make sure this blindfold is on tight."

Becky watched his eyes, but there was no expression, no kindness. Becky pulled Lizzie by the hand into the room, closed the door, and sat her on the bed. Lizzie began to cry.

"Why won't you let me see my daddy? Why don't you like my daddy? What did my daddy do to you? Why are you keeping me here? Why won't you let me go?" Her voice become louder and louder with each question. Becky kneeled in front of Lizzie and held both her small hands in hers.

"Honey, listen. I don't like this any more than you do,

but if everything goes like it's supposed to, you'll see your daddy tonight."

"Really?" She whispered the word, then a smile covered her face. "I get to see Daddy. Really?"

"Shhhh." Becky lifted Lizzie back on the bed and laid her back. "I need you to be really quiet for the next little while. My friend's very upset right now." Becky tied the ropes around her wrists and slipped the rope around the bedpost. "He wants to make sure you get back home and it would really help if you could stay quiet back here. Can you do that for me?"

Lizzie nodded as Becky tied the second rope. "It's all going to be fine. You just have to believe it."

She patted Lizzie on the head and walked back into the main room, shutting the door behind her. The room was darker than just a few moments earlier and she went to the window. Gray storm clouds drifted above the shack.

"Is there something I can do to help?" She turned to look at Dennis at the shack's open door. His fingers were flying over his Blackberry keys.

"No, thanks." His reply came quickly as if he hadn't really heard her. She walked across the room and put her hands around his waist from behind. He didn't stop typing, so she laid her cheek on his back.

"I put Lizzie's stuff in her backpack." He nodded, but didn't reply. She glanced at the cooler and saw the restaurant bag. One of the fry boxes had tipped over and the soda can sat unopened.

She walked over and picked up the bag. "Aren't you going to eat your dinner?

"I'll eat when I'm done with this." His fingers clicked across the keys.

"I don't want to eat alone. Can't you put that down for a few minutes?"

He turned on her. "No, I can't put it down." His voice was guttural. "I have to finish sending this e-mail and then I have about thirty others I have to read." He walked toward her, his voice getting louder with each step. "Just because I'm out here with you and the kid doesn't mean I can let my work at the firm pile up. I work for a living, you know? Now just sit down and eat your damn sandwich."

He turned back to the doorframe and went back to his typing. Becky's vision blurred with tears and she started to answer him, but anger overtook her. She picked up the bag of food and threw it at him, hitting him in the back of the head.

"What the hell?" He grabbed the back of his head and looked at the food scattered on the floor.

"I'm done."

Becky leaned over and put the two *People* magazines on the couch into her backpack, then scooped up two t-shirts and a pair of socks and stuffed them in. Standing tall, she turned to him. "I've had enough. I'm leaving."

"What are you talking about?" She pushed her way past him and stepped down from the shack into the grass and spun around.

"I've had it, Dennis. I've had it." Months of anger and fear released as she screamed. "You tell me about this plan to hurt Luke and make a million dollars that you want me to work on with you. So I do as you ask and take Lizzie from her father's house in the middle of the night and keep her here tied up for days on end in this nasty ass shack. You told me that we'd be together after this is over and that you want to be with me, but every time you're here, you end up yelling and screaming at me and hitting me and it's not worth it, Dennis." She took a deep breath and said in a lower voice, "It's just not worth it."

She watched his expression soften. "Becky, come on.

Don't be like this."

"No!" She screamed, backing away from him. "I'm done." She turned and started walking in the direction of the parking lot. She heard him running through the tall grass, then felt his hand on her arm.

"Becky, please stop." His tone was softer. "I need you."

She shook his hand off as hard as she could. "You only need me to finish this job. You don't really love me. You never did. I know that now."

She started to run, but he quickly caught up to her. He grabbed her arm and turned her to face him. She swung her arm back, then slapped his face as hard as she could, but instead of hitting her back, he pulled her close to him, wrapping his arms around her.

"I've been an asshole. You're right. I don't deserve you."

He lifted her chin and saw tears in her eyes. "I'm sorry I haven't told you more often how I feel about you and I'm sorry if I've snapped at you. I've been under so much pressure from the firm and other things. But that's not your fault. I need you with me." He held Becky to his chest and whispered in her ear, "After this is all done, we'll be together. We'll go somewhere away from all this stress and maybe get married. I love you, Becky."

The tears fell free as she put her arms around him. She breathed in his cologne and let his last words sink in. It was true. He did love her.

"I love you, too, Dennis." She tucked her head under his chin and felt his chest muscles tighten against her cheek. A light breeze had been blowing, but the winds now gusted around them. Looking up, she saw the clouds were now dark gray.

"It looks like it's going to rain."

"Shhhh." He was listening to something in the distance.

A moment later, she heard the sound of dogs barking from the woods behind the shack.

"I don't like the sound of that," Dennis said, pushing her toward the shack. "We need to get out of here."

42

Stepping into the kitchen, a zillion thoughts raced through Luke's mind. Nick and his men were at the park searching for Lizzie. They now had the name of a college student whose phone had been used to make the ransom calls. She was a student of Claire's and the person she had called most since Lizzie's disappearance was Claire's husband. Both were suspects, but still, no one knew where Lizzie was being held.

He looked into the dining room and watched Claire struggle to stand, and the truth hit him like a brick. His girlfriend's husband had kidnapped his daughter. The woman he had been dating for a month and was falling in love with was married to the man who was holding his daughter hostage this very minute.

"Honey, are you all right?" Maria laid her hand on his shoulder and looked up into his face.

"This is my fault." Luke leaned against the wall and his legs felt like Jell-O. Maria guided him into a kitchen chair and he watched Claire as she looked around the room. Their eyes met and she stood and began walking toward him. Before she could reach him, an FBI agent approached her and holding her arm, motioned for her to come back with him to the couch.

Luke turned to Maria, who had pulled another chair next to his and sat down. "If I hadn't fallen for a married woman, none of this would have happened. Lizzie and I would be at the park together on the swings or she'd be riding her bike in the parking lot. But because of me—"

"I need you to stop talking like that."

"Mom, if I had acted like a responsible father and put Lizzie first instead of dating the first woman I met, my daughter would be here instead of...God, what kind of man does that?" He looked into the living room and watched the same lost look cross Claire's face as she watched him.

"The kind of man who tries the best he can, but who is a victim of evil." Maria took both of his hands in hers. "You're the kind of man who's not going to rest until his daughter is safe in his arms and I know that's going to be very soon."

He looked at his mother and saw a quiet peace. He heard her words, but her certainty confused him. "How can you know that? How can you say that? We have no idea where she is."

"I can say it because an hour ago, we didn't know who had her and now we have a pretty good idea. I can say it because well-trained professionals like Nick and his team found the two people who either have her or know where she's being held. And, because of modern technology, we know the approximate location of the second ransom call. Now, I know you want all the answers now, but I say this is all going to work out."

"What in the world could make you say that and believe it so strongly?"

"You were probably too young to remember, but we lost Tom when he was four." She sat back in her chair and crossed her arms. "He was gone for five hours." She held her hand up when Luke started to speak. "I know being lost and being taken are two very different situations, but I'm telling you that I remember the guilt and the pain that you're feeling now just like it was yesterday. And you know what I did?"

"You prayed."

"Damn right I did. We gave the police our most recent picture of Tom and they started interviewing neighbors. I knelt down in the living room and prayed for your brother's safety. I couldn't go anywhere, so I figured prayer was the only thing I could do to help. Next thing I knew, about a dozen neighbors and family members were in the living room praying for Tom with me."

"I don't remember this."

"You were probably two. Your father and I asked everyone that called to pray for Tom and for the police. We finally found him about a mile away at dusk. He was playing at St. Catherine's School about a mile from our house. He had been playing on the slide and swings on the playground and while chasing his ball, he'd fallen down a small flight of stairs that led to a basement storeroom. Then it started to thunder and he sat down to wait out the rain.

"I had called the convent and Sister Mary Agnes went out to search the school property and found him. Other than a skinned knee and a few scratches, he was fine."

Luke looked into his mother's eyes and saw determination and faith. She had always been faithful to the church, but it brought her peace and serenity that he'd never known.

"So you've been here?"

"I prayed for strength and help and I asked my friends and family to do the same and I got what I needed: my son back. I think you should try it. We're going to need all the help we can get in the next few hours."

જ જ જ

Two bolts of lightning lit up the gray sky, one right after the other as Becky entered the shack, stepping over the fast food bag and fries that had spilled out. She watched as Dennis closed the door behind him.

All the arguments and stress and crying and loneliness of the past months slipped away when she remembered his eyes when he'd told her he loved her just now. She'd known it all along. How could she have yelled at him and threatened to leave when it was so obvious that he needed her and was under so much stress? She berated herself for not understanding him.

A crack of thunder filled the room, but it couldn't cover Lizzie's shrieks.

Becky moved quickly to the back of the shed and opened the door. Lizzie's blindfold had slid off her left eye and she met Becky's stare. Lizzie stopped crying for a moment and tried to catch her breath.

"I thought you said I was going to see Daddy?"

The nagging questions of why they were doing such an awful thing to such a cute little girl needled Becky's brain, but she pushed it aside as she remembered Dennis' urgent need to leave. She picked up Lizzie's backpack, then kneeled on the splintered wood floor and looked under the bed for any clothes left behind.

"You will, but right now, we have to go for a ride with my friend."

Becky took the blanket off Lizzie and started to fold it.

"I don't like your friend. Where are we going? When can I see my daddy?"

Fresh tears rolled down Lizzie's cheeks.

Becky leaned her elbows on the edge of the bed. "I don't know," she heard herself say in an angry tone. She took a deep breath. This was not Lizzie's fault.

"Honey, all I know is we're leaving in a minute and I've got to get your stuff together."

Becky wanted to know what Dennis was planning, but at the same time, she didn't. In any case, the plan seemed to be falling apart and she wasn't looking forward to driving with Dennis in this storm. She just wanted this all to be over so they could be together. But first, she had to make sure nothing was left behind.

Another lightning bolt illuminated the room and a second later, thunder boomed loud enough to make her jump. The storm must be right above us, she thought. A moment later, she heard heavy rain hitting the roof.

"I don't want to go. I want to see my daddy." Lizzie started thrashing in the bed, kicking her legs and flipping her head from side to side. The blindfold flew off both eyes now and Lizzie continued to scream, "I want my daddy. I want to see my daddy."

Becky felt every nerve in her body alive with tension and worry. If Dennis came in and saw Lizzie like this, there was no telling how he'd react.

She put down the blanket and sat on the bed. Becky untied her hands and pulled Lizzie onto her lap, wrapping her arms around Lizzie and resting the little girl's head on her chest while putting the blindfold back on. The whole time, she watched the door for Dennis.

"Shhhhh. Come on, come on, calm down. There's no use getting so upset."

Becky rocked back and forth until Lizzie quieted some. "We're going for a ride and we need to go now. I need you to be good so you don't upset my friend. Hold onto my hand, okay?"

She stood and held onto Lizzie's small hand, guiding the blindfolded girl toward the door. But before she could reach the door, it swung open and Dennis filled the space, his eyes wide, looking past them and searching the room.

"Have you got everything?" He didn't wait for her to answer. "Come on, we've got to go." He grabbed Lizzie's hand from Becky and pulled her out of the room, causing her to stumble and fall. "Come on, stand up." He yanked on her arm, pulling her to a standing position.

When Lizzie had trouble standing, he pushed her to Becky. "I don't have time for this." He started pulling the drink cooler toward the door by its handle.

"Becky, get both your backpacks. I'll drag this to the car." He looked back to see Becky kneeling on the floor.

"What now?" he bellowed.

"She's got a cut on her knee."

"She'll be fine. Just pick her—"

"You go." Becky screamed at him, continuing to hold onto Lizzie. "We'll be there in a second." They stared at each other for a moment, then Dennis shook his head and walked out the door, bumping the cooler down the outside steps.

Becky realized Dennis had cleaned up all the food from the restaurant and she began to look for something to wipe Lizzie's cut.

She saw something white under the couch and pulled out a napkin. Holding Lizzie on her knee, she dabbed at the cut. Seeing it wasn't deep, she stood and took Lizzie's hand.

"C'mon. Let's run to the car before the rain gets worse."

43

ᒎᒎᒎ

Nick closed his cell phone and said a silent prayer of thanksgiving for the call from Annie, then he called through dispatch to all the officers involved to line their cars along the road in front of the Gordon house on Collins Road. Nick's men were arriving quickly. He had also called in Officer Kava and his bloodhound partner, Tito.

Nick reached into the car and pulled out a map of the state park that a trooper had handed him as he'd left Luke's condo. He spread the map on the hood of the car. The park was mostly wooded acreage with trails near the back. Near the entrance was a lake and open fields that families could use for impromptu baseball or football games. The main park entrance was three miles away on another road. The men gathered around Nick and he faced the group.

"Okay, listen up." A lightning bolt lit the sky and a second later, thunder rumbled. The Gordons' house sat on the only cleared land on the park side of the road, but tall pines surrounded the house, almost concealing it from view. "I just got a call from a citizen with a good tip on one of the only uninhabited structures in this area. It's a maintenance shack about a half mile into this wooded area straight ahead." Nick pointed into the densest part of the woods next to the Gordon home.

"I have reason to believe that's where the child is being held. This is the back of Johnson State Park. The entrance to the park is three miles away on Smith Road, so the majority of us are going to move through these woods to the shack."

He held his picture of Lizzie in the air.

"This is the girl we are looking for: Lizzie Rosentino. We think she is with Dennis Kincaid and Becky Overton, both white. Kincaid is in his late thirties, blond hair, blue eyes. Overton is eighteen, long brown hair and is probably caring for the child. Kincaid may be armed. Our main objective is Lizzie's safety. Monitor your radios and call in anything suspicious."

He pointed to three of his men and motioned for them to come to the car and pointed to the main entrance on the map.

"I need you three to take your cruisers and move to the front of the park and block the entrance. Check every car that comes in or out of the driveway."

The three officers ran to their cars and turned them around heading in the opposite direction. He pointed to Kava.

"You and Tito take the lead through the woods. The rest of us will follow."

Suddenly, a car squealed into the Gordons' driveway eighty feet in front of Nick. Annie jumped from the driver's seat and shouted at him. "Nick, the shack is this way." She pointed toward the back of the Gordon property.

Nick ran to Annie's car.

"You're sure about this shack?"

"Yeah. I remember it like it was yesterday. You can go through my parents' yard. They're out of town, but I know they'd do anything they could to help Luke. It's a more direct route than through these woods," she said, pointing at the woods next to the house.

"Okay." He turned to the men. "We're going through the back of this property," he pointed to the Gordon house. "It's quicker access."

Kava reached into a pouch tied to his belt and pulled out a child's t-shirt. He held it out for Tito to sniff. Nick stepped aside as Tito and Kava started toward the back of the house with the other men behind them.

Nick turned and saw Maria standing next to the passenger door. She watched the men go behind the house, then took Nick's hands in hers and looked into his face.

"Go. Find Lizzie. Do whatever you have to do to get our baby back safely." Looking into her face, Nick felt a renewed confidence.

"Don't worry. We'll get her back."

"I know you will."

He turned and ran after the men, the map clenched in his hand.

༄ ༄ ༄

The canopy of oaks and pines kept most of the rain off Dennis and the lightning lit the trail just enough to avoid the rocks and tree roots. Looking back into the clearing, he watched Becky walking quickly across the field with Lizzie on her hip, blindfolded.

"C'mon, we got to move," he yelled to her.

She finally caught up to him and they moved through the low brush. The storm was moving north and the lightning strikes were more than a minute apart now, so Dennis turned on his flashlight.

"Turn on your flashlight," he said over his shoulder. "The trees are thicker up here. You've got to be able to see."

Suddenly, he realized he didn't hear her. Turning around, he saw her fifty feet back and Lizzie was standing next to her. Becky was crouched down, looking through her backpack.

"What are you doing?" he yelled.

"My flashlight is at the bottom. I'll have it in a second."

"C'mon, we don't have time for this." He waited for a second, then walked back, crouched down, picked up Lizzie and continued toward the car. Lizzie struggled against Dennis, reaching her arms toward Becky's voice, screaming and kicking her legs.

"Dennis, bring her back here." He turned to see Becky walking toward him with the flashlight in her hand.

"I've got it. Let me have her. I found it."

"I've got her. We've got to get to my car. This place isn't safe anymore." He heard leaves crunching behind him as she quickened her pace.

"You're scaring her. Give her back to me."

"She's fine. Just come on. Hurry up." A moment later, he heard Becky cry out and then the sound of something hitting the ground. Turning around, he saw her lying on her stomach, her foot stretched across a tree root about an inch off the ground. He walked back to her and put Lizzie down, leaning close to her face. "Don't you move," he told her.

"What now?" He shook his head and ran his hand over his face. "Roll over."

Becky rolled onto her back. He took her hand and pulled her to her feet in one swift movement. As soon as she put weight on her right foot, she crumbled, almost hitting the ground a moment before he caught her.

"You've got to be kidding." He stared at her foot, then her face. "You're telling me you can't walk now?" She wiped spots of dirt from her cheek as she leaned on him.

"Just help me to the car. Lizzie can walk herself."

"No, she can't," he screamed at her. 'She's blindfolded. Jesus Christ, what a great help you are. Now I've got two children to get through the woods." He picked up Lizzie, flipping her to his left hip, then took Becky's left arm. "You're going to have to hop. The car's right through this last bunch of trees."

A hundred thoughts raced through his mind as they made their way through the last of the brush. He just knew they had to move and move quickly. He sensed something had changed. And there was only an hour until Luke would drop off the money, so he had to stay close.

Coming out from under the canopy, Dennis saw his car a hundred feet away. The drizzle turned to heavy rain. Becky was getting tired, her pace slowing as she held tightly onto his arm. They finally reached the car and he opened the back door and put Lizzie on the seat.

"Slide over."

Lizzie did as she was told and Becky slid in and pulled Lizzie close to her side. He slammed the door and walked to the driver's door. Starting the car and slamming it into reverse, he pulled out of the parking spot. He put the car in drive and the tires spun on the pebble parking lot as he pressed hard on the gas. He heard Lizzie cry softly as the car swung out of the park onto Smith Road and headed north toward the highway.

ও ও ও

Nick stepped around the back of the Gordon home and watched his men make their way down the wet, muddy, leaf-covered hill at the back of the property. At the front of the pack, Tito had his nose to the ground leading the men toward a wired fence that divided the Gordon property from the park.

Nick picked the clearest route he could find and followed the men, occasionally holding onto a pine tree to keep from sliding. He caught up to the group as they were climbing over into the park. The ground leveled about thirty feet past the fence.

Looking back toward the road, he could barely make out the house through the thick branches. He followed the group to a stream measuring more than two feet in width. Tito jumped the stream and picked up the scent in the foliage on the other side.

Ten minutes later, Nick looked fifty yards ahead of Tito and saw a clearing and a dilapidated wooden shack. They were walking directly toward it.

Nick pointed to different groups and to different sides of the building and the men sprinted into place, covering the sides and rear of the building. Tito raced to the front door of the shack and Kava held Tito in place while an officer kicked in the door.

Tito walked in with his nose to the floor followed by Kava and Nick with their weapons drawn. There was a couch and small table, but otherwise, it was empty. The dim light from the one window showed that the floorboards in front of the couch were wet. The dog walked through the room and scratched on a door at the back of the structure.

Nick walked forward, opened the door and cleared the room. This room was darker than the front room. A small window near the ceiling was closed and covered with a dark piece of cloth duct-taped to the wall. The room was at least ten degrees warmer than the front room. Tito walked over to an iron frame twin bed and leaned down, sniffed underneath the frame and started barking again.

Nick walked over, got on his hands and knees, and looked under the bed. A small stuffed bear lay on its side in the dust.

"Detective Capriotti, we need you out here."

Nick turned toward the voice in the front room, then turned to the officers behind him. "Bag this for evidence." He stood and walked into the front room and breathed in the cooler air as he walked to the couch.

"We found this under the couch." A state trooper pointed at a crumpled fast food napkin with a large spot of blood under the restaurant's logo imprint. Just then, Nick's cell phone rang. He pulled it from his pocket and flipped it open.

"Capriotti."

"Sir, this is Bentley. We're up at the front entrance to the park. We just finished interviewing two hikers who said they saw a man, young woman and child matching the descriptions of Kincaid, Overton and Rosentino. The hikers had just pulled their car into the front parking lot when it started raining and were about to back out and leave when they saw the three come out of the woods and get into a black Mercedes. They said the girl was blindfolded. The car left the park and headed north toward the highway about ten minutes ago."

"Listen, Bentley, I'm sending two troopers and an FBI agent through the woods toward you." He spread the park map on the couch and motioned for the troopers and agent to look, then marked the shack with one finger and the park entrance with the other.

"I want you to walk quickly toward the hiking trail, then around the right side of the lake toward the woods. Meet them at the edge of the woods with your flashlight to mark the way and bring them back to your car at the front of the park.

"Then I want you and your men to exit the park and head north toward the highway. I'm putting out a Be On The Lookout alert for a black Mercedes on I-77 and Smith

Road north of the park. These hikers didn't happen to get a license plate number, did they?"

"No, sir. They just watched, thinking it was a family trying to escape the rain after a picnic. They only realized after they were gone about the blindfold."

"Okay. Thanks." He hung up and dialed the dispatcher, giving Dennis' car information and asking that all units, both city and state, watch for this car and communicate if they saw it.

Closing his phone, Nick looked again at the napkin. A spot of the blood was fresh. Nick closed his eyes and whispered to himself.

"Hold on, Lizzie. We're coming."

44

The wipers could barely keep up with the steady pounding. The rain was coming down in sheets. Dennis leaned closer to the windshield and squinted, trying to make out the middle line of the road. Lightning strikes lit the sky several times a minute, illuminating the two-lane country road, but after the strikes, it was near zero visibility.

"Where are we going?" Becky's voice came out as a squeak. Dennis quickly glanced in the rearview mirror and saw that she was sitting in the middle of the seat, hugging Lizzie close to her chest. The car swerved slightly, approaching a bend.

"I don't know for sure." The clouds seemed to open as a deluge of rain hit the windshield, blocking Dennis' view completely for a moment. He passed the only visible streetlight and was plunged back into darkness. Pines and oaks lined the road and created a canopy high above the cement. The thick branches were still thickly covered in leaves, which in dry conditions would only let in small spots of light, but with the heavy clouds and curtains of rain, Dennis had to rely completely on his headlights.

He couldn't explain why had felt he had to leave the park so suddenly. He remembered being outside the shack arguing with Becky one minute, then the next feeling like a hunted animal. Then hearing the dogs in the distance, he knew in his gut that they had found him. He had worked too hard to let the cops ruin his plans now, so close to the finish. He still had an hour until Luke dropped the money. This could still work; he just had to lay low for a while.

"I want to see my daddy." Lizzie's voice was not much more than a whisper.

"Shhhh, honey. Let my friend drive." He watched in the mirror as Becky ran her hands over Lizzie's hair. "You'll see your daddy soon enough. You'll be home soon."

"Why do you have to keep talking to her like she's your kid? What? Do you think you're her mother or something?"

"No, Dennis. I don't think I'm her mother. Her mother died a few months ago in a car accident."

"How in the hell could you know that?" Dennis breathed a little easier as the rain let up slightly and he saw a sign for the intersection with I-77. He looked at Becky in the mirror and saw her eyes mist.

"Are the two of you having girl talks at night that I don't know about? Do you both get into your jammies and whisper and giggle all night?"

"No." She was quiet for a minute, then wiped the corner of her eye with her finger. "She told me earlier today. She moved here with Luke about a month ago."

Dennis heard her response, but couldn't answer. He was approaching the highway ramp and had to decide quickly whether to take the north or south ramp. His initial thought was to head south and take one of the state routes, but then he realized they would have to pass the park's exit and the cops might be waiting for him there.

But they were only about fifteen miles south of the North Carolina state line and the city of Charlotte. If it was just South Carolina authorities looking for him, he could drive over the state line and hide out there for an hour, then come back into the state on a smaller state route. He swerved the car onto the northbound entrance ramp and smiled as he watched the gray clouds move to the east, leaving a lighter gray behind.

"Well, I tell you what. You and your little friend sit back there and whisper to each other all you want. I am going to find a place to wait this out, then we go back and get my money and everything will be great."

"What if the police are waiting for you at the drop-off point? I just don't know if this is such a good idea."

"Like I said, I think you and your little friend should just sit quietly and let me drive." He knew he could only take her talking for a little while longer. His patience was wearing thin. They were only eight exits from the state line. "The weather's letting up. Why can't you give me a break for just one second?"

He watched in the mirror as Becky put her head down close to Lizzie's. What he didn't see was the state trooper's car in the grassy median.

∾ ∾ ∾

South Carolina drivers and rainstorms do not mix. The fact was more evident every day to South Carolina State Trooper Shawn Kelley, as he drove south on the highway and pulled into the "emergency only" median that connected the northbound and southbound lanes of the interstate.

The median was hidden by forty-foot pines. This allowed troopers the element of surprise when tagging speeders. Most cars didn't see the lane until they spotted the trooper's car pull out and hit the lights and sirens.

Shawn's stomach growled. He didn't usually work nights, but he'd been sick with the stomach flu for three days and had switched with another trooper so he could sleep late today. He hoped the night would be uneventful, but so far, he hadn't gotten his wish.

He'd been in this spot two hours earlier when dispatch called all vehicles in the area to a multi-vehicle crash on a two-lane state route a few miles north. An SUV had taken a curve too fast and slid into the side of a pickup truck. The car behind the pickup slid under the truck's bumper. Amazingly, no one was killed, but several people had been rushed to the hospital with broken bones. He hoped that would be the big excitement of the night. All he wanted was to finish his shift and go back to bed.

He drove up to the northbound lane and parked. Shawn leaned back in his seat and checked his laptop. A Be On Look Out was at the top of the messages. It was about the kidnapping of the little Rosentino girl. He had heard talk around the station that afternoon that a ransom demand had been issued. The BOLO mentioned a black Mercedes and included the car's license number.

Shawn pulled down his visor and ran his fingers over the picture of his five-year-old daughter. She was probably lying in her bed, being read to by his wife. It was the same book every night. A story about a duck leaving the farm, then finding his way back. He tried to imagine her being taken and shook his head to get rid of the thought. Lizzie's father must be going crazy right now.

The vehicle that moved across his field of vision was just a blur. Shawn flipped on the lights and siren, shifted the car into drive and hit the gas. Turning the wheel hard to the left, he pulled onto the shoulder. After clearing the lane, he accelerated quickly and found the car in question in front of him. It was a black Mercedes with plates matching the BOLO.

Shawn picked up his car radio and told dispatch he had Dennis' car in sight and that he was in pursuit in the high speed lane. He gave his location on the highway and heard the dispatcher alert authorities in North Carolina that the car was within ten miles of the state line. Shawn could make out the shape of someone in the back seat, but couldn't determine who was driving.

He moved his car within two car lengths. At that point, the driver hit the gas and increased the distance between their cars. Shawn told the dispatcher that he needed backup. The driver of the Mercedes was trying to escape and Shawn was keeping close to the Mercedes, despite the steady rainfall.

Shawn watched the back window and after a few moments, he saw the person in the back seat turn and look out the back window. It was a woman, which meant that Kincaid was driving his own car. He still couldn't see the child, but at six years old, she would be too short to see through the back.

Again, he moved within two car lengths of the Mercedes. Checking his speedometer, he saw they were traveling at ninety miles per hour. A second later, Kincaid turned the wheel to the right and swerved across two lanes and took the westbound exit ramp. Shawn reacted quickly and followed in pursuit, telling the dispatcher that the Mercedes had exited the highway and was driving west on State Road 90, heading toward the warehouse district.

45

⋘⋙

Claire breathed a sigh of relief as the FBI agent finally stood from the couch and walked to the other side of the living room to consult with his supervisor. Every fiber of Claire's being ached as she leaned back into the couch and closed her eyes.

She'd spent the last hour telling the agent everything she knew about Dennis, his friends and what she knew of his business. His questions helped her realize how little she knew about his life. The idea sank in that they had led separate lives for years and she finally had to admit it. She couldn't wrap her mind around the idea that Dennis was connected with Lizzie being kidnapped.

Even if he wasn't the mastermind, he was still involved and was in a relationship with Becky. One of her own students was Dennis' lover and they took Lizzie and were causing all this pain. Dennis was the man she'd loved completely for more than a decade and he was the one causing Luke the worst heartache of his life.

Opening her eyes, she watched Maria in the next room speak to Luke, then glance in Claire's direction and stand

and walk toward her. Claire felt her stomach turn. There was no question that Luke hated her, and now his mother was coming to lower the boom. Claire wanted to stand and run from the room, but her body was frozen. All she could do was watch Maria's face as she approached. Maria sat down next to her and laid her hand on Claire's shoulder.

"How are you doing?" Claire was stunned to hear the compassion in Maria's voice. She couldn't take her eyes off Maria's face. Her eyes were droopy, as if she hadn't slept in days, but her smile was warm and real. Claire couldn't find the words she wanted and lowered her head. Maria's voice was soft and close to her ear.

"Listen, I can't say I know what you're going through, but I can tell you that no one here blames you. No one." Claire let the words wash over her. Warm tears leaked from her eyes as her chest tightened.

"How can you say that?" she whispered, glancing up at Maria. "My husband is a prime suspect in Lizzie's kidnapping. Dennis, the man I've lived with and been married to for more than ten years, stole Luke's daughter and has put her in horrible danger. How can you say no one here blames me?"

Maria looked over at Luke, then back to Claire's damp face. "First, we don't know for sure that Dennis took Lizzie." Claire shook her head and cried fresh tears. Maria spoke with more certainty. "It might look like that is certain, but we only know for sure that he knows Becky. Second and more importantly, you're divorcing him. You realized that the marriage had died and you made a powerful decision to make a better life without him."

Claire looked across at Luke and their eyes met for a moment before he looked away. "I shouldn't be here. Luke's got enough on his mind without me here." She looked down at her hands. "I don't belong here."

"You're not going anywhere." Maria lifted Claire's chin and locked eyes with her. "If your husband is involved with Lizzie's kidnapping, that's him, not you. I need you to understand that no one here blames you. I don't blame you." Maria paused, then continued. "I think you love my son and you feel you've let him down."

Claire started to disagree, but realized Maria was right. Glancing toward Luke, she whispered, "I do." She felt Maria take her hands and turned to see a smile on Maria's face. The reality of how much Luke meant to her stung, but she knew it didn't matter.

"He's not going to want to see me or talk to me." She shook her head. "Why am I still here? This is crazy."

"You're here because you love my son and he loves you too. But you're also dealing with the reality that your husband is not the man you thought he was and you're grieving."

A sudden burst of movement came from behind Luke. The FBI agents, sheriffs and marshals all gathered together around the map on the table. Luke jumped to his feet. Maria and Claire ran into the dining room.

"Yes, I understand," said Schultz, as he peered at the map closely with his cell phone to his ear. "I see it here. We're on our way." He closed the phone and started gathering maps and documents.

"What is it? What's happening?" Luke said as he pushed past the men to Schultz's side.

"Sir, there's been a break in the case and I need you to stay here and wait."

"He's taken her somewhere new, is that it?" Luke was half screaming. "He's moving her and you're on his trail, is that right? Tell me, damn it! Where is he taking Lizzie?"

Just then, a squeaky sound came from the radio of one of the officers in the room. "This is trooper seventy-five fifteen. Black Mercedes just took exit ten of Interstate

Seventy-seven. Mercedes turned west. I am in pursuit."

Claire watched Luke as he pushed through the men and headed toward the front door.

An FBI agent started after Luke. "Sir, I need you to stay—" but the door slammed closed and they heard a car start outside. The agent spoke to the room.

"Kincaid's on the road with Lizzie." He pointed to two of his agents. "You two stay and monitor the radios. The rest of you, let's go."

Maria and Claire stood back as the men left the condo. Suddenly, the room was quiet, except for the occasional codes coming from the radio on the table.

Maria grabbed Claire's hand and headed for the door. "C'mon, you drive. You know the area better than I do."

∽ ∽ ∽

For the first time since he'd found Lizzie's bed empty almost thirty six hours earlier, Luke felt there was a possibility that he'd find her and she wouldn't be harmed. But the storm clouds, which had been varying shades of gray throughout the day, were now black. Lightning streaks lit the sky to the east two or three times a minute and Luke flipped the wipers on high as a crack of thunder boomed straight overhead. Images of Lizzie flipped through his mind, but also images of Claire. He'd watched her while she talked to the agent, wanting to talk to her, but not knowing what he would say.

He knew one thing: his mother was right. He did love her. He just couldn't think of that now. It hurt too much.

Through the storm, he saw the sign for Exit 10 and moved into the right-hand lane. Turning west, he heard a siren and moved to the shoulder as a state trooper sped past.

Pulling back onto the road, he tailed the trooper's car. Both vehicles raced up and down hills, rain hitting the windshield in sheets. Luke noticed a convenience store on the right side of the road with two sheriff's cars in the parking lot. They had traveled about a mile from the highway and he wished he knew the area better.

As Luke began to wonder if the trooper in front of him was on another call, the trooper suddenly turned left into an industrial complex. Following the patrol car through the opening of the ten-foot chain link fence, Luke felt like he was in a television police drama. There were one-story office buildings straight ahead of him and to the right stood a warehouse at least three stories high. Surrounding the building were state trooper vehicles, sheriff's cars and other unmarked cars, all with lights flashing. Men in various uniforms were running in every direction, all with bulletproof vests. Luke pulled over to the left, parked and got out.

"Sir, you can't be here." A trooper wearing a fluorescent yellow raincoat and matching hat walked toward him, waving a glowing stick at the gate opening. "You're going to have to leave, sir."

"You don't understand. I'm her father."

"Sir, you're going to have to leave now." The officer stood five feet from Luke, rain dripping from his yellow hat.

"I'm Luke Rosentino. My daughter's in there." Fear and anger bubbled inside Luke as he took a step toward the officer.

The trooper lifted his radio from his shoulder and said "I need backup at the front gate," his eyes never leaving Luke's. The officer laid his hand on his taser. "You shouldn't be here, sir. You need to leave."

"I've got it, Kelley. Thanks." Luke heard a familiar voice from over the trooper's shoulder. Nick walked up from behind the trooper, said something in his ear and pointed toward the building. Reluctantly, the trooper walked back to his vehicle.

"You shouldn't be here, Luke."

"Does he have Lizzie in that warehouse? Answer me honestly."

Nick looked down at the ground, shaking his head. "You're not supposed to be here, Luke. This will get ugly."

"Answer my question, Nick. Does he have my daughter in that building or not?"

Nick thought of Maria and breathed deep.

"Yes, a trooper followed Dennis' car from the highway and into this complex. By the time he caught up with the car, Dennis had taken Lizzie into the warehouse."

Luke watched as a sheriff's car with SWAT on the side entered the compound. Nick turned Luke away from the building and walked him toward his car.

"Look, Luke, we got a full operation here. We've got canine units, sheriff's office units, FBI, snipers and our SWAT team on site and we know Dennis and Becky are in this building with your daughter. Police have the building surrounded. There is no way out. This is going to end soon, but I need you to not be here." Luke started to speak, but Nick continued.

"Let us finish this. I guarantee you this is the best team in the country. They will get your daughter out unharmed." He stopped and looked Luke in the eye. "You just have to trust me a little longer."

When Luke didn't respond, Nick continued. "There's a convenience store about a half mile down the road. The county's set up a command post inside the store. I'm going to call my guys over there. I need you to wait with them for news."

Luke looked back at the building, at the officers with their weapons drawn and the SWAT team huddled together.

Nick closed his cell phone. "Officer Kelley will drive you there."

"Nick, kill the bastard if you have to. Just make sure Lizzie's safe."

46

∽ᔷᕲ

Dennis was relieved there were no employees in the warehouse as he and Becky walked past row after row of metal shelves filled with oversized wooden crates.

The storm was in full force and the clamor of the rain of the metal roof was almost deafening. Inside the front door facing the parking lot was a small office with metal tables and metal folding chairs tucked under and old computer monitors on top. Forklifts sat parked along the front wall. Metal support beams were spaced fifteen feet apart, reaching to the ceiling.

Dennis had toured this property a few years earlier with a client. Tonight, when he saw the trooper pull out of the median and start to tail him, he'd remembered the property and swerved to take the exit. Reaching seventy miles per hour on the back roads trying to lose the trooper, he had the car airborne. Once Dennis lost him, he pulled in behind the building, ran inside and locked the door.

Dennis stood in the middle of the building and realized how quickly his plan had unraveled.

The two million dollars was supposed to be dropped off in an hour, but he had no way to get to it. The building was surrounded by sheriffs and troopers and they knew he was involved in the kidnapping. He'd tried to contact Rodney by cell phone, but he wouldn't answer. There had to be a way to get the money from Luke and get it to Rodney. Dennis had tossed ideas in his head for the past hour, but every idea relied on him getting out of the warehouse.

Lizzie's crying and whining was rubbing on Dennis' last nerve. It hadn't stopped since they'd left the park. She was practically wrapped around Becky like a pretzel and the two of them whispered together all the time.

The pounding behind his eyes plus Lizzie's crying was enough to make him want to bang his head against a wall.

"For God's sake, can't you quiet her down?" He gave Becky a desperate look over his shoulder. He watched as Becky whispered in Lizzie's ear and Lizzie wrapped her arms around Becky and buried her face in Becky's neck. He had to think about his next move.

"What about the ransom for Lizzie?" Dennis cringed at the whininess in Becky's voice. "We've only got forty-five minutes."

He turned on her. "You don't think I know that?" Screaming, he lost all his control. "Every God-damn cop in the state has this building surrounded and I'm trying to think of a way out, but I can't think because all I hear is your whiny voice. Just please shut up for a few fucking minutes!"

He looked around the building for a way out. A small front door next to the office led to the front parking lot. There were no skylights and the only windows were near the top of the walls on the far sides of the building. They were twenty-five feet off the floor and there weren't any shelves near them for access. He could see the patrol car's lights reflecting off the inside walls of the warehouse, so the front entrance was out. There were four loading dock doors. His car was parked outside the last one, but he could hear police outside those doors. The warehouse was connected at the long end to the office building next door, but he'd tried that door and it was locked, and there were no keys on the wall or in any drawer he could find.

If he didn't get two million dollars to Rodney by tomorrow morning, his reputation and his business would be ruined. His embezzlement ten years earlier would become public knowledge and he would lose everything and definitely go to prison.

Suddenly, the answer came to him. It was the only way out. Just then, his cell phone rang. He quickly pulled it from his pocket.

"Dennis Kincaid." He prayed the other voice would be Rodney, but it was a much deeper voice.

"This is Special Agent Roberts. I'm a hostage negotiator with the FBI. You need to know that the building is completely surrounded and there is no way out. We might be able to help get you out of this situation, but you have to work with us. The safety of everyone inside and our officers is our top priority. We need to know that everyone inside is safe."

Dennis laughed.

"You want to help me? You're the fucking cops! You don't want to help me. You would just as soon storm the building and take everyone out."

"We're here to help you."

"You want to help me?" Dennis laughed loudly into the phone, then shouted, "Leave me the hell alone," and hung up.

ℳ ℳ ℳ

Claire pulled into the convenience store parking lot. She and Maria walked toward the store, but they were stopped by an officer at the door.

"I'm sorry, but you can't enter the store, ma'am."

Maria stepped forward. "Listen, my granddaughter is being held in the warehouse down the street and this is my daughter," pointing to Claire. "We've been at the command post all day and we followed Detective Schultz here."

"I'm sorry, ma'am. This store is being used by authorities. No civilians inside."

Maria stepped up to the officer. "What's your name, son?"

"O'Brien, ma'am."

"Well, Officer O'Brien, I suggest you get on your radio and check with Detective Schultz or Capriotti about us. We'll wait."

He stepped inside the store and Claire watched him speak to Schultz. She looked down the street toward the warehouse. She couldn't see the building, but she could see the police car lights reflecting off the trees across the street.

I shouldn't be here, she thought. My husband is the one that's causing all these problems. Luke hates me and I don't blame him. I'm doing nothing but causing heartache by being here.

"Maria, I—"

"Shhh, here he comes."

O'Brien opened the door and came out with Schultz. They walked up to Maria and Claire, just as a patrol car pulled up to the store. Luke stepped out of the passenger side, and looked right through her as he approached Annie. Claire swore she felt the temperature drop as he passed her.

Schultz stepped toward Claire. "I just got word from Nick and the negotiator. They want you over at the warehouse."

"They want me?"

"That's what Nick said. Officer Kelley will drive you over."

A few moments later, she was in the front seat of a patrol car. They pulled out of the parking lot and drove the half mile to the warehouse. As they rounded the bend, Claire saw the building. There were at least two dozen cars in the parking lot and police officers in vests behind the cars with rifles aimed at the building. Closer to the building was a van with SWAT painted on the side. Men in helmets and vests stood to the side of the building in a group, rifles in hand, watching Nick and a few FBI agents standing by another van in front of the building.

The officer pulled up next to the van. Nick turned around, saw Claire and opened her door. She swung her legs out and realized her whole body was trembling. Nick took her hand and helped her out.

"Are you okay?"

"They said you needed me. I don't understand. What can I do?"

Nick tapped on the shoulder of the man behind him. The man turned around, took his headphones off, then looked at Claire. Nick did the introductions.

"Special Agent Roberts, this is Claire Bennett. Overton is her student and Kincaid is her husband."

Roberts shook Claire's hand. "I hope you can help us."

It didn't make any sense. None of this was making any sense. "Nick, I shouldn't be here. That's my husband in there making death threats and causing Luke all this heartache." Her chest was tight and she was short of breath as tears filled her eyes. "Dennis stole Lizzie because of me."

Roberts turned back toward the warehouse and Nick walked a few steps away with Claire. He turned to face her.

"We want you to talk to Becky and try to reason with her."

"What? Why would she listen to me? She's obviously in love with Dennis. She's not going to listen to me. I'm Dennis' wife. I'm sure she hates me."

"Did you ever tell her your husband's name?"

"What?"

"All those times you talked to Becky, did you ever tell her Dennis' full name?"

Claire thought of those afternoons and the times in the hospital after Becky's failed suicide attempt.

"No. I always called Dennis 'my husband,' but I never said his name, not even first name."

"So she probably doesn't know you're his wife. I'm sure he never brought up your name. And you and Becky still have a good relationship?"

"Yes. Our last conversation was about her writing. I told her she has real talent."

Nick pointed to the warehouse. "I think you have a chance of helping us end this."

Claire thought back to all the nights that Dennis lied about overnight trips and how Annie had seen him and Becky in his car at the restaurant. Anger bubbled so close to the surface, but her thoughts of Becky were stronger, and she realized that finding out about Dennis' lies had freed her. She remembered how she had let Dennis rule her life for so long. Becky was just a young girl.

"All right, I'll help."

Nick walked with her back to Roberts. Nick nodded to Roberts, who handed Claire a headset with a microphone attached.

"Tell me when you're ready and I'll call Becky's phone. Dennis will answer, but I'll get Becky on the line. You stay quiet until you see me nod at you."

Claire nodded and put the headset on. A second later, a dial tone, then Dennis answered. His voice shocked Claire to her core and she had to fight not to make any noise. He sounded desperate to her and she closed her eyes and tried to close her mind to his voice and think about Becky. The young traumatized, shy, scared girl that she had seen come to life in the past weeks needed her help.

"Roberts, I said leave me alone," Dennis said in a low voice.

"I want to talk to Ms. Overton."

"She's got nothing to say to you."

"Mr. Kincaid, we're trying to help you. I just want to make sure she and Lizzie are physically okay. I'll only talk to her for a minute."

The line was quiet for a moment, then Claire heard him say in a muffled voice, "The cops want to talk to you. Make it quick."

"Hello?"

"Ms. Overton, this is Special Agent Roberts with the FBI. Can Dennis hear my voice?"

"No."

"I have someone here who wants to talk to you. Just listen. Only answer in yes's and no's for the safety of you and Lizzie."

Roberts nodded at Claire. She took a deep breath.

"Becky, it's Professor…it's Claire."

"How—"

"Professor Rosentino is a good friend of mine and I've been with him all day. Please just listen to me. Are you and Lizzie okay?"

"Yes." Her voice was softer and shaking.

"Becky, I know that Dennis is the man you wrote the letter to. I know he's the man you fell in love with and he's the man who broke your heart."

The line was quiet, then a tearful "yes" came across the line.

She felt Nick's hand on her shoulder and continued.

"Becky, this entire building is surrounded by police of every level. There is no way out. I need you to think of Lizzie. Think of how you were treated as a young girl and all the harm that was imposed on you. Don't let that kind of violence happen to Lizzie. Be her protector. Can you do that?"

"Yes." Becky was openly crying now.

"Remember how we talked about being strong women? Remember that day in my classroom when I told you what a good writer you are?"

"Yes."

"Becky, you have so much to offer this world. Think of all our talks and remember that you are a strong woman who has survived a terrible childhood. Use that strength to protect Lizzie at all costs."

"Okay."

"Is there any way you can help us get Lizzie out of the warehouse?"

There was silence on the line for a full minute with Becky crying softly, then, "No."

"What the fuck are you saying to her? She's crying like a baby in here." Dennis' voice hit Claire's ear and she held her breath.

"Sir, we're just checking on the child." Roberts nodded at Claire and she took off the headset and handed it to Nick with shaking hands.

"You did good," he whispered.

ℬ ℬ ℬ

Dennis watched Becky walk back to Lizzie and hug her.

"My main goal is that everyone in that building comes out alive," Roberts' voice said on the cell phone.

This could work. Dennis walked away from the two of them.

"Special Agent Roberts, is it?"

"Yes."

"I'm thinking you and I could work something out."

"I'd like to think that's true."

"We both want to avoid having a bloodbath." He walked farther away from Becky and Lizzie. "I don't think there's any reason for it."

"I agree. This can be settled with no violence," Roberts said.

"Well, I'm in somewhat of a bind. Now that the ransom money's not been dropped and I can't reach it and hand it off, information about me is going to be disclosed to the media later this week." He looked around the room.

"Plus now, my face will be plastered across newspapers with headlines like 'Baby Stealer' and 'Kidnapper.' My law firm is going to close, I'll be put on trial and probably sent to prison for years for this and other things. I need for that not to happen."

Roberts was silent for a moment.

"I don't know what you want me to do."

Dennis looked back at Becky and Lizzie. "I need to leave the country and I need you to make that happen. I want a plane arranged for a flight to Mexico."

Roberts replied instantly. "I can't let you leave, Dennis. We need to work something out here. Since you know the ransom isn't going to work, let's work on getting Lizzie sent out. You don't need her anymore and her father would really like to see her."

"Her father would like…why do I give a rat's ass what *her father* wants?" Dennis kicked at one of the crates. "Her father is dating my wife. He can fry in hell as far as I'm concerned."

"Okay, I understand." There was silence, then, "You don't have any children, right?"

"No, I don't."

"I'm sure she's been crying a lot these past two days, huh? That's a lot of tension, even if Becky's been caring for her more than you have."

"How'd you know that?"

"It's an easy assumption," Roberts said. "A busy man like you is used to dealing with adults, not small children." Dennis thought about it.

"What's your point?"

"All I'm saying is now that the pressure of the ransom is off, how about we work toward you sending Lizzie out?"

"He'd love that, wouldn't he? Mr. History Professor wins again. A month ago, he strolls into that college, meets Claire and feels he can take her from me." He walked back toward the girls and met Becky's quizzical look. "We'd only been separated a couple of weeks and he's already at my house, kissing *my* wife. And then it turns out his family's loaded. Of course, I'm going to take advantage of the situation. It serves both him and Claire right." Dennis sat down next to Becky on the crate. "So how is that plane looking, Roberts?"

"I don't think I can help you with that, Dennis."

"Well, then I don't think I have anything else to say

to you." Dennis pushed the 'End' button on his phone and took a deep breath.

"Your wife's name's Claire?" Becky glanced sideways at Dennis. He turned to face her.

"Yeah. Claire Bennett. Why?"

He watched as Becky processed the information, then struggled to speak. "She's my English professor," she said in a strangled tone.

Dennis put his face in his hands and shook his head. "You've got to be kidding me."

"No, she was wonderful to me the first few weeks of school. She even sent in a story of mine to a national writing contest. She said I have talent."

He looked at her young face and realized what a mistake he'd made. Becky was so innocent and gullible. This whole weekend, she'd huddled close to Lizzie, like a mother hen protecting her young. She didn't actually have the drive and motivation he'd seen the first weeks of her internship. She'd worked harder than any other intern that summer, staying late to work on projects with the other lawyers, reading legal journals and always listening and watching.

"I thought you wanted to be a lawyer. You were so driven at the firm."

He watched her eyes search his, as she took his hand in hers. "I just wanted to be near you. I knew it the moment I saw you. All those hours with the other lawyers after work; I told them all I wanted to work with you on a case. You're so strong and smart and," she wrapped both her hands around his, "you said you loved me."

"What?"

"I know you do. I understand. You have so much tension in your life, but if we go away together…if we get out of here and go to Mexico, we could start a new life together."

Dennis pulled his hand back and slid away from her. Standing up, he took Lizzie in his arms and backed away from her.

"Babe, if *we* get out of here, I'm going to Mexico by myself."

47

"What do you mean, you're going to Mexico?" The question came out as a shriek. "This whole weekend, the whole time we've had Lizzie, the whole idea was for us to leave the country together with the ransom money. But now, you say if we get out of this warehouse, you're going to Mexico by yourself? What about me? What about us?"

Becky stared at the man she'd loved for months. She'd dreamed about living with him, making love with him, even marrying him. He seemed so different from any man she'd ever known, but he wasn't. Looking into his face now, she saw it. He was just like her father.

The realization struck her like a slap in the face. She'd spent so much time daydreaming about the good times they'd had, but in reality, she'd been hanging on to a fantasy. Scenes from their relationship flashed through her mind. When Dennis wasn't in need of sex or some favor he knew she'd do, he treated her like her father had at home. It was like she didn't exist, like she was a piece of furniture he could kick when he was frustrated.

She'd wasted so much time loving him and planning

her future around him. She never stepped back and realized that he wasn't interested in making plans with her. She walked toward him and Lizzie.

"How could I have been so stupid?" she screamed at him. Lizzie started to cry and reached out for Becky, but Dennis held her close to him. "How could I have believed that one day, you would love me like I loved you?"

Just then, his cell phone rang. He looked at the number and cursed as he put it to his ear.

"I told you I don't have anything to say to you, Roberts." He stepped backwards away from Becky with Lizzie in his arms. "Unless you've got a plane for me, we've got nothing to discuss."

"Listen, Dennis, I don't have the authorization to get a plane, but I am working on something with my team. It might take a little while so I'm asking for your patience."

"I don't think so. The plane was my last chance out of here alive."

"Listen, the men out here are working on my command. Nothing will happen unless I give the order. If we work together, we can make this happen. Nobody needs to get hurt. All I want is everyone safe, both inside and outside."

Dennis turned his back on Becky and said in a softer tone, "You've got to help me, Roberts. I'm dealing with a child and a crazy woman here. Anything would be better than where I am now. I'm thinking I should just shoot them both."

"You son of a bitch," Becky screamed behind him. "I am not crazy. I have done every thing you've asked me to do and you still treat me like dirt." She looked down, saw a mop and small metal bucket next to the wall. She kicked the bucket, he turned and it hit him in the shin. "No wonder Claire kicked you out. You're a poor excuse for a man, you piece of shit."

Dennis put the phone on a nearby crate and pulled a gun from the back waistband of his pants. He turned around and pointed it at Becky with his right hand and held Lizzie against his left hip. He walked up to Becky and placed the barrel of the gun against her forehead.

"Shut up! I have had enough of your fucking mouth. I want you to shut the fuck up and let me think or I will put a bullet right between your fucking eyes!"

Becky's eyes widened and she couldn't breathe. She looked at Lizzie, whose eyes were focused on the gun and Becky acted without thinking.

"Give her to me. This is between the two of us. Give her to me."

Dennis turned his body slightly, keeping the gun to Becky's head, and Lizzie held her arms out. Becky took Lizzie, stepped back several steps and lowered Lizzie to the floor. She looked back at Dennis. His arms were stretched straight in front of him and he was holding the gun with two hands, aimed directly at her head.

"I don't want to shoot you, Beck, but you are driving me fucking crazy!" His face was flushed and she saw beads of sweat on his forehead. "I am out of fucking options. I need to get out of here. I need to get the hell out of here."

"Please put the gun down," she said softly. "Please."

"SHUT UP! You never know when to shut up!"

Suddenly, Dennis' cell phone began to ring. He spun around and fired two shots at the phone. The bullets hit the crate and the phone flew in the air. He began to turn back to Becky.

The sniper's bullet hit Dennis in the forehead and he fell onto the cement floor.

48

ော

Luke knew snipers were in position, but it didn't register until he heard on an officer's radio that Dennis had been shot.

Luke ran to Nick with terrible images racing through his mind.

"Is Lizzie okay?"

"I'm sure the sniper only got Dennis. Negotiations had ended and Dennis was being extremely violent. We heard him threaten to shoot both Becky and Lizzie. The sniper was given authorization to shoot when possible. He took the shot through a second-floor window across from the warehouse. I'm going to the warehouse now. You need to stay here. I'll bring her back to you." He took Luke by the shoulders. "This may not be over yet. I need you to stay. Do we understand each other?"

"I get it. I'll stay here."

Luke watched Nick run down the road toward the warehouse parking lot. He couldn't stop shaking. Every muscle in his body wanted to run after Nick, but they were so close to ending this. If he ran after Nick and there was gunfire and he was hit, then what would happen to Lizzie?

He got down on his knees in the parking lot and put his hands together in front of him and whispered to himself.

"Dear God, please help my little girl. I know she's going through the worst experience of her life right now and I'm asking you to be there with her. Guide the police to her and let them find her unharmed so they can bring her back to me. I know you gave her to me to care for and I feel I've let you down these past few weeks, but I ask that you give me the chance to raise my daughter and love her every day."

Luke heard someone walking toward him. He opened his eyes and watched a trooper approach him.

"Mr. Rosentino, the scene is secure. They're bringing your daughter this way."

Luke ran across the parking lot toward a female officer carrying Lizzie in her arms. Lizzie's head lay on the officer's shoulder. They met at the edge of the road and the officer said softly in Lizzie's ear, "Your daddy's here, baby."

Lizzie turned her face to him and he held his arms out to her. She reached out for Luke and for the first time in thirty-six hours, he held his daughter tight in his arms. The sirens and talk over police radios were all muted as he held her tight, her arms around his neck. He felt her body shake with fear and heard her cry, and he rocked her and walked the parking lot, feeling her tears on his neck and running his fingers through her hair.

"I've got you. I've got you. It's all over, baby. It's all over. Nobody's going to hurt you ever again. I promise that. I won't let anyone ever hurt you again."

She cried into his shirt.

"I wanted to come home, but they wouldn't let me. They said you had to pay first." She lifted her head from his shoulder and he wiped her tears away with his fingers.

"I know you wanted to, honey. I'm so sorry I couldn't

get to you." He felt all the air rush out of his body as he brushed her bangs from her forehead. Warm tears blurred his vision. Lizzie wiped his tears with her hand.

"The police have been helping me look for you since the moment I saw you were gone. I'm so glad we found you, baby."

She put her head on his shoulder. He felt a cool breeze hit his face and looked across the parking lot toward the store. Maria was walking toward them.

"Look who's here," he whispered in her ear. Lizzie looked up and she quieted down just as Maria reached them. She put her hands on either side of Lizzie's face and kissed her several times.

"She's all right?"

Luke realized he hadn't thought of any injuries and motioned for one of the officers nearby to call for a paramedic.

"Are you okay, honey? Does anything hurt?"

"I'm fine, Daddy. They didn't hurt me. They just yelled a lot." She looked toward the warehouse, then back to Luke. "Daddy, why did he hate you so much? He said he took me because he hated you. Did you do something mean to him?" Her eyes bored into him and he looked at Maria for help.

"No, honey, Daddy didn't do anything mean to that man," Maria said softly as Luke kissed Lizzie's cheek. "He was just a terrible man. We're just so glad you're back with us and that you're safe."

Luke put his arm around Maria and whispered in her ear, "I don't know what I would have done if you wouldn't have been here. Thank you so much." They shared a glance and Maria watched as Nick approached them.

"Honey, I want you to meet Detective Capriotti. He's a policeman and he's been looking for you with all these men and your dad since yesterday morning.

Nick came over and took Lizzie's small hand in his and kissed her fingers. "You're just as pretty as your picture."

∾ ∾ ∾

The ambulance drove past Claire as she stood at the edge of the store's parking lot and watched the vehicle swing into the warehouse driveway. She started walking toward the warehouse, but felt as if she was walking in a fog. Nothing made sense. Every part of her universe had changed in two days.

She had only learned a few hours earlier that Dennis was involved in the kidnapping of her friend's daughter, and with his girlfriend, one of Claire's students, had kept the girl hostage for almost two days. A few moments ago, she heard over a police radio that a sniper had shot the kidnapper. As the thoughts tumbled through her mind, she felt lightheaded and leaned against a light pole.

How could this be happening? Just two months ago, she was living with Dennis as husband and wife. A month ago, she'd discovered his affair, kicked him out and started her own life and become friends with Luke. Now, the man she'd married ten years ago and loved with all her heart was lying on the floor of the warehouse, injured or killed by a police sniper during a kidnapping standoff.

And Becky...that beautiful young girl had written a heart-wrenching letter to a man who turned out to be Claire's husband. The man that Becky almost killed herself over was Claire's own husband.

And the most insane part was that Dennis took Lizzie to hurt Luke. Her husband was so angry that she didn't forgive him for his affair and let him move back into her life and home that he stole the daughter of her friend. Claire knew how power-hungry Dennis had always been, but she had never seen such an evil side of him.

She realized she was standing in the middle of the warehouse parking lot. Police officials passed her, spewing words like "lunatic" and "maniac." Police officers and FBI agents crowded near the front door of the building.

Her eyes were suddenly drawn to the blue uniforms of the officers walking out with Becky in handcuffs. Her head was down, but suddenly, she started screaming and crying and tried to move back into the warehouse. As she turned, the light hit her just right and Claire realized the front of Becky's shirt and her arms and legs were covered in blood. The officers pulled Becky away into a waiting police car.

Claire's legs gave way and two nearby officers grabbed her arms and led her to a police cruiser by the road. They opened the back door and let her sit on the back seat with her feet on the ground.

"Here, ma'am, put your head down between your knees." One of them brought her a bottle of water. Her stomach was churning and her head was spinning. Then a woman's voice came from behind the men.

"I got this, gentlemen. Thanks for your help." That voice. Claire looked up slowly and saw Maria in front of her.

"What are you doing here?" Claire cried, fighting the nausea that was washing over her. "Why are you over here with me? My husband kidnapped your granddaughter and was going to do God knows what to her. This whole ordeal you and your family have gone through the past two days is because of my husband. You should hate me."

The two women stared into each other's eyes, then Maria crouched down in front of Claire.

"My son has his daughter back. He's across the street holding her hand as a paramedic is checking her out. They're a family again. They're back together. Luke's almost whole again."

"But my husband—what?"

"Luke is almost whole again."

"Almost?"

"He needs you, Claire."

"Maria, please. There's no way your son ever wants to speak to me again. Even if you forgive me, which I doubt, there's no chance of him forgiving me."

Maria put her fingers under Claire's chin, raising her face.

"I know my son loves you." Claire tried to lower her eyes, but Maria met them and locked on.

"He told me about you the day after he 'ran into' you on campus. He couldn't stop talking about you. At first, I thought he was just infatuated with someone new, but when I got here and saw the way he looked at you, I knew. There's an excitement in his voice that I hadn't heard in years."

A warm tear escaped Claire's eye and rolled down her cheek.

"I also believe that God put you here to help our family recover from this ordeal. We'll get through this together. Luke knows you wouldn't have any part in causing that much pain to anyone. You're not wired that way."

Claire stood to hug Maria, but she felt a shiver pass through her body as she heard an officer walking past say the sniper was successful. Dennis' body was in that warehouse and she was a widow.

"Right now, though, you have to grieve for your husband."

Claire leaned against the back of the patrol car and tears flowed as she sobbed on Maria's shoulder.

49

ഗാഗ

The ringing wouldn't stop, but there was no way for Claire to get to her Blackberry at the bottom of her purse. Rushing down the hall toward the ground floor elevator, she grabbed the English II workbook just before it slid off the pile she was carrying.

"Wait, hold that elevator." The student's eyes widened as he threw his hand out to stop the doors from closing.

"Thanks," Claire said, stepping in and shifting the stack of books on her arm. "It's definitely been one of those days where you can't..." Glancing at the student, she saw the iPod earbuds and realized she was talking to herself.

A few moments later, the elevator doors opened at the English department floor and she left the student bopping his head to what looked like a hip-hop beat.

One of the professors had taped paper Thanksgiving turkeys to every office door and Claire realized how much she had to be thankful for this year. Her classes were going well, no professors had threatened to quit this month and there was talk of her continuing as department chair indefinitely.

"Hey, stranger, how about lunch?" Annie leaned out of Claire's office just before she reached the doorway.

"God, you scared me." Claire walked in and set her books and purse on her desk and flopped into her leather chair. "I could probably do lunch. Sit down; I've got a couple of e-mails to return first."

Annie sat and pulled her legs up into her lap Indian style and grabbed the daily paper from Claire's briefcase. After glancing over the front page stories, she put the paper down.

"Boy, I'm glad we're in education. All we have to worry about is teaching these lunkheads the English language and history of our people."

Claire laughed. "You mean our Einsteins?"

"Right. Einsteins, gems, whatever you want to call them." Annie held the paper in front of her face, then put it back in her lap.

"So, have you talked to Luke lately?"

Claire shot her friend an inquisitive look, than glanced back at the computer monitor. "No, I don't see the point. He's never going to speak to me. That whole experience is over. It's better if I just stay out of his way."

Annie sprang up from the chair and walked to the doorway. Claire looked up to see Annie motioning to someone in the hall.

"See, I disagree and so does he, but I'll let him tell you that part."

A moment later, Luke entered the room. Claire met his eyes and felt herself shrink into the chair. She'd tried for two months to avoid running into him just for this reason.

Annie started out the door, then turned. "I'll meet you in the cafeteria, Claire. Oh, and I just realized I forgot to tell you both about my date with Nick last night."

"Nick, the cop?" Claire felt her brain couldn't

comprehend anything other than Luke's being in her office right now.

"Nick Capriotti, the very same. Dinner last night, details for you both at lunch." She turned to Luke. "Bring her to her senses, please. I'll save you room at the table." She glared at Luke, then practically skipped out of the room.

Claire stared at Luke for a moment, unsure of what to say. But he seemed to have his speech memorized. He smiled as he walked toward her, shaking his head.

"I have always wondered about that child."

Claire smiled, but felt like bolting for the door. He was trying to make this so easy, but it wasn't. There was so much pain to get through.

"You're probably wondering why I'm here. I know you've been avoiding me. I've watched you turn the other way when you see me on campus."

Claire stood and came around her desk. "I didn't want to bring up any bad memories. I caused so much trouble for you. I'm trying to do what's best for you and Lizzie."

Their eyes met, then he looked down at the floor as he continued to approach her. "I think it's time you heard this from me instead of my mother or Annie or anyone else. Maybe then you'll believe it." He stepped right in front of her.

"I never blamed you."

Claire felt her chest tighten and her voice didn't work when she tried to speak.

"You had nothing to do with Lizzie being kidnapped." His eyes pierced hers. "I know you're going to say that Dennis was your husband. I get that. But you and he were from different planets, different worlds. He planned the whole kidnapping with Becky after you kicked him out. You stood by me the whole time. How could I blame you?"

He was now sitting on the edge of her desk, facing her with his feet spread apart as he'd done several times before the kidnapping. He bit his lip, took her hands in his and continued.

"I love you, Claire. I've loved you since I met you. I think fate put us together and tested us early to see how we'd survive the hard times. I'd say we did pretty well." He paused for a few seconds, then said in a softer voice, "My only question is...do you love me?"

She stepped in between his feet and kissed him. She felt his arms surround her as he held her tight. His kiss was soft as she ran her fingers through the hair on the back of his head. She could get lost like this.

"I take that as a yes," he murmured. She nodded and kissed him again.

"Okay, then. We've got to go." He pulled her by the hand toward the door. "Making Gordon wait for lunch is a really bad idea."

LaVergne, TN USA
20 October 2010
201559LV00004B/1/P